THE HUNTED

MIKE MORRIS

A NATHANIEL RANE NOVEL

by Mike Morris

For Tee, Dee, and Zee.
Forever and always.

Then

1

Rane

Rane lay on a cold stone floor, dimly aware of the sounds of fighting far away. Something warm and sticky covered his eyes. Blood. His blood.

It was hard to work out what was happening, remember where he was. Someone cried out in pain. He didn't know who. Could've been him. Why was it so hard to think?

He moved his hand. Dragged it more like. Managed to wipe the blood from his eyes and get them open. It took a while to focus, move past the swirling spots and dark shapes, get the world to stop spinning. All he could see was the stone floor—cold, grey, polished. Covered in blood. Was that his blood?

Darkness tugged at the edges of his mind, telling him to stop, give up, rest for a minute, an hour, a lifetime. Where was *Kibon*, his sword? He could hear it calling him.

Promising to make the pain go away, save him, if only he could hold it.

He lifted his head, saw the sword only inches away. So close.

Kibon meant 'hope' in Naijin. Now, it was all that was keeping Rane alive.

A wave of nausea slammed into him. He blinked more blood from his eyes. It was coming from somewhere, leaking out of him. He wondered how much he'd already lost. How close he was to dying.

He reached out and dragged *Kibon* to him, felt that beautiful pulse of magic the moment he held the hilt, a counter for the pain. Not nearly fast enough though. By the gods, no. Not for the pain he was in.

A battle raged somewhere. He could hear it. The roar of war. Gunfire and cannon fire. Screaming and dying. He turned his head, trying to see something—anything— and was rewarded with more pain for doing so. He might have passed out again. He didn't really know, except he'd opened his eyes again, blinking more blood away.

That was when he saw her.

Myri. His friend. His comrade in the Legion of Swords. Once even, his lover. Now, she stood by the window, watching him, smiling at his pain, lost to the Taint.

It all came back to him then. Myri had found him and told him that the magic that the Legionnaires had used to win the war was now turning them into monsters. Their Lord General, Jefferson, had promised to cure them from the curse if only they could meet to him at their old castle in Orska. Myri and Rane had trekked halfway across the country to get there—only to find it'd been a lie.

The Lord General had planned it all. He'd wanted to

create a secret army with supernatural powers, killers loyal only to him.

He'd tried to make Rane one of his monsters, but Rane had fought back, resisted. But Myri ... Myri had already been on the edge when they'd arrived at the castle. It hadn't taken much to turn her. To make her one of them. Tainted.

Once, Myri had been one of the deadliest warriors he'd ever fought beside. Now she was a monster with inhuman speed and strength, and Rane had no idea how to stop her.

Rane tried to move, couldn't, and slumped back on the ground, face down in his own blood. He caught his reflection in *Kibon*'s blade, mad-eyed, a black mark on his forehead. Had he been shot?

He pulled *Kibon* tighter to him, both hands wrapped around its hilt. Pulled the magic from it as if he was breathing air into his lungs. Energy rippled through his body, pushing back the fog, softening the pain, healing his wounds.

Myri—beautiful Myri—tutted. "I told you it'd not kill him."

Gregor, another Legionnaire—another comrade lost to the taint, sat on the bed, reloading a pistol. He looked over at Rane and laughed. "I know but it was fun to try."

"Bastard," spat Rane.

"Language," rebuked Gregor. "Remember, you're an officer."

Gritting his teeth, Rane managed to push himself up and get his legs back under him. He swayed for a moment as he sat up, but *Kibon* sang with power, demanding revenge, filling Rane with all the magic it contained, healing him. Making him strong again.

He staggered to his feet.

Gregor raised the pistol once more. "Try and stay dead

this time." He pulled the trigger and the gun spat its bullet. But Rane wasn't going to get shot a second time. He swerved, and the bullet smashed into the wall behind him.

The Tainted weren't the only dangerous ones in the room. Not the only one with powers.

Rane came at them, closing the gap in a couple of strides. He was fast, faster than any normal man could hope to be. Faster than they thought he'd be. He brought *Kibon* down in a sweeping arc. Gregor threw his pistol to one side and tried to draw his own sword—but he was too slow, too late.

Rane put all his strength into the blow. *Kibon*'s razor sharp edge did the rest. He barely felt any resistance as it entered Gregor's shoulder, none as it carved a path through the Legionnaire's body before slipping out just above the hip. Blood sprayed and splashed, so red against the stone. More energy rushed through Rane as *Kibon* fed on the man's soul. The last of his pain disappeared.

A shadow crossed his peripheral vision. Myri hissed as she lunged at Rane's heart, and he only just managed to stop her thrust in time.

He went low, aiming for Myri's leg, but her black blade interrupted *Kibon*'s path. She countered with impossible speed, driving her sword up, hoping to split Rane in two, forcing him to flip out of the way. Rane struck back, swinging *Kibon* at her neck. This time it was Myri who skipped back, trying to gain some space. Holding her sword horizontally across her chest, she retreated into the center of the room, and Rane followed.

He moved to the left, hoping to get behind her guard. Myri countered by twisting her body so she faced him side-on. Rane feinted a strike at her head, drawing her attention, then switched, aiming for her stomach. She dropped her sword down over her shoulder, taking the sting out of his blow but not doing enough to stop him from drawing blood. Even though it was just a scratch, the sight of it made Rane smile.

Perhaps he could win this.

Myri launched a series of overhead strikes, fueled by rage and hatred. He blocked them, feeling the force of each one vibrate through *Kibon* and into his arms. She came again, but Rane stepped out the way of her and slashed at her back as she passed. She screamed as his sword bit deep, and Rane felt another pulse of pleasure as *Kibon* absorbed her blood.

Rane pressed the advantage, but Myri's leg shot out, slamming into his chest, and sent him flying. He bounced back to his feet quickly, fueled by Kibon's magic, and blocked Myri's next blow. Steel sang against steel as their swords clashed. Her movements grew faster and faster until they fought in a blur. Her sword was everywhere, blocking, striking, slashing. She was tireless, and it was taking all Rane had to keep up with her.

Myri caught Rane on the forearm, cutting deep, and then she sliced a gash across his chest. She slammed her elbow into Rane's jaw, and he only just blocked the sword strike that followed. Her sword skittered along *Kibon*'s edge, sparks flying as the two blades kissed, drawing them together. Rane slammed his head into hers, crunching her nose. As she staggered back, Rane drove his sword into her gut.

Her scream came straight from the underworld, harsh and hateful. She punched Rane, sending him sprawling. He was back on his feet in an instant, only too aware his sword was in her and not in his hand. All she had to do was walk away, take it out of his reach, take it more than twelve feet from him, and all its magic would be undone. The wounds it had healed would reopen. He would die in seconds.

But Myri's black blade was inches from his face, holding him at bay. With her other hand, she reached for *Kibon* and dragged it slowly out of her. Blood gushed from her stomach as she threw the sword to the floor. She pressed her hand against the wound, wavering on her feet, but she never once took her eyes off Rane, not giving him a chance to reach *Kibon*.

"This isn't the end of it," she spat. For a moment Rane thought she was going to attack again, but she raced towards the window and, before he had a chance to react, threw herself through it. Glass shattered in a thousand directions as she disappeared into the night. Glass tinkled like falling rain against the ground below when Rane reached the window.

Myri had to be dead.

A fall like that would kill anyone—even a Legionnaire.

But no body lay on the ground below.

Rane staggered back, reeling from the madness of it all. How had she survived? How had she escaped?

"I will find you," whispered Rane. "I promise I'll put your soul to rest."

He owed his friend that much. Once he'd dealt with Jefferson and the other monsters in Orska, he'd hunt Myri down—and kill her.

Now

2
─────────

Rane

Nathaniel Rane crashed through the trees, not daring to slow down or stop. Not if he wanted to stay alive. He chanced a glance back, saw the flickering torch lights of his pursuers. So many of them and getting closer by the second. All with swords in their hands and hate in their hearts. Hate for him.

"Where are you, monster?" The high priestess's shrill voice cut through the darkness. "You can't hide from Odason's Children!"

Odason's Children. They were the All-Father's most blessed, His chosen, or so they'd have the world believe. Rane knew different. They were the Soldiers of the Inquisition, killers one and all, happy to burn anyone for just thinking impure thoughts, and more than happy to torture and kill a Legionnaire. The more bloody the work, the more holy they found it.

They had hounds with them too, snapping and growling, straining against their leashes, Rane's scent in their keen noses.

The night was against him. Unseen roots threatened to trip him. Branches lurched out of the darkness to slash at his face. Even the muddy ground sucked at his feet, draining his energy and slowing him down.

Rane staggered to a stop against a tree, breath rasping, and watched his pursuers continue to spread out through the woods. The Inquisition had been on his trail for days now, ever since he'd been recognized in a small town farther north. They'd chased him relentlessly through the Ascalonian countryside, giving him no time to rest or eat. Now, cold and exhausted, he had no idea how much longer he could stay ahead of them.

The trail of torchlights spread both east and west, forming a skirmish line as far as he could see in either direction. Hundreds of them. If he wasn't careful, they'd close around him like a fist, until he wouldn't be able to wriggle free.

There was no more time to rest. He adjusted his pack on his back and reached up to grasp the hilt of the sword next to it. A thrum of energy passed through him, enough to waken his mind and pump enough blood through his legs to get moving once more. With nothing to eat for days and only snatched mouthfuls of water when he could find it, his sword's power was all that was fueling him, but even *Kibon*'s magic was dwindling. It had been months since the sword had tasted blood. Soon its charge would be as exhausted as he was.

And that was a good thing, he told himself. Better to die human than die a monster.

The sword growled in his mind. It didn't agree. It didn't want to be trapped in its scabbard while Rane ran like a dog.

Especially when all he had to do was unsheathe it and his problems would be gone—the cold, the tiredness, and, of course, his pursuers. How easy would it be to cut them all down? To send them off to meet their god they cared so much about?

Kibon would make short work of them.

Rane could be free.

If he killed them all.

He stopped, and his hand reached for *Kibon*'s hilt once more. He could almost taste the joy that would bring. After all, how many of his comrades had the Inquisition killed across the five nations? How many of his fellow Legionnaires had they executed in front of jeering mobs?

To kill them would be justice. It would be right.

No.

He shook the thought from his mind and forced his legs to move once more. Forced himself to run. He wasn't the killer the sword wanted him to be. He wasn't the monster the Inquisition believed him to be.

Not yet.

He knew the sword couldn't be trusted. No matter its name, it didn't offer him hope. It promised only damnation. Like so many of his friends and comrades in the Legion of Swords.

There was a good reason why he was hunted, why his friends had died.

He was cursed.

Cursed by Babayon.

The mage had fused the souls of every Legionnaire to their swords in the final days of the great war against the Rastaks and their demon allies. It had been a desperate gamble to stop the five nations from being destroyed. And it worked.

Babayon's magic had made each member of the Legion stronger, faster, and all but impossible to kill. Since that fateful night, Rane had been stabbed in the gut, in the chest, shot in the head, and much more besides, and yet the wounds had healed every time.

With their new strength, the Legionnaires had waded in amongst their enemy and slaughtered them, winning the war and bringing peace back to the five nations of Ascalonia, Fascaly, Nortlund, Naijin, and the Souska Islands.

But little did any of the Legionnaires know at the time, there was a terrible price to be paid for such power. The swords drained the souls of those they killed and, as a result, corrupted the Legionnaires until they, too, became monsters far worse than any they'd fought in the war.

The taint was marked by a growing black stain across the steel of the Legion swords until they were darkness made tangible. Once the blade was black, the Legionnaire was lost. The curse had consumed his best friend, Marcus, and his comrade and former lover, Myri, and so many others Rane cared about.

He'd been lucky. He'd discovered the consequence of Babayon's magic before it was too late. His sword was blemished but not black. If *Kibon* wasn't fed blood, then the curse wouldn't progress. If it wasn't fed, its hold on him weakened. If it wasn't fed, he had a chance to find a cure. Rane had not used the sword in combat since he'd killed the Lord General and the Tainted at the castle in Orska.

And his sword didn't like that.

Kibon wouldn't fall silent. It talked to him constantly, tempting him and urging him to let loose, to kill, to welcome its power. It knew his weaknesses and niggled away at them, so much so that, on occasion, Rane thought he would go mad.

He'd destroy the damned thing if he could, but that, too, was impossible. The moment the blade was broken, its magic would come undone and all his old wounds would reopen. He couldn't be more than twelve feet away from the sword if he wanted to stay alive.

As much as he hated it, Rane was stuck with *Kibon* until he found Babayon and forced the mage to reverse the magic. Then he'd save himself and any other Legionnaires who had yet to fall to the curse.

Of course, he had to live long enough to find the mage. And that was starting to feel like an impossible task.

Rane glanced back. The torches were getting close. Far too close.

"Stop running, monster," shouted the priestess. "There is no escape from Odason's wrath."

The hounds grew louder, full of excitement at closing in on their prey.

"This way!" shouted a man. "He's this way!"

The zealots were only fifty yards away, through the trees. They barged through the bushes, snapping branches, not caring about the noise they made. They hacked at the undergrowth with their swords, carving a way towards Rane.

Something hurtled towards him, small, low to the ground. Rane turned as it leaped, got his arm up as he saw the flash of teeth, heard the snarl. Memories of demons flashed through his mind—and all the fear that came with them.

But it was only a dog.

The hound bit down on Rane's arm. Its teeth pierced his sleeve, sinking into flesh. He snatched at the knife that he kept tucked away on his belt at the small of his back and stabbed the hound in the side. Once, twice, three times. Hot blood gushed over his hand, and then the pain in his arm was gone. The hound fell to the ground.

Ran stumbled forward, hoping the bites weren't serious, that he wasn't losing too much blood. The sword would heal him—but it needed time. He couldn't get caught. He...

The ground sloped suddenly, throwing Rane off-balance. He went down, slipping and sliding in mud. He snatched out with a hand to steady himself but found nothing to grasp but more dirt. He tumbled, hit his head against a rock, knocked his hip against a tree stump.

The mud carried him down, faster and faster, flipping him around, then knocking him this way, then that. He saw a root, grabbed at it, got a hold and felt his shoulder wrench as his momentum stopped for a single heartbeat—then the root snapped and he was falling again, bouncing and battered, picking up speed. He tried to dig his feet in, clawed with his fingers, but he kept going, kept sliding.

The ground disappeared. Rane had a heartbeat to realize there was nothing beneath him when he dropped.

3

Rane

Water smashed into Rane's back, knocking the air from his lungs, swallowing him up, ice-cold, black as death. He went down, down, bubbles all around him, a fading light above. He had no idea how deep the water was or if he even had the strength to swim up.

Even *Kibon* felt heavy on his back, pulling him down as he flapped about in the water. His ass touched the bottom. Rane got his feet under him, pushed up and swam. One heartbeat, two heartbeats and his head broke the surface.

He gulped air, went back down, then back up. He saw the river bank, kicked out and started swimming out of pure instinct. He would've dumped his pack if he didn't think he'd drown trying to get it off his back. Instead, he floundered through the water, getting colder by the second, his clothes and his pack becoming heavier by the moment.

His boot scraped the ground just as he was starting to sink again, and Rane stumbled forward. Somehow it was even colder out of the water, but he waded ashore. Once on dry land, he sank to his knees, gasping and shivering and utterly spent.

He reached up over his shoulder and touched *Kibon*, grateful he'd not lost the sword in the river. A slither of magic ran up his arm. It stopped the bleeding from the dog bite and took the edge off his battered body, but that was all.

I must be fed if you want more, growled the sword.

High above Rane, the dogs howled and barked, more frenzied by the moment. They had his scent and wanted his blood. Soon they'd find a way down to the river.

He had to keep moving.

Rane got to his feet, staggered on. He splashed through the shallows, letting the water wash his scent away. There was no need to be quiet.

He just had to get away.

Kibon told him he was a fool. Running was weakness. A true warrior would stand and fight. A real man would show the Inquisition the folly of pursuit.

But Rane didn't listen to his sword and its lies. Killing had too terrible a price.

Instead, he shivered and shook as he made his way along the river, not even sure where he was or what direction he was going, not caring as long as it was away from the bloody dogs and the Soldiers of the Inquisition.

He ducked under an overhanging branch. Wet leaves brushed his face as he pawed them out of the way. His ears rang with barking and shouting from above. At least they were up there and he was—

Something smashed him in the face, knocking him off his feet and onto his ass.

He looked up, dazed, the world spinning, blood running from his nose, and saw four of Odason's Children standing over him. One had a long staff in his hands and a smug grin on his face.

"Don't move, monster," said Smug.

All four of them looked identical, their heads shaved almost to the bone, their white, holy robes concealing armor. No one went up against a Legionnaire with just cloth over their heart. Smug's friends carried double-edged swords with the confidence of veterans and a zealot's belief.

"Mother Hilik said we'd get lucky down here," said the second man. His nose had been broken at some point and not properly set. They stepped forward, shifting weight as they prepared to fight. "They always run down the rivers."

Rane held up both hands. "I don't want to fight you. Just let me get to my feet."

"Demon," spat the third man. A scar ran down the left side of his face from brow to chin. "Don't think you can trick us."

"I say we just kill him now," said the fourth, lingering behind the others, less conviction in his voice.

"I don't want to hurt you," said Rane—though *Kibon* thought otherwise. The sword wanted blood. It wanted death. Rane could feel the fierce longing building inside the weapon, feel the power the blade promised. "I've done nothing wrong. Let me pass."

"We'll let Odason decide your innocence," said Smug. He shifted the long staff to one hand and delved into a bag on his hip. He pulled out shackles and chain. "Put these on, monster."

"No," said Rane.

"Do as he says," said Broken Nose, stabbing his sword forward.

Smug and Broken Nose stayed where they were while Scarface and Cautious splashed through the water to his rear.

Smug rattled the shackles once more. "Put them on—or face Odason's justice."

Kibon burned on Rane's back. It knew how to escape. It knew what to do. Images flashed through his mind. He could see the sword's arc, cutting through them one by one. Their blood joining the river's current as *Kibon* cleaved a path through them.

But Rane would not become a monster. His head dropped, shoulders sagged. "Give me the chains."

Smug looked to Broken Nose for a moment and got a nod back. "Watch him," said Smug, but his grin grew even wider now he knew he'd won. He stepped forward, his long staff pointing straight up as he offered the shackles and chains with the other hand. "Put your hands out."

Rane did as he was told, offering them just above his head, wrists together. Smug had to take another step forward and rattled the shackles in Rane's face.

Rane grabbed them and yanked the man forward, throwing Smug off-balance and over his shoulder. Rane was on his feet a second later and stamped down. His boot smashed into Smug's teeth, putting an end to his smile once and for all.

Rane moved on, swinging the shackles hard and fast. Broken Nose tried to stab at Rane, but the iron manacles were quicker. They cracked into his jaw, spinning him sideways, sword flying from his hand as he collapsed in the shadows.

Rane swapped the chain to his left hand and snatched up Broken Nose's sword out of the water as he turned to face

Scarface and Cautious. They stared at him wide-eyed and open-mouthed as their friends lay at his feet.

"Monster," said Scarface. "Monster."

"No one's dead yet," said Rane. "You can still run."

Kibon hissed on his back. This wasn't what it wanted. It had no time for mercy. *Kill them.*

"Monster!" screamed Scarface and charged at Rane. Rane flung the chain out like a whip, the end snaking around Scarface's legs. With a yank, the soldier went down hard. He managed to raise this head in time for Rane to kick him unconscious.

Cautious was smarter, waiting for his friend to go down, rushing in the moment Rane turned his back. Rane dropped the shackles as he turned and brought his borrowed sword up. The two blades clashed, steel sliding against steel, locking together. They pushed against each other, noses almost touching. Cautious grabbed Rane's sword arm, tried to pull it to one side. Rane punched him with his left hand, good and hard in his side, feeling ribs break despite the man's chainmail. Cautious grunted in pain, eyes bulging, and Rane struck again for good measure. The tension in the two swords slackened at once, and Rane hooked the soldier's blade away from his hand, leaving Cautious weaponless.

"No!" spluttered Cautious.

"Yes," said Rane. He smashed the pommel of his sword into the man's nose.

Rane stood over the felled men, chest heaving, throat raw, anger boiling. *Kibon* hissed in his ear, adding fuel to the fire raging inside Rane. *Kill them. A dead enemy is one less to worry about. Better to be safe than leave them alive.*

But Rane wasn't the man his sword wanted him to be.

Slowly, he became aware of the rest of the world again,

the shouts, the barks, and Mother Hilik's shrieks. Four downed men didn't mean his troubles were over.

He threw the borrowed sword into the stream and set off once more, moving quickly, watching for more traps as he went, eager to get away from this Mother Hilik and the rest of her Soldiers of the Inquisition.

The darkness swallowed him up as he moved farther away from the shouting and the dogs' barking. Cold water soaked through his boots, but he cared not. It washed his scent away too.

Rane followed the river as it twisted and turned through the countryside until it found another river to merge into. Rane stuck to the banks where the water was only up to his knees. He had to go slower now, wading, avoiding any splashing as best he could. His pursuers were no more than a distant clamor, but he still didn't feel safe.

Until he could find a cure, he would always be the hunted.

4

Sarah

Sister Sarah looked down at her four brothers, Harold, Roon, Jonas, and David, with a mixture of pity and contempt. They had been tested by their encounter with the monster and were found wanting. How could the men's faith have been so obviously weak? How could they wear the cloth of the Inquisition and claim to be Odason's Children if they did not believe enough to defeat one monster?

The four men knelt with their heads in prayer, surrounded by ten of their brothers and sisters, still bearing the bruises and cuts of their encounter with the monster. Occasionally, one would look up, see the array of swords pointed at them, and then return to his prayers.

The sun had risen by the time Mother Hilik arrived. Birds sang under a glorious blue sky and leaves rustled in the autumn breeze. It was a beautiful day for bloody deeds.

"My sons, my daughters," said Mother Hilik, her thumbs hooked into her belt. A tall, broad woman, her head was shaved on each side, like all priestesses, the skin of her scalp tattooed with sun rays that spread down her neck. Chainmail glinted at her throat, but her armor was covered by the heavy white robes they all wore. Her sword, *Odason's Wrath*, hung at her hip, and Sister Sarah felt a touch of fear at the sight of it. She'd seen many die on that sword's sharp edge.

"Mother Hilik," chorused the Soldiers of the Inquisition together, and they bowed their heads.

They moved to one side so she could stand before the shamed men. "It is a dark day indeed that finds us here," said Mother.

Harold was the only one of the four to look up. Blood was crusted around the nostrils of his broken nose, and his eyes had started to blacken. "Please, Mother Hilik, we did our best."

"You encountered the monster, did you not?" said Mother.

"We did," said Harold.

"And yet you did not capture the monster."

"We tried. As Odason is our witness, we tried."

Mother backhanded Harold across the cheek and sent him sprawling in the dirt. "Do not say His name. You have lost *that* right."

Harold had the sense, at least, to hang his head in shame at Mother's words.

Mother turned her back on the four men. "Have we found the monster's tracks?"

Brother Norris stepped forward, bowed. "He ... it used the water to evade the dogs. We believe it reached the main river nearby, the river Tylin. Our brothers and sisters are searching the banks in both directions, but we have yet to pick up the monster's trail."

"Send word to every village or town near enough to be at risk. Warn them the monster is loose and tell all to be extra vigilant," said Mother.

"As you wish," said Brother Norris.

Mother held up a finger. "And remind them that the penalty for harboring a monster is death by burning. Anyone or any place tainted by the monster's presence will be purified."

Sister Sarah winced at that command, then prayed no one saw her weakness. She understood the necessity of putting tainted places to the torch, but it was not something she was ever in a hurry to see again. Her own village had been purified by fire when she was a young girl, and she still felt the loss of her friends and family.

Harold, Roon, Jonas, and David heard Mother's words and understood what it meant for them.

"Mother, please," said Harold, raising his hands in supplication.

"We are still pure," begged Jonas.

"We will catch the monster, Mother," said Roon. "Give us another chance."

Mother ignored them. She turned her gaze to Sarah. "Prepare the pyres and be quick about it. I wish to be gone from this place by noon."

David lunged forward on his knees and grasped the hem of Mother's robes. "Mercy, Mother—" His smashed teeth garbled the rest of his words.

Odason's Wrath was out in a flash. David screamed, his severed hands on the ground before him. He stared at the bloody stumps of his arms, whimpering. Mother turned to a nearby brother as she flicked the blood off the edge of her sword. "Cauterize the wounds. I will not have him bleed to death before we can cleanse his soul before Odason."

Two soldiers snatched up David and dragged him away, kicking and screaming. The three remaining brothers sobbed on their knees, whispering prayers to Odason even though they knew He was even less merciful than Mother.

Sister Sarah bowed. "With your leave, Mother."

"Go," replied Mother. "You have work to do."

Sarah left and set about calling other brothers and sisters to help. Four stakes were driven into the open ground, close enough that the brothers would be touching shoulder to shoulder once they were bound in place. Firewood was gathered and stacked around the base of each stake, then layered high until it was enough to get a good fire going, enough for the flames to catch on flesh.

Brother Finn caught Sarah's eye, and he waved her over with the slightest of gestures. She went to him. "Yes, Brother?"

He looked around but no one was close enough to hear. "Should we dampen some of the wood, Sister?"

Sarah looked at Finn. She'd not served with him before, so she could not be sure of his motives. To dampen the wood would produce more smoke. More smoke would kill the condemned faster. It would be a mercy. However, if she agreed and he then told Mother what she'd done...

"No, Brother Finn. Our brothers must stand judgement before Odason. He will judge their strength and see if they are worthy of a place in His golden halls or whether they must spend eternity in Heras's kingdom."

"Yes, Sister. As you wish."

"No, Brother. I merely do Mother's biding. It is her wish and Odason's command that we follow."

Finn bowed, his cheeks red. "Of course, that... that is what I meant."

"Carry on," said Sarah. She watched the brother scuttle off. For a moment, she thought of mentioning his words to Mother but quickly dismissed the idea. To witness four of her fellow soldiers die was enough for one day.

Tired, she rubbed the stubble on her head. She'd hated her hair when she was younger—the other children would tease her for its flame-red color—but now she could barely remember what it looked like. It had been shaved for fifteen years now, and she doubted she'd even seen a mirror in that time either. To care about one's hair was vanity after all, and that was not something a Soldier of the Inquisition had need for.

Sarah glanced over at Mother. The woman stood to one side, her arms crossed, watching Odason's Children at work as they prepared to move on in their pursuit of the monster. Sarah hoped to one day have Mother Hilik's strength and resolve. The woman hadn't slept for at least a day and a night, and yet she still had boundless energy.

Once the pyres were ready, no time was wasted in bringing Harold, Roon, Jonas, and David out and binding them to the stakes.

Brother Nicolai waited with a burning torch while Mother stood in front of the condemned, oblivious to their cries and please. The rest of the Children lined up alongside and behind her.

Sarah wished she didn't have to watch, but this, too, was a test of faith, a reminder to be strong. Mother would not take kindly to any who might leave or look away. Sarah wished the condemned would show some measure of strength now, in their final moments. Odason was watching, and the brothers' shame would follow them for eternity.

But the question that always haunted her on such occasions—how brave would she be in their position?—came
back to her now. She wanted to believe she would be strong,
silent, accepting of her punishment, and happy that she
would, eventually, take a place by Odason's side in his great
halls. But the fear was always present—that she, too, would
cry, weep, and plead for mercy that would not come.

Sarah wished she'd wet the wood after all. For her own
benefit more than theirs. She didn't want to watch and listen
to them burn for a moment longer than she had to.

"Sister Sarah." Mother's voice rang out.

Sarah lifted her head. Mother hadn't moved, hadn't
taken her eyes off the men at the stakes. She wasn't looking
at Sarah. "Yes, Mother?"

"Take the torch from Brother Nicolai. You shall have the
honor of lighting the pyres."

"Yes, Mother." She stepped forward, heart racing. Was
Mother aware of her thoughts? Why had she been called
out? Every step was a conscious effort. She couldn't rush,
couldn't dawdle. Eyes were on her, judging her. She kept her
back straight and her chin up. She couldn't show weakness.

It seemed to take forever to reach Nicolai and take the
torch from him, avoiding his eyes as she did so. Out of
everyone there, he knew her best. He was her only friend
within the order. And she couldn't let him see her nerves.

With the torch in hand, she walked towards the
condemned. The flame danced in the breeze, warm against
her skin, but not as warm as it would be for Harold, Roon,
Jonas, and David.

"No, Sarah," called out Jonas. "Don't do this. I beg you."

"Odason the Mighty," called out Mother as Sarah passed
her. "Odason the Wise. Our All-Father. Cast your eye upon
us, your Children on earth."

Sarah walked on. She had to start on the left, with Harold. To do that, she had to walk past the other three.

"Please, we did no wrong," cried Roon. "No one could stop him. No one."

"Odason," continued Mother, "judge these four men. Look into their hearts as we test them with pain. If their faith in you is strong, then welcome them to your great halls with mead and venison. But if their faith is weak, then cast them from your door. Let their pain and suffering last an eternity in Heras's depths."

Roon shook against his bonds, weeping like a baby.

"Don't do this, Sarah," said Harold. "You don't have to do this."

Sarah stopped and looked Harold in the eye. "I do."

"No."

She placed the torch amongst the kindling of Harold's pyre, watched the flames rush from her torch to the wood. It took no time at all.

Sarah withdrew the torch, walked down to Roon, repeated the action. By the time she reached Jonas, Harold was screaming. By the time she reached David, Roon howled alongside Harold. The smell of roasting pork filled Sarah's nostrils, but she placed the torch into the pyre at David's feet.

She left the torch there and returned to her place in the ranks, the cries of the condemned filling her ears. Sarah was only vaguely aware of tears running down her cheeks, but she could not wipe them—that would bring attention to something most might not have noticed.

Sarah watched Mother Hilik instead, who stood unmoving, her face slightly raised to the heavens. There was a reason she was beloved of Odason. No one was as strong, as righteous, as Mother Hilik. Sarah wondered what thoughts went through her mind as she watched the fallen burn.

Even without wet wood, it didn't take long for the four men to die. Sarah doubted any of them would be dining with Odason that night, such were their screams.

At Mother Hilik's command, the audience dispersed and began their preparations to move on. Scouting parties still roamed in every direction looking for tracks, but Mother had prayed earlier and she wanted the main body of soldiers to head northeast after the monster. Wagons were loaded, armor, guns, and swords checked, horses and oxen readied.

Of course, Sarah had nothing of her own, like most of Odason's Children. A water skin hung across one shoulder, and her sword was sheathed against her left hip. Her meals would be provided to her when it was time to eat, and she would collect her bedroll from a wagon when it was time to sleep. She had no need for any possessions for they encouraged greed and jealousy, made a person weak to temptation and lust.

She'd just helped load another water barrel into a wagon when Brother Nicolai approached.

"Sister," he said. His blue eyes found hers, and she could've sworn she saw a twinkle in them— a hint of mischief.

"Brother." Sarah tried not to blush. This wasn't the place for such thoughts.

"Mother would like to see you."

Sarah gave a start at the message. "Is something wrong? Have I..." She stopped herself. Took a breath.

"Everything's fine," whispered Nicolai, his lips barely moving. His fingers brushed her hand, then he turned. "Follow me."

Sarah followed, reassured by his touch. Mother waited near the head of the column. She did not ride a horse or travel by wagon. She always walked with the rest of Odason's Children, no matter the terrain or the miles that needed to be traversed.

She smiled when she saw Sister Sarah. It was a tight smile, barely a flash of teeth against her dark skin. It had no warmth that Sarah noticed.

Sarah bowed. "Mother."

Mother looked past her, at Nicolai. "That will be all for now."

Sarah waited while Nicolai left, her emotions in turmoil. She didn't want to be alone with Mother. What had she done to be singled out in this way? Three times in one morning? Had someone spoken out against her? She had done nothing—said nothing—that she could think to warrant Mother's displeasure.

"You look worried, girl," said Mother, her voice soft. She stood so close that Sarah could see the small age lines around Mother's eyes and mouths. It made her look older and even more serious.

"I am just honored that you wish to speak to me, Mother," replied Sarah, grateful that her voice didn't crack.

"You did very well today. Many would've struggled with what I asked of you."

"It was Odason's will."

"Even so. How long have you been with the church?"

"Since I was four. Some fifteen summers."

"Where were you during the war?"

"In Chandra, Mother. I helped tend to the wounded."

"So you were there when the magic was done."

Sarah nodded. "I was. We all thought our victory was a miracle at first." She'd watched the Legion rush out and destroy the Rastak hordes, kill their monsters and save them all. "We should've known that it was falsely won."

"Evil often hides itself under the pretense of good. The Legion unleashed such magic that night that the world is still cracking under its weight. Odason's Children are all that prevents it from falling into eternal darkness."

"We shall not fail," said Sarah. Standing so close to Mother, Sarah's belief in her words was eternal, fierce. Mother made everything seem possible. Despite the fact that, for all the Inquisition labored, there were more and more monsters in the world each day.

"I have been a high priestess for longer than you have served the church," said Mother. "It was a role I did not want nor ask for, and yet I have never shirked from doing the duties given to me by the All-Father, no matter how distasteful they may appear to be."

"You are an inspiration to us all, Mother," said Sarah.

"Bless you, child, for your kind words." Mother reached out and tilted Sarah's chin so their eyes met. "Unfortunately, I am getting old and, though my mind is willing to serve Odason until the day I die, my body is not quite so capable."

"Mother, I—" Sarah was lost for words. Mother looked far from frail. She looked formidable.

"There is no need to flatter me. I speak the truth." Mother let go of Sarah's chin. "I believe in honesty at all times as Odason preaches—especially with myself. I have run our order, under Mother Singosta's guidance, for nigh on thirty years. But I am only mortal, and, one day, the All-Father will call me to His great halls. Now, what has this to do with you, you ask yourself?"

Sarah nodded. "I do."

"I need a successor, Sister Sarah. I need someone I can

train to one day wear the sun marks and lead Odason's Children as I have in our war against the ungodly."

Sarah held her breath.

"I want you to be the high priestess of our order after me," said Mother. "I know you do not want nor ask for this responsibility, but Odason Himself has chosen you. So, what say you? Will you accept this honor?"

"I do." The words floated free. How could she say no?

Mother smiled once more, her dark eyes fixed on Sarah. Like a snake before a mouse. "Excellent."

5

Rane

Rane crouched in the shadow of a tree and looked down at the inn. It sat on a well-traveled cross-road that brought traffic from the cities of Napolin, Grinon, Salor, and Linon to its doors. Not that there was anyone out on the roads now. Not after dark. Anyone with sense was behind four walls and a locked door or hunkered down for the night with wagons circled and guns at the ready.

Only outlaws and monsters roamed the night. Some would say Rane was both of those things.

It had been a week since he'd last seen any sign of the Inquisition, but that didn't make him any less wary. Their numbers only seemed to be growing as the state of the world got worse. Bracke, Jotnars, and Valkryn had become all too common a sight across the five nations, terrorizing communities and attacking travelers, and only the Inquisition had the will to hunt them down. But their favorite prey were still Legionnaires, Tainted or not, and Rane knew that Mother Hilik would not give up her pursuit of him.

So why was he thinking of going into an inn full of people? Better to stay out in the wilds and out of sight.

Rane's stomach growled in answer. It had been too long since he'd eaten a proper meal or had a proper night's rest. He needed both desperately.

The inn was worth the risk.

It was a decent size, big enough to have lodgings in addition to a common room to eat and drink in. The stables at the back were substantial too, large enough to take a coach party or two. In a way, that comforted Rane. The busier it was the better. It would be easier to hide in a crowd than if the inn only had one or two customers.

Yellow light spilled from the windows, and Rane could hear laughter drifting up the hillside. How long had it been since he'd heard someone laugh?

How long had it been since he'd laughed?

Back when Kara was alive?

He shook the thought from his head. There was no point dwelling on that now. On her. It changed nothing.

Rane took a deep breath and stood up. He checked that there was nothing about him that would reveal him to be a Legionnaire. His sword was wrapped up in some rags he'd found that disguised its distinctive shape. Someone might assume it to be a sword but no more than that. His pistols were in his pack. His Legionnaire's great coat was long gone, lost after the events at Orska.

The truth was, after months of being hunted, he looked nothing like the man who'd once commanded armies. As a Legionnaire, he'd always been meticulous about his appearance and keeping his uniform as spotless as the war allowed. Now his clothes were only fit for burning and his hair and beard unkempt.

And that was a good thing.

The noise and the heat hit Rane as he entered the inn with an almost physical force. The place was even busier than he'd expected, with some fifty to sixty people inside, and it made him pause for a moment, doubting his decision. Faces glanced his way as he loitered in the doorway, so he forced himself onward. The patrons turned back to their own conversations soon enough after they saw the long-haired stranger was no one of interest.

He made his way across the main eating and drinking area, observing the customers as he passed. There were people of all ages and nationalities enjoying the inn's hospitality. What looked like a family from Fascaly had the largest tables nearest the fire—a man with his wife and two teenage girls sat around one table, while four men who looked like their servants sat at the other. Rane also saw a Nortlunder or two elsewhere in the crowd. He'd not seen one since the war as they preferred to keep within their own borders. Some older men stood by the bar, most likely locals from the nearby farms, but there was certainly no one who would pose a threat to Rane that he could see.

Rane found an empty table in the far corner of the inn and sat down. He kept his head down and placed his sword and pack out of sight. He'd have preferred to sit nearer the fire, but, after weeks tracking through forests, he was just happy to be out of the cold and away from the wind. He had a price on his head after all.

A serving girl approached, unfazed by the long hair and untidy beard. "Can I get you something?"

"Some food, please, and some ale." His voice sounded

strange. He'd not spoken to anyone since he'd fought the soldiers on the river bank.

The girl arched an eyebrow. "It'll cost you half a bronze bit." It was a cynical look for one so young, but she already knew trust wasn't a thing to be taken for granted. A truth probably learned the hard way.

"Of course," Rane said with a smile and produced a full bronze coin. He flicked it on the table. She scooped it up in her hand before it had time to settle.

"I'll be back with your change. Food won't be long." She turned and headed back to the bar and the kitchens.

Rane sighed and closed his eyes, feeling the warmth working its way across his skin, tingling as it fought the entrenched chill. He was tired and ached from sleeping outdoors for so long. He was getting old for a life on the run.

A memory of a cottage by a stream flashed through his mind. A beautiful wife with a growing stomach. A different life—stolen. He opened his eyes, eager to banish those thoughts back to the recesses of his mind, but he was too slow. The old pain had reawakened. Worse than a thousand sword cuts. Kara. His only love.

It'd been six months since she'd died. Killed by bounty hunters after the reward on Rane's head. She'd been pregnant at the time, so he'd not just been robbed of her life. He could still remember their excitement at starting a family, the dreams they'd had in the beautiful cottage Rane had built.

His hand slipped to the chain on his wrist and Kara's locket. Rane rubbed the small silver disc with his thumb. It made him feel closer to her once more, as if some part of her spirit lingered within it.

Her death was something else for which he blamed

Babayon. It was the mage's actions—his magic—that had brought the bounty hunters to Rane's door.

Rane looked around the inn, as if he'd see the mage sitting at one of the tables. A foolish hope but a hope all the same. Even after all this time, Rane was sure he'd recognize the man in an instant. It was his eyes that Rane remembered most clearly, how the shadows never seemed to leave them and the sense he was looking straight through you.

Of course, the mage wasn't there amongst the traders, the hunters, the locals, and the travelers. He was far away and hidden for now.

Rane looked down at the scar that ran across his right palm, vivid white against dark, road-stained hands. His mark. They should've known such magic would demand a terrible price. They were fools to allow Babayon to fuse their souls with their swords.

You're a fool for wanting to stay a man, whispered *Kibon.*

Rane glanced down at the concealed sword. He could feel its hunger pulsating, its need to take lives. It didn't care if they were innocent or not. It just wanted souls. It wanted to turn Rane into a monster.

He couldn't let that happen.

A bowl was placed in front of Rane, bringing him back to the present. Half of his bronze coin was dropped next to it.

"Bear stew," said the serving girl before putting down a heel of bread and a jug next to it. "Bread. Ale."

"Thank you," Rane replied.

"Get you anything else?"

"I'd like a room if you have one—and a bath."

"That'll be a bronze and a half."

Rane produced another coin, put it next to the half she'd

returned. Again they vanished into her apron a heartbeat later.

"I'll let you know when it's ready." The girl raced back to the bar under the watchful eye of the man working behind it—her father, Rane thought, based on their similar features. He was a big man with arms the size of tree trunks and a scowl that looked engraved on his brow, but the love he had for his daughter shone through in the way he looked at her.

The food smelled wonderful, the meat dark in a rich gravy with the odd vegetable lurking within. Rane hadn't eaten a hot meal in days, and it took all his will power not to just shovel it down. Instead, Rane took small mouthfuls, savoring the flavor, taking his time and chewing slowly. Whoever had made the stew had added some delicate herbs and spices that elevated the quality of the food past what he'd come to expect in an out-of-the-way inn.

He used the bread to soak up the last spots of gravy, ensuring nothing was wasted, even licking his fingers after he'd finished. It never failed to amaze Rane the difference a full stomach could make. Warm, well-fed—he almost felt normal again. The ale was the right side of bitter, as well-brewed as the food was cooked.

Rane glanced over at the mountain of a man behind the bar. The innkeeper certainly knew what he was doing when it came to his food and drink. With talent like his, he could've made serious money on a well-travelled road. He was wasted here, hidden away in the middle of nowhere, but no doubt he had his reasons for where he'd chosen to settle down.

Rane stretched his legs out and wished he was closer to the fire. No matter. He had time to let the heat soak into his bones. He wasn't going anywhere for a while.

Rane finished his ale, and the girl appeared a second later. "Would you like another?"

"Please."

She had her hand on the mug when the door opened. The whole inn fell silent again as heads turned. This time everyone kept staring.

Three men stood in the doorway. Large fur cloaks covered their bodies and hoods hid their faces, but Rane knew trouble when he saw it. So did everyone else because the room remained silent, all eyes on the newcomers. Even the serving girl backed away towards the bar, holding Rane's mug tight to her chest, her eyes wide and bright.

Release me, hissed *Kibon*.

The men walked to a table occupied by a man and a woman near the fire. They stood over them, staring at the man and, when he looked away, they moved in even closer. One of the newcomers laid his hand on the woman's shoulder and let his fingers work their way down towards her breast, sucking his teeth as he did so. The man shot up from his chair, but the newcomer had a knife as big as his arm out and ready to greet him.

"Have the table," said the man, and the newcomers laughed while the man helped the woman from her seat.

"She might not fuck you now," said one of the newcomers as the pair shuffled away, faces flushed, the woman's hands clenching her skirt. "Especially now she knows real men are here." With the table to themselves, the newcomers shrugged off their cloaks and sat down.

Rane felt his pulse quicken.

They were Rastaks, his old enemy. They still wore scraps of their old armor, and there were plenty of weapons on show. Two of them had black circles tattooed around their eyes, each interrupted by a single line that ran down their foreheads to their jawline. It was the mark of Heras, the goddess of death, and only the deadliest Rastaks were allowed to bear her ink. The third, the one who'd confronted the man, bore no tattoo but had a mad gleam to his eyes all his own. He' shaved his head, leaving only a long strip interwoven with feathers, bones, and trinkets running down the middle. He looked around at the other patrons staring at him still and bared his teeth in response. It was an old Rastak challenge, and, to emphasis the point, he slammed the long knife into the table before he sat down.

"Ale," shouted one of the tattooed men, waving a hand at the bar. "Quick." He spoke the common tongue with a heavy accent, but the threat hidden in his words was plain to hear.

The man mountain behind the bar wiped his hands on his apron and glared at the three men. "I don't want no fighting in here. If that's what you want, then find somewhere else."

The Rastak laughed. "We just want a drink." He looked around the bar, trying to meet the eyes of anyone in there. Heads dropped in reply.

Shaved Head spat on the floor. "There's no one here that could fight us. You're all too weak and pathetic."

Rane kept his head down, his shoulders slumped, trying to look like the others as he fought the urge to confront the three men. He hated Rastaks. He'd spent far too many years fighting them from one end of the continent to the other. Too many of his friends had died by their swords and the demons they'd brought with them.

Kibon could feel his hatred too. It practically hummed with excitement at Rane's feet, full of longing. *They deserve to die. Kill them. Kill them now.*

It was easy to imagine the sword in his hand, hear its song as he pulled it from its scabbard. Oh, how easily he could kill the Rastaks. Three strokes of his fine sword and he could sleep well that night, knowing he'd rid the world of such scum.

He took a deep breath. That was *Kibon* influencing him. The Rastaks might have been his enemy in the war, but that fight had ended long ago. He had no reason to kill them. They were only after something to drink—just like Rane.

The innkeeper took the three jugs of ale over to the Rastaks himself, letting everyone see his full height. Rane wouldn't have been surprised if he had Nortlunder blood such was the size of the man. He slammed the ales down, then leaned on the table so the Rastaks could see the thickness of his arms. "Leave my guests alone or you'll have me to deal with."

Shaved Head picked up his jug and drank, never taking his eyes off the innkeeper. He drank until the jug was empty, then slammed it back on the table, just as loudly as the innkeeper had. "Another," he said and smiled.

"Show me your money," said the innkeeper.

One of the black eyes threw a handful of coins on the table.

The innkeeper looked down. "Some of these have got blood on them."

"Do you care?" asked Shaved Head.

The innkeeper hesitated for a moment, glaring, but then he scooped up the coins as quick as his daughter. The Rastaks laughed as he made his way back to the bar.

The serving girl brought over another jug of ale to Rane. "Sorry about them."

"Rastaks come here often?" asked Rane.

"Once in a blue moon. There's always trouble at some point. Da normally can handle them though." She sighed.

"Your room's ready if you want to go up and get away from them."

The Rastaks' laughter grew louder, and people from other tables were starting to head upstairs or make for the door. "You'll not have any business if everyone leaves," said Rane.

"Better that than dead customers."

"Tell your da that if he needs any help, just ask. I've dealt with Rastaks plenty of times before." The moment he said the words, he regretted it. He was supposed to keep a low profile. Offering to fight Rastaks was hardly that. But he also knew trouble when he saw it, and he knew he wouldn't be able to stay out of it if the Rastaks were itching for a fight.

"You fought in the war?"

Rane nodded.

She glanced back at the bar. "So did Da. He was at Candra near the end. Me and Ma never thought he was going to make it back to us."

"They were bad days."

"Aye—so Da says. " She paused. "I'll tell him what you said. My name's Lisa by the way."

"Nathaniel," replied Rane.

"Enjoy your ale, Nathaniel," said Lisa.

Rane watched her walk back to the bar and speak to her Da. He looked over at Rane while she spoke, and the two men exchanged nods. Rane settled in to watch and wait.

It was late enough that many of the patrons slipped away to wherever they were sleeping that night, while the Rastaks told war stories in their own tongue. Rane seemed to be the only customer who understood the language. He did his best to ignore it. Most of it was just drunken soldier talk and a lot of false bravado. They blamed their army's defeat on everyone but themselves.

It was only when they talked about their great leader, Mogai, that Rane started paying attention. Back at Orska, Jefferson had claimed Mogai was alive and reassembling his army. That was the Lord General's justification for condoning the magic that was corrupting his Legionnaires. Jefferson wanted monsters to fight monsters.

Apparently the dark-eyed Rastaks had heard Mogai was back too. "We should go home," said one. "Rejoin the army."

"I'm not going back to die for another's man ego," sneered Shaved Head. "And from what I hear, he's not the man he used to be. He's already lost control of the demons that Heras gave him. The Bracke are running wild and growing in number by the day. Even the Jotner have had enough and returned to the mountains. If we couldn't win with their help, how are we going to win without them? No, better we stay here and rob these fools."

"Are you sure?" asked the other dark eye.

"Look at them. Fat and lazy with gold in their pockets," said Shaved Head. "They won't even put up a fight when we take their women. Why travel north for Mogai's promises when we take all we want here?"

The others toasted him with their ale jugs and slapped Shaved Head on the back.

The Fascalian family had enough of their noise and, with a word from the father, all four stood up to leave.

Shaved Head had other ideas. He grabbed the father's arm as they passed the Rastaks' table. He nodded at the man's wife and children and sucked his teeth. "How much for your women?"

The man tried to pull his arm free but the Rastak's grip was too strong. "Leave me alone," the Fascalian said loudly, as if that would make a difference.

It didn't. "I give you a silver coin each for the young ones.

The old hag I take for free. She is only good for satisfying my horse."

"How dare you," said the Fascalian, trying and failing to free his arm.

Two of the man's servants stepped forward to help, but the other Rastaks stood and showed their weapons before they could take two steps. The servants stopped.

Pick me up. Free me, urged *Kibon.*

No, Rane wasn't going to get involved.

Shave Head pulled the Fascalian closer. "I'll give you two silver coins and your life. Take my offer before I decide not to be so generous."

"Oi," shouted the innkeeper, coming around the bar, a cudgel in his hand. "I warned you."

Shaved Head sent the Fascalian sprawling as he, too, stood. The scrap of the chair legs on the floor echoed around the inn. "And your daughter? How much for her?"

"Why you—" The innkeeper rushed over, cudgel raised.

Shaved Head snatched his knife from the table and readied himself for the Innkeeper's attack.

He didn't see Rane come up behind him, *Kibon* in hand but still in its steel scabbard. Rane brought the sheathed weapon down on Shaved Head's wrist. The bone broke on impact with a loud crack. The knife went flying as Rane scooped the Rastak's legs from under him. He hit the floor hard, and Rane smacked *Kibon*'s pommel in the middle of his forehead. Shaved Head didn't move after that.

One of the Black Eyes roared as he turned on Rane. *Kibon* hissed free of its scabbard, eager to taste blood, but Rane stopped the stroke an inch from the Rastak's throat.

The man froze, his eyes fixed on the mottled steel before him.

"I suggest you take your friend and leave," said Rane. "No one wants to see you die in here."

The Rastak stared at Rane, panting in rage as he tried to work out if he could kill the man before him.

"You heard the man," shouted the innkeeper. He pointed at the door with his cudgel. "Get out of here."

Kibon lingered at the black eye's throat. Rane held the blade rock steady despite the urgings from the sword to take the Rastak's life. He kept his eyes fixed on the Rastak's, waiting for the first sign that the man was dumb enough to attack. "Don't do it."

"I know what you are," said the Rastak, curling his lip.

"Then you know you can't beat me. I'm offering you your life. Take it."

The Rastak glanced at his friend, got the slightest of nods back and the fight went from both of them. "We go," said the one facing Rane.

"Good choice," said Rane, but he didn't lower *Kibon*. He could feel the sword's fury in his hand. Yet again, this was not the outcome it wanted.

The dark-eyes picked up their cloaks and then their friend and dragged him out of the inn. The innkeeper went to the door and bolted it behind them as quick as he could. He walked slowly back to the bar then, filled a jug with ale and drank it down in one. Once the jug was empty, he carefully placed it on the bar. Only then did he look up and catch Rane's eye.

"Thanks for your help. Three of them might've been too much for me on my own." He grinned and let out a long sigh.

"I'm glad I could help." Rane already had *Kibon* back in its sheath, but it was all too late. He'd drawn it without thinking. Everyone had seen the sword. The Rastaks wouldn't be the only ones who knew what he was. Someone there could tell the Inquisition. What a fool he was. With the inn locked up for the night, at least no one would leave before morning. He was safe until then.

"Your room is on me tonight," said the innkeeper. "I'll have Lisa get your bath ready."

Rane nodded. "Thank you."

Once the innkeeper returned to the bar, the Fascalian father approached. He gave a slight bow, nervous eyes darting everywhere, and there was a flash of white teeth through his black beard. "I just want to add my thanks."

"No need," said Rane. He sat back down at his table and placed *Kibon* at his feet. He wished he could cover it again but that would have to wait. He could still feel the tingle of the hilt in his hand, the power it promised. By the Gods, he wanted to hold it again.

"Can I buy you a drink at least?"

Rane shook his head. "I'm calling it a night—but thank you for the offer."

"You just passing through?" asked the man.

"Why do you ask?"

The man quickly held up his hands. "Didn't mean no offense. It's just that me and my family ..." he glanced back at his wife and daughters, "... we're heading up to Napolin, and I was wondering if you were heading that way too. If you are, and fancy some company, you could travel with us. We could do with someone to look out for us. The roads are dangerous these days and the men I have ... well, you've seen for yourself how useless they are. I'd pay you for your time, of course."

Rane looked at the man, wondering if there was more to his offer now he'd seen Rane's sword, some trap perhaps, a way to earn the Inquisition's reward, but he didn't look like he had that sort of cunning. "Why are you going to Napolin?"

The man pulled a chair over and sat down at Rane's table without asking, then realized what he'd done. "Do you mind ...?"

"Sure."

The man held out a hand. "My name is Christoph."

Rane shook it. "Nathaniel."

"I was born in Napolin. Most of my family are still there. I moved south before the war, set up a trading company in Salvator, got married, had a family." Christoph shrugged. "But the war ... and everything since ... We thought it best—safer—to move back home and be with my family. Work with them. The city has its high walls and the river and the sea to protect it. Maybe they'll keep the monsters out."

"Long journey to get there," said Rane.

"And dangerous. Tonight's not the first time we've had some sort of trouble. Before, my men did their jobs and we passed on without any real problems. But now, I think, things will be worse." Christoph took a deep breath. "Someone told us there are packs of Bracke roaming the Steppes now. It's probably a rumor but ..." He held up both hands.

"You have guns?"

"Two of my men do. A rifle and a pistol and some ammunition."

"Hopefully the number of Bracke have been exaggerated," said Rane. "If that's the case, and your men are good shots, you should be fine."

"I would feel happier if you were to join us," said Christoph.

"I'm sorry. I prefer my own company."

The man looked crestfallen. "I understand. I'm sorry to have bothered you."

"You didn't, Christoph. Have a good night."

"You also." The man returned to his family with a shake of his head.

In another life, perhaps, Rane would've helped him, but to travel with people was too risky a choice, even if they did have good intentions.

He picked up his sword and pack and headed up to his room. A bed sat in one corner and a bath in the other. Steam rose invitingly from the water.

Rane bolted the door shut, placed his pack on the floor and *Kibon* on the bed. Staring at it, he replayed the encounter with the Rastaks over again in his mind. He'd just acted on instinct. Truth was he was disappointed the Rastaks had backed down. He'd wanted to fight, wanted an excuse to kill them. At the time, he'd not even thought about the danger that would've posed to his soul.

Still staring at the sword, Rane undressed and climbed into the bath, letting its warmth embrace him.

He closed his eyes.

You can't fight me forever, whispered *Kibon. You can't stop your destiny.*

6

Rane

R ane was up and dressed while the new day was still only a distant hint away. The bath had been wonderful, but the bed had proven too uncomfortable after so long sleeping on the open ground or in a pile of hay. In the end, he'd slept on the floor between the bed and the window with a blanket pulled over him and *Kibon* tucked under his arm. Every creak and groan from the inn had him awake, listening to see if someone would try his door, but no one did.

Now it was time to go, before anyone else was awake.

He was just putting his jacket on when he heard a carriage approach at great speed. Rane peered out the window and saw a passenger stagecoach pulled by four horses. A driver and a guard sat in the driver's box, with two other guards riding their own horses. There was a dead body strapped to the back of the coach.

They pulled to a hard stop outside the inn, brakes squealing and horses protesting, and one of the riders was banging on the inn's door a heartbeat later, loud enough to wake everyone.

So much for Rane's quiet departure.

He thought about waiting in his room until he could slip away when the inn grew busier. But he could hear shouting downstairs from the new arrivals. Something had happened to the coach and Rane wanted to find out what.

He wrapped *Kibon* back up in the cloth he'd used to disguise its shape. It had felt so good in his hand the previous night. He could still feel the promise of violence thrumming through his veins. But there was no forgetting the sight of the black stains that ran along its length either. It had been six months since he'd last drawn it. Had the stains grown in that time? Was that even possible? It looked like at least half of the sword was blackened. He was halfway to becoming a monster.

By the time Rane made it downstairs, the common room was nearly full, people either drawn down by the ruckus of the coach's arrival or the smell of the food. Rane sat at the same table as the previous night and, once more, placed his sword and pack beside him.

The coach party had claimed a couple of tables near the fire, and an audience had formed all around them. Rane spotted Christoph and his wife amongst them. One of the arrivals, perhaps the driver, was talking in a rush while gulping down a jug of ale. "Didn't think we were going to make it," he said. "Not all of us did."

"Bracke," said another—one of the riders. "We tried shooting them, but there were too many. We just rode as hard as we could. They took down two other coaches and four guards."

"Saved our lives that did—they were too busy eating the others to worry about us," said the driver. "We're only here by Odason's good graces."

"And this was out in the Steppes?" asked Christoph.

"Yeah," said the driver. "About two days in. They were just hiding in the grass. Didn't see them before they were on us."

Christoph exchanged worried looks with his wife. "How many would you say there were?"

"Too many," said the driver. "Could easily have been a hundred of them."

"More," said one of his companions.

The news rippled through the inn, enticing quiet cries of shock and horror. Christoph had to be helped back to his table by his wife.

"Morning," said Lisa, appearing at Rane's table. "Did you come down to see what the fuss was all about?"

"Sounds like they had a bad journey," said Rane.

"Doesn't sound much better where they came from either."

"Where was that?"

"Napolin. They've got some news sheets with them, and it's all grim tidings."

"I wouldn't mind having a look, if that's possible," said Rane

"I'll bring one right over." She gave his shoulder a squeeze. "With some breakfast on the house."

"Thank you."

A few minutes later, Lisa brought Rane a plate of bacon and fresh bread along with the news sheet. It had been printed on cheap paper in Napolin a few days earlier. Half the ink had smudged where it had passed around plenty of people already, and, after a quick glance through it, Rane wished he hadn't asked to read it as well. Everything in it was bleak: the return of Mogai and what that meant for the five nations, executions of some noted Legionnaires by the inquisition, the increase of Bracke, Jotnar, and Valkryn, food shortages everywhere, interruptions to trade—it went on and on.

Rane was about to throw it away when an article caught his eye. It was about a series of murders in Napolin. The victims had all been mutilated before death, and some had been attacked in locked rooms many stories above the ground, with no sign of how the murderer had gained entrance. People were being advised to stay in after dark and make sure all doors and windows were locked.

He read the article again and again, knowing, somehow, that this was the work of a Tainted Legionnaire. Memories of the horrors his friend Marcus had committed came flooding back. He'd taken endless lives and mutilated the bodies before Rane and Myri had stopped him.

Rane ate his breakfast but he couldn't taste the food. His eyes kept drifting to the news sheet. In the end, he folded it up and placed it inside his pack.

He glanced around the inn and saw that Christoph was in a heated conversation with his family and retainers. They caught each other's eye and Rane gave a nod of acknowledgement.

It was enough of an invitation for the Fascalian to make his excuses to his party and come over. "Good morning, Nathaniel. Did you sleep well?"

"I did, thank you."

"Thank you again for last night. I couldn't help but think how badly things could've turned out if you'd not interceded."

Rane held up a hand. "It was nothing."

Christoph smiled awkwardly. "My offer still stands if you'd like to come with us to Napolin."

"You're still going?" asked Rane. "I heard what the driver said ..."

"We both knew there were Bracke on the Steppes."

"But in those numbers. It'll be suicide trying to get through."

Christoph ran his fingers through his beard. "Could I join you for a moment?"

"Please, sit."

Christoph settled into the chair opposite Rane. "I wasn't exactly honest with you last night."

"In what way?"

"Our reasons for going to Napolin. It's true my business in the south has suffered, but that's not why we're relocating." He glanced over at his family. When he turned back to Rane, there were tears in his eyes. "It's my daughter, Saphie. My youngest. She's dying."

"I'm sorry to hear that."

"She's only fifteen summers, but she's got a rare blood disease. Our family doctor didn't know what to do, and he reckons she's only got months at best to live."

Rane looked closer at the girl and noticed the shadows under her eyes for the first time, her prominent cheekbones, the tightness around her mouth.

"But there's a man in Napolin. A doctor," continued Christoph, "who apparently has great success treating such blood diseases. If we can get Saphie to him, there's a chance he can save her."

"But getting there ... you're putting all your lives at risk."

"I can't just give up. We have guns. I have men who can protect us. And now we know the Bracke are out there—they won't catch us by surprise."

"Have you ever encountered a Bracke?" asked Rane, his voice quiet.

"No." Christoph's chin dipped as he broke eye contact.

"I have, and they are the most vicious creatures you could ever imagine. We called them devil dogs in the war but even that doesn't do them justice," said Rane. "When they stand up on their hind legs, they're almost as big as a man. They like to jump on you and pin you to the ground with their razor-sharp claws. Once you're trapped, it's over. They'll rip you to shreds. Your only hope is to keep them at a distance and kill them before they get close, and that's easier said than done. I've seen them rip through ranks of soldiers—men and women who knew what they were doing, armed with guns, swords, and spears—just like that." Rane clicked his fingers, making Christoph jump.

The man wiped a tear from his eye. "Odason will protect us. We're good people."

"I know you are but, in my experience, Odason's not going to be much help if the Bracke turn up."

"If you were to come with us ... you know what we're facing. You've killed them." Christoph gripped Rane's hands. "You could be the difference."

Rane sighed. "I can't talk you out of going?"

"No."

"And you know what I am?"

Christoph took a deep breath, looked around as if to check if anyone else was listening, then leaned closer. "I ... I saw your sword last night," he whispered.

Rane straightened as *Kibon* hissed in his mind. "And?"

"Legionnaires help people in need."

"I haven't been one of those for a long time. Some would say I'm a greater danger than the Bracke."

"You saved my life last night. You wouldn't have done that if you were evil."

"The Inquisition would burn you just for saying that. If they find out I've traveled with you, they'd burn your whole family with you."

"I won't tell them if you won't?" Christoph tried a smile and failed. There was no hiding the fear in his voice and the desperation in his eyes. "Please. My daughter deserves a chance to have a life."

Rane glanced down at the news sheet once more. If this was the work of a Legionnaire, he had to do something to stop whoever it was. He had to go to Napolin one way or another. Perhaps it would be better for everyone if he traveled with the Fascalian's family. "Okay. I'll come with you."

Stunned, Christoph stared for a moment, then a smile of genuine delight eased his features. He shook Rane's hand. "Thank you. Thank you. Thank you."

"When are we leaving?"

"In an hour, I think. If that's alright with you?"

"I'll need some of your powder and bullets."

"Yes, yes. Whatever you need."

"Good. One hour then."

Christoph nodded. "One hour! Fion, my wife, will be very happy!" The man returned to the others with almost a spring in his step.

Rane sat back and wondered if he'd done the right thing. To ride knowingly into a pack of Bracke? With people who knew he was a Legionnaire? It went against everything he'd done to stay safe since he'd become a wanted man.

However, traveling by coach had its advantages. He'd be able to put a greater distance between himself and the Inquisition faster.

And what if they did make it? He looked at the news

sheet again. Was he really going to hunt this murderer—
who might be a Tainted Legionnaire? If so, they'd be
stronger than him, deadlier. Rane had only beaten Marcus
by sheer luck and with Myri's aid.

He'd be on his own in Napolin.

It was utter madness.

Then he saw the faces of Christoph's family. His wife was
beaming. So were Christoph's daughters. They had their
belief back. Their hope.

Everyone needed some of that.

And Rane couldn't take that from them. He'd sworn an
oath long ago to protect those weaker than himself, and he
knew Christoph and his family would never make it to
Napolin without his aid. Truth was, they might not even
make it even with his help.

He had to go, no matter the risk to himself.

The rest of Christoph's companions weren't quite so
happy to hear that Rane was joining the party. The two
guards, in particular, threw Rane hard looks as Christoph
introduced them when the party gathered outside the inn,
but he'd already seen their mettle the previous night against
the Rastaks. He only hoped they'd be braver when they
reached the Steppes. It would take everyone working
together to get past the Bracke.

Christoph was oblivious to any tension. "This is Carl,"
he said, introducing the bigger of the two guards. The man
had a nose that had been broken more times than he could
probably remember and a shaved head that showed off a
nasty scar off to one side—all signs that he liked to fight but
maybe wasn't so good at it. He carried a flintlock rifle in one
arm. "And this is Harken." The smaller man pushed back
greasy, blond hair from his face, and looked Rane up and
down. His lip curled in distaste. A pistol was strapped to his

chest and two knives hung off his belt. Perhaps he was braver when armed than he had been the previous night.

Rane smiled. "Pleased to meet you. I'm Nathaniel."

Both men just stared back as if Rane were a bug to be squashed.

"This is Jak, my driver," continued Christoph, indicating a man who looked well into his later years. The man had been checking the wheels of the stagecoach but stood up at the mention of his name.

"How do?" said Jak. "That's my son, Droon, on the other wagon."

There was no doubting Droon's parentage. The younger man was a wrinkle-free version of his father. Both wore their hair tied back in a bun, but Droon's was black to Jak's silver. Both had goatee beards and the same blue-grey eyes. The lad was checking the baggage and supplies tied up in the cart of the second wagon. He looked up at the mention of his name but quickly went back to his task.

"Hello," said Rane.

"Nathaniel will be riding beside you, Jak," said Christoph. "Some extra protection for us while we travel across the Steppes."

"You don't need extra help," said Carl from behind them. "You got us."

Christoph kept his smile but arched an eyebrow as he looked over his shoulder. "Like we had you last night, Carl?"

Carl shut up then and had the good graces to look embarrassed. "We didn't have our guns with us last night. That won't happen again."

"I'm sure it won't, Carl. That's why you've still got your jobs. But, when it comes to my family's safety, I think a little extra protection works wonders."

Carl nodded. "You're the boss."

"I am, Carl. I am."

Carl spat on the ground and walked off.

"Get the horses ready," called Christoph after him, then turned back to Rane. "The man's all bluster. He's just upset that he might have to share the bonus I promised everyone if—when—we make it across the Steppes. He won't let us down when the time comes."

Rane nodded. "I'm sure." He watched Carl and Harken return to their horses and thought he might have to reappraise whether he should be worried about them. They both looked like they'd be happy to shoot Rane in the back. "You said last night you had some ammunition?"

"That's right—powder and bullets. Jak can sort you out." Christoph signaled the driver to join them.

The big man jumped down from the box seat and jogged over. The man had greasy hair touching his shoulders and weathered skin from long days in the open. A large knife was fixed to his belt. "Yes, Mr. Christoph?"

"Nathaniel needs some powder and shot."

Jak nodded. "No problem. This way, Nathaniel." The man was all politeness but there was an edge to his tone that Rane took an instant dislike to but he also knew that a life on the run made him weary about anyone he met.

Rane followed Jak over to the main coach. It was a well-crafted wagon, designed to carry up to six people in relative comfort. There was even glass in the windows.

"I keep everything up in the driver's box with me," said Jak, climbing up. He lifted a cloth to reveal a padlocked trunk just behind his seat. "Can't have anyone dipping in when they feel like it."

Rane watched him produce the key from his pocket and unlock the box. Inside were several powder horns and lead bullets. Rane opened up his own pack and pulled out his pistols and holsters.

"Bloody hell, they're nice," said Jak. "Must be worth a fortune."

"They are," said Rane. "They were made by the gunsmiths of Eldacre."

"Why'd you keep them hidden away in your bag?"

Rane smiled. "I've not had any ammunition for them for months now. Seemed pointless to wear a weapon I couldn't use."

"Well, let's change that," said Jak. He passed Rane a powder horn. "You got a pouch for the bullets?"

"I do." Rane delved into his bag once more and found the small leather pouch he'd once used for such a purpose.

Jax scooped a handful of bullets and slipped them into the pouch. "There you go. I've not got any wadding though to stop the bullets rolling out the barrel."

"I can sort that out. Bullets and gunpowder might be in short supply, but old bits of cloth are easy to find." Despite not using the pistols for months, he'd kept them clean and ready, so Rane wasted no time in loading them. He poured fresh powder into the flash pan and closed the frizzen to keep it safe, then poured powder down the barrel, followed by one of the balls wrapped in a square of cloth from the inside of his pack. He pushed the ramrod down to compact everything as tightly as possible in the barrel before plugging everything in place with another piece of cloth. Once both pistols were ready, Rane strapped on his holsters and slipped the guns in place.

For a moment, he almost felt like a Legionnaire again.

"You need anything else out of your pack?" asked Jak. "If not, I'll strap it to the rest of the luggage if you're done."

Rane placed the powder horn and the bullet pouch into

the pack and held up the bag, well-worn and dirt-stained by months on the road. There were four ornate travel cases fixed to the coach's roof already—most likely Christoph's family's most important possessions and a couple of sacks of lesser quality. Jax tied Rane's pack to the sacks rather than the luggage.

Jax chuckled. "At least your gear and mine look like they belong together. Can't be doing with all that fancy stuff myself."

"Does your son have a rifle or pistols on the other wagon?" asked Rane.

Jak laughed. "Droon? No. He's lucky I trust him with a knife. If I gave him a pistol, he'd shoot his own bloody head off first chance he got—or worse, he'd shoot me."

"Might be worth giving him some lessons over the next few days," said Rane. "If what that other coach party said was true, we'll need everyone who can hold a gun."

Jak waved a hand. "Don't believe all you hear in an inn. Those men were just trying to get some free drinks and a bit of sympathy. I've driven the Steppes plenty of times. There's nothing to worry about." He leaned in and dropped his voice to a whisper. "But I'm glad their tales got me an extra bonus for just doing my job."

"I hope you're right."

"Listen, Carl and Harken might look like grumpy sods, but they're good men. I've known them a long time, and they've never let me down. Both of them know how to point a pistol or rifle at someone when it matters. And we've got you on board too. So there's nothing to worry about."

Christoph helped his family into the coach, then climbed up onto the doorstep. "We're ready to go now, Jak. Lead us on."

"Right oh, Mr. Christoph," said Jak. "Settle yourself down and we'll be off."

Rane sat down next to the driver and propped *Kibon* in the crux of his arm. He could feel tingles of excitement in the sword. It knew there would be bloody days ahead.

Jak flicked the reins, and the horses pulled the coach forward, toward whatever unknown horrors waited on the road ahead.

7

Rane

The two wagons moved slowly along the road, heading north. Rane scanned the ground on either side out of habit more than concern. The ground was rough and uneven, the grass coarse and discolored from a hot, dry summer. There were a few lonely shrubs and bushes but nothing that would hide a threat to the party.

A crow watched from a nearby tree and squawked as the first coach drove past, but that was all the life he saw.

Grey clouds rolled overhead, promising rain later, chased along by an autumn wind, with a cold bite that made Rane grateful for his heavy coat and cloak.

Every now and then, he could hear coughing coming from the inside of the coach. It had to be Saphie, fighting whatever illness was plaguing her. The coughing sounded wet and harsh, a sign that whatever the disease was, it had reached her lungs. A worrying sign. Not many recovered when that happened.

No wonder her father was determined to reach Napolin.

Rane had never been a father. His child had been lost when Kara died, still in her womb, but Rane could understand that parental bond, the sacrifices one would be willing to make for one's child.

Still, it was a dangerous path they were on.

Rane thought about the three Rastaks from the night before. Somehow, he felt they hadn't seen the last of them—they could either make an attempt to rob the wagons on the road or more likely, if they had any sense, they would report Rane to the authorities in return for the reward money.

Not that many people would want to give so much money to Rastaks. Go to the wrong place and they could just as easily end up swinging on a rope as they could end up rich.

Still, whatever their intentions, their conversation and the reports in the news sheets confirmed one thing—Mogai was alive and trying to rebuild his army. The Lord General hadn't lied about that.

The five nations had only defeated Mogai because they'd come together as one and the Legionnaires had given their souls to stop the Rastaks. Now, all the countries were in disarray, the Legion hunted and executed, and demons were everywhere.

If Mogai could raise an army and invade, who would stop him? Had Rane cursed his soul just to delay the inevitable? By Odason, he hoped not.

"Are you some sort of wandering sword-for-hire, then?" asked Jak, snapping Rane out of his thoughts.

"No. No, I'm not. I'm just wandering. I don't normally take on work like this," replied Rane.

"You wandering to any place in particular?"

"Not really."

"Footloose and fancy free," laughed Jak. "I like that."

Rane thought about the price on his head, the people who wanted to kill him, his dead wife, and his cursed sword. "Not so free."

"Well, doesn't sound like you've got someone waiting for you to get back, ready to take what little money you've made straight out of your pocket like I do. I love my wife but, as Odason is my witness, she's a hard one to keep happy. She doesn't trust me to keep a coin to myself, says I'd spend it all in one night down our local inn the first chance I got." He shook his head, then laughed again. "I'm not saying she's wrong—I mean, that's exactly what I would do. Plenty of times she's burst into The Four Elms and dragged me home."

"Perhaps she's doing it because she loves you," said Rane. "Protecting you from yourself."

"Protecting me from fun more like. And she has Droon to watch over me while I'm away. He makes sure I don't decide to go on a 'wander' myself." He nudged Rane with his elbow. "Good job I love her, eh?"

"Indeed."

Jak gave him a look. "You're not very chatty, are you? It's going to be a long bloody journey sitting next to me if you're not going to say more than one word at a time." He held up a hand. "I mean, if that's your thing, it is what it is. I can make do. I understand. But I reckon we've got at least a week sharing this bench. It might help the time pass a bit quicker if we could have a conversation or two."

"I've been traveling by myself for a while now. I've not really spoken to anyone for a long time. I'm out of practice," replied Rane.

"Well, that's a relief. I thought I was going to have to tell you to travel with Droon. That boy's really got nothing to say —well, not to me he hasn't. Plenty to say *about* me, though, to his mother. He's dropped me in it up to my neck a good few times, has that boy. Good job I love him—otherwise I would've wrung his neck by now."

"You driven for Christoph for long?"

"I've known him a while. Done a few short trips, but nothing like this one." Jak shook his head. "Poor sod."

"Why do you say that?"

"This isn't the first of his children that's got sick. He had a son too, couple of years older than Saphie, but he caught this same disease when he was the age she is now. Mr. Christoph tried everything, he did. Absolutely everything. Threw a lot of money at the problem." Jak leaned closer to Rane. "And when I say 'a lot', I mean a lot."

"What happened?"

Jak sniffed. "None of it worked."

"The boy died?"

"Did he ever." Jak puffed out his chest. "The boy was a strapping lad—tall, well-built—but, by the end? I could've picked him up with one hand. All skin and bone he was. Took Mr. Christoph over a year to get over it—not that I'm saying he ever did. Losing a kid? That haunts you."

"I can imagine." Ran thought of Kara. Her death had left a hole in him that he thought could never be healed. There wasn't a day when she wasn't on his mind. It was strange, though. Her face was blurry, faded, as if he couldn't see her directly, but her spirit was as clear as ever. Stronger even. Without thinking, Rane rubbed her locket. By the Gods, he missed her as much as he ever had. Perhaps more so.

Jak leaned closer, dropped his voice to a whisper. "Blamed himself for the lad's death—so when Saphie got sick, he sent word far and wide, offering everything he had for a cure, and that's how he found this man in Napolin. I just hope he can do what he says he can do."

"You have doubts?"

Jak shrugged. "For the money Mr. Christoph is offering, I'm willing to risk getting eaten by Bracke. Other people out there might be willing to say they can walk on water if it was to get them a couple of bags of gold—doesn't mean they can do it."

"Is Christoph carrying that sort of money on these wagons?"

"Nah. That would be madness. We'd have robbed him of it all on the first night if that was the case!" Again, he held up his hand. "Only joking, of course."

"Of course."

"He's got promise notes. Left money with a lender back in Gormun so he can give the note to the man's partner in Napolin and get the gold back."

"A good system."

"Well, it certainly keeps us honest. Makes sure we get him where he needs to go. He can't have any ... accidents on the road—if you know what I mean."

"I do," said Rane.

"Good job we're the trustworthy types, eh? Of course, if we find where he's got the promissory notes ..." Jak winked and followed it with a chuckle.

Rane wasn't so sure the man was joking. He glanced over at the riders on either side of the wagons, then at Droon on the coach behind. Trustworthy wasn't the word Rane would use to describe the men. They looked far from it, in fact.

Maybe he shouldn't worry about the Rastaks coming back. Maybe he should keep an eye on those around him first.

Jak kept talking away while the wagons rolled on for the rest of the morning, bumping and rattling along the northern road. Rane nodded when he could and replied when he had to, but Jak wasn't that annoying. In the meantime, Rane watched the horizon for anything that looked like trouble, but, for all intents and purposes, they were alone in the world.

They stopped around midday for a small meal. Immediately, the hired hands gathered together by the wagon to eat while Christoph and his family ate by the stagecoach. Rane didn't feel like he really belonged with either group so he walked away from the road while he chewed the bread and ham he'd been given. His gaze was drawn back the way they'd come. The road was one straight line back to the horizon, and the inn was lost in the distance behind that.

"Excuse me, Mr. Nathaniel?"

Rane turned to find Christoph's wife, Fion, standing behind him. "Please, it's just Nathaniel."

"Nathaniel." Fion nodded. She was a handsome woman, with long, chestnut hair and a warm smile. "It feels quite peaceful here, doesn't it?"

He nodded. "It does."

"You must think us mad, making this journey."

"You have a very good reason."

Fion glanced back at her family. "We do. No parent wants to see their child die."

"Hopefully all will be well when you get to Napolin."

"Yes, indeed."

"Was that your daughter I heard coughing?"

"The dry air seems to aggravate her." Fion looked back at her family for a moment, her smile wavering on her lips. Saphie was much paler in comparison to the others, her brow knotted. "Poor thing."

"How long has she been sick?"

"A good few months now. It started off with just a small cough, and she was just tired all the time. But we knew the signs, and Christoph already had people looking for doctors …"

"That was fortunate."

"It was, but sometimes I look at her and think we should've stayed at home and just made her last days as comfortable as possible—not dragged her halfway across the country, hoping we'll find a cure."

"For what it's worth, I think you've made the right choice."

"I hope so. Still, it always feels like we're running out of time."

"I know that feeling only too well." For six months now, he'd been searching for Babayon, and he'd yet to find a single clue as to his whereabouts. If he couldn't get the mage to free his soul from his sword, Rane would turn into a monster. His soul was damned.

"How do you find the strength to keep going?"

"Because the only thing certain in this world is what happens if we give up," said Rane. "If we keep going—no matter how little time is left to us—there's always hope that we'll be successful in what we're trying to achieve."

"That's exactly what I needed to hear, Nathaniel." Fion squeezed his arm. "Anyway, I just wanted to say thank you for coming with us. You're a good man."

Fion left him then, and Rane finished his meal, wondering how long he could stay good. How many lives could his sword take before he turned into a monster? Perhaps, if it was just him afflicted with the curse, he could've found a quiet place to build a home and see out the rest of his life alone. But there were others out there—other

Legionnaires—who needed a cure too, and he couldn't give up on them.

In many ways, Christoph and his family weren't much different to Rane. In an unsafe world, only the prospect of a greater tragedy forced people to travel so far from all they knew, holding onto hope as best they could.

He brushed the crumbs off his hands as he headed back to the others. Carl, Jax, and Harken were still muttering to themselves, but Droon was rummaging around on the back of the luggage wagon. He gave Rane a wary look as he approached.

"You lost something?" asked Rane.

Droon looked up, scowling. "What?"

"Have you lost something? You were checking the luggage before we left the inn as well."

"Just doing my job," the lad spat back. He had his shoulders back and his chest out, trying to look tough.

"Never said you weren't." Rane smiled, trying to ease the tension in the man, but Droon already had his head down.

The coaches moved on again shortly after. Jak jabbered away the whole time, more to himself than to Rane, and he seemed quite content with the odd word or two Rane interjected.

For his part, Rane was happy to watch the countryside roll past. It been a long time since he'd travelled in this part of the world, and there was a wildness to it that appealed to him on a very primal level. Trees stood in defiance to the winds that tried to uproot them and the hot summers that tried to turn them to tinder. The bushes and scrubs were short, stubbly things, full of thorns and prickles, forcing their way up through hardened dirt to claim their spot in the world. Even the wildlife seemed to be made of determined survivors, willing to live off what they could scavenge.

Saphie's coughing continued as they rattled along, getting worse as the day drew on. Listening to it broke Rane's heart, and he could only imagine how Christoph and Fion felt.

A few hours on, Jak pulled the coach to a halt as they approached a crossroads. "Mr. Christoph," he called. "Could I have a word?"

There was a shuffling of feet within the coach, then the door opened and Christoph's head appeared. He smiled, but Rane was starting to notice the tiredness behind it. "Jak, my good man, what can I do for you?"

"Best I show you." The driver clambered from his seat and dropped to the ground. Christoph sighed and followed, then glanced up at Rane, who got the impression he wanted him to come too. Rane nodded back and climbed down. They followed Jak to the crossroads. The northern road stretched on ahead, while the other road cut to the northwest.

"What is it?" asked Christoph again.

"This road is the most direct route to Napolin," said Jak, pointing straight ahead. "Goes right through the heart of the Steppes. Four days, maybe five, we're in Napolin, all being well."

"That's the plan," said Christoph.

"This road," said Jak, pointing northwest, "takes us through the Steppes as well but along the borders, then turns back on itself to Napolin. Might be worth taking it. If the Bracke are out roaming, we might miss them going this way."

"How long would it take us to reach Napolin if we did that?"

Jak shrugged. "Just over two weeks."

"That's twice as long. I'm sorry but no, that's out of the question."

"We'd have a better chance of making it," said the driver.

Christoph shook his head. "I thought you didn't even believe in the Bracke. I thought you said they were exaggerating the danger."

"I don't believe in the Gods either, but I'm not going to do anything to piss them off if I can help it."

Christoph turned to Rane. "Nathaniel, what do you think?"

"Jak has a point. It would be safer. The Bracke are probably hunting the main road and the buffalo that roam the grasslands. We might miss them going the longer way where's there's less food for them to hunt. The question is: can we afford to take an extra eight to ten days to get Napolin? Do we even have supplies for a longer journey?"

"Supplies aren't an issue. Time is. Each day, my daughter gets sicker," said Christoph. "The sicker she gets, the harder it will be to cure her. We have to get to Napolin as quick as we can."

"So there is no choice," said Rane. "We go straight."

Jak shook his head. "The boys won't like that."

"I said I'd give you all an extra bonus," said Christoph. "You all gave your word to get us to Napolin."

Jak pointed down the other road. "That way will get you to Napolin."

"Not in time," replied Christoph, through gritted teeth.

"And what happens if you die out on the Steppes, eh?" said Jak. "We'll all be out of pocket then, even if we get the rest of your family to this fancy doctor."

"We'll have to make sure that doesn't happen," said Rane, stepping forward.

Jak jabbed a finger towards Rane. "You can guarantee that, can you?"

Kibon stirred at the threat in Jak's voice. "I'll do my best—as *I've* promised. I think you and your men should do the same."

"You think you're really special, don't you?" The two men stared at each other, neither moving. Rane could see the uncertainty grow behind Jak's glare. The driver knew he'd not win in a fight with Rane but he didn't want to back down either. Rane could see out of the corner of his eye the man's hand drifted towards that big knife of his on his belt.

"Don't do anything stupid," said Rane. "Pride isn't worth dying for."

Kill him, urged *Kibon* but his sword never had any time for peace.

"My wife can cash my promise notes," said Christoph, stepping between them. "Whatever happens, you'll get your money."

"If things get bad out there," said Jak, not taking his eyes off Rane, "we'll have to renegotiate this bonus."

"I'll see you looked after," said Christoph. "Now, can we get moving again?"

Jak stepped back, sniffed, then spat. Only then did he look away from Rane. He gave Christoph a mocking salute. "Right away, sir. You're the boss."

They all returned to the stagecoach. Once Christoph was settled back with his family, and Rane and Jak returned to the driver's box, Jak got the horses moving.

For a moment, neither man spoke but Rane could sense the man stewing over what had happened.

"I was thinking of the boss as much as I was myself," muttered Jak eventually. "Going the long way would've been safer for everyone."

"I know," said Rane.

"No point earning a big fat bonus if I'm not around to spend it."

Rane arched an eyebrow and smiled. "I thought your wife wouldn't let you spend anything."

Jak roared with laughter. "Too bloody true. In fact, sometimes I think I might be better off dead, the way she goes on at me. Let me tell you about the time ..."

Rane leaned back and crossed his arms, *Kibon* by his side, and let Jak's voice drift off into the distance.

They pulled the wagons off the road as the sun set, and, for a while, everyone was busy making camp or tending to the horses or their own needs. Rane helped build the fire, watched by Christoph's two girls and Fion. The girls were wrapped in traveling cloaks while Fion had a knitted shawl to help keep her warm. Saphie's coughing seemed to ease once she was out of the stagecoach and not moving, but the day's journey had left her pale and there were dark rings under her eyes.

"We haven't been introduced yet," said Rane, once the fire was underway. "My name is Nathaniel."

Fion smiled. "This is Saphie and Rache."

"Hello," said Rane.

The girls gave him tired smiles.

"It's been a long day for them—for all of us," said Fion, pulling her shawl tighter around her shoulders.

"They both look a lot like you," said Rane. He picked up *Kibon* and rose to his feet. "Who's oldest?"

"Saphie is," said Rache, pointing at her sister with her thumb. "I'm the cleverest."

"No, you're not," said Saphie, with a roll of her eyes.

"Father said I was," retorted Rache.

"He was joking," said Saphie. Her voice sounded exhausted.

"Now, girls," said Fion. "Help me get dinner ready, Rache, instead of squabbling with your sister. We've got hungry people to feed."

"Do I have to? Why is it always me that has to do it?" The girl crossed her arms.

"You know why," said Fion, calmly.

Rache glanced at her sister. "It's not fair." But she jumped up all the same.

"Ask Droon for the pot," said Fion.

The girl stomped off without another word.

"I'm sorry about that," said Fion.

"Don't apologize," said Rane. "It can't be easy on her."

"She's lost her brother, now her home, and everyone's attention is on Saphie," said Fion.

Rache was back with Droon in tow before Rane could reply. The lad carried the cooking pot and a basket with meat and vegetables.

"I'll be back in a moment with the sticks to set the high bar up, ma'am," said Droon.

"Thank you." Fion turned back to Rane. "We'll call you when the food's ready. It's nothing fancy, but it'll be hot and filling."

"I'll be grateful for anything. A hot meal can seem a luxury these days." Rane wandered away from the fire and then out of the camp. Night had all but settled, but most of the day's clouds had passed on without leaving any rain. Stars shone bright from horizon to horizon.

There was an old saying in the Legion—'the heavens don't care who you are'. It reminded the troops to not rely on anyone or anything other than themselves. Not to look to Odason or the fates for any special favors. Standing there, at that moment, Rane felt the weight of those words. How could any higher power see a speck like him when the heavens were so vast? Why should they even care what happened to him? Or to anyone?

He was alone.

Without his wife, his child, his friends.

Cursed.

When the time came, would he even have a soul to go to the afterlife? Would he die a man or would he be a monster?

Would Kara even recognize him when the time came?

What if his damnation wasn't just ephemeral but for eternity?

By Odason, it made his head hurt just thinking about it. And what good did it do?

Then Saphie started coughing. The chatter in the camp behind Rane died while she hacked away, trying to clear her lungs. He listened, feeling guilty for his worries when that little girl had real, immediate concerns.

It was a reminder of the oath he'd made as Legionnaire, to help those in need. It was why he had fought in the war. It was why he'd allowed Babayon to use his magic on him. It was a reminder of how he should live his life moving forward.

Odason knew there were enough people in this world who needed his help.

8

Sarah

T he mood within the Inquisition was surly as they entered the village of Lipstock. They'd been chasing the monster for over a week now with nothing to show for it except growing frustration.

Sister Sarah had barely left Mother Hilik's side in that time. Ever since Mother had said she wanted Sarah to succeed her, every waking minute had been spent in lessons and discussions with her. It was exhausting. Sarah had to watch everything she said in case she got an answer wrong or uttered anything that might change Mother's view of her. Others were treating her differently too, despite nothing being officially announced. Brothers and sisters who she'd once considered friends went out of their way to either avoid her or, if that wasn't possible, they acted as if she were already high priestess.

Sarah wished Mother had never considered her for the

position. She wished she could've refused without her life being forfeit as a result. Mother had been right after all, being High Priestess was not what Sarah wanted nor asked for.

If only she could find a moment to speak to Nicolai. She could relax in his company at least. They could ... No. That would have to stop. A high priestess could not have friends, let alone ... She couldn't even bring herself to think the word.

Still, when she looked his way and he looked back, she could barely control the emotions he stirred up in her.

"Sarah!" Mother's voice cut through her thoughts.

"Yes, Mother?" Sarah felt her cheeks redden.

"What is this village called?"

"Lipstock, Mother." They could just about see it, a growing shadow across the road.

"Perhaps this is where the monster is hiding." Mother sounded tired but there was an edge to her voice too. A touch of anger perhaps.

"It is a godly village, Mother. I would hope they would not give any of the damned shelter."

"We must keep our eyes open," said Mother. "Look for any signs of the monster's corruption. Even if he is not hiding here, he could've infected it with his presence just by passing through."

"Yes, Mother." She prayed to Odason that wasn't the case. If it were, the whole village would be purged. Hundreds could die.

The village of Lipstock was protected by an eight-foot fence of wooden stakes and a gate of oak that was quickly opened once the Inquisition drew near. The villagers even managed to line up along the main path to the market square to welcome Odason's Children as they entered

Lipstock. Some fell to their knees as Mother lead her soldiers into the village. Sarah tried to count the villagers as she passed them but, in the end, had to guess at a number. All told, she reckoned there were around two hundred of them—and all their lives hung in the balance.

Their temple to Odason was on the northern side of the market square. It was only a small building, perhaps only big enough for half the villagers to attend service at any one time, but Sarah could see care and thought had gone into its construction. Hand-carved crows perched on each corner, looking over the village, and the world tree, which connected Heras's kingdom and Odason's great halls to the mortal world, had been etched in intricate detail into the temple's doors. One glance at Mother, though, was enough to tell Sarah that she wasn't impressed as she called a halt in front of it.

The village priest, an old man with long white hair and beard, bowed to Mother in greeting. "You honor our small village with your visit, Mother."

Mother looked over the temple. "Does everyone in your village pray, Brother?"

The priest looked around at the Inquisition gathered in the square, no doubt seeing their weapons more than their faces. Sweat appeared on his brow and his voice shook. "We ... we are godly people here, Mother. Everyone is a true believer. Our temple is small, but everyone attends—"

"If we weren't in a hurry, I'd ask you to prove that point," said Mother.

The priest paled. "Mother, I wouldn't—"

Mother held up a hand. "We are in pursuit of a monster, Brother. A Legionnaire.

The priest looked around as if he expected to suddenly see the monster appear. "A Legionnaire? Here?"

"Has he passed this way?" continued Mother. "Has someone in your village given him succor?"

"We ... we have had no s ... s ... strangers pass this way, Mother. None what-so- ever," said the priest, going even paler. For a moment, Sarah thought he was going to fall to his knees. Thank Odason, he didn't. Mother would see that as act of guilt.

"No strangers, Brother?" said Mother. "No one has come to trade in your market or drink in your inn? I find that so hard to believe."

"Before Odason Himself, I speak the truth."

"We shall see," said Mother and Sarah's heart sank at those words. If there were questions to be asked, there would be flames before the day was out—and deaths a plenty. She ran her gaze over the villagers, seeing only frightened people, their faces worn down by hard work in hard weather, scraping by with far too little food and even less coin. Their only interest in the Gods was to ask for help with the harvest and protection from whatever horrors might come their way. They were simple people with simple lives—until the Inquisition arrived to upset it all. How many were praying in that instant, begging Odason to send His Children elsewhere? Anyone with any sense, certainly.

Had it been like this when the Inquisition had arrived in her family's village? She remembered so little of her life before the church. In fact, she barely remembered her parents. Only her father's dirt-ingrained hands and the smell of his sweat and the warmth of her mother's embrace, the feeling of being loved by them both. Young as she had been, she had no sense that her family or anyone in her village had been corrupted in any way.

No one had ever told her what her village's crime was and why it had to be purged. Sarah had never asked. To do so was to suggest she questioned the church's decision and, therefore, Odason Himself. *That* behavior ended up in one place only—the fire.

A finger brushed hers. She glanced to her left, saw Nicolai standing beside her, his eyes fixed straight ahead, giving away nothing. She wanted to return the touch, but knew she couldn't. His contact with her could be explained as an accident, but a second touch would be seen as intentional by anyone watching. And they would report it, especially if they didn't want Sarah to have her position of authority.

Sarah took a deep breath and concentrated on Mother and the priest.

"Can I show you inside?" asked the priest. "You'll see everything is well-looked after, Mother. A temple to be proud of."

"Pride is a sin," said Mother, with a sharpness that all felt. She stepped past the priest and entered the temple.

Sarah was going to follow when a man caught her attention—not that he was trying to be noticed. Far from it. He was tall, thin, with a heavy black mustache under prominent cheekbones, and he looked as guilty as a man could possibly look as he edged his way back through the crowd.

"Brother Nikolai," said Sister Sarah quietly. "The man—black mustache—trying to leave."

"I see him. Leave it with me." Nicolai stepped forward, two other brothers falling into place behind him with barely a signal. They moved quickly, their advance well-drilled. The mustached man didn't even notice them until they were upon him. Then he squeaked as the brothers snatched him up and carried him back through the crowd.

Mother turned as the villagers parted way for Nicolai and his prisoner to come through. "What do we have here?"

"This man was trying to leave, Mother," said Sarah. "I thought his actions were suspicious."

Mother raised an eyebrow. "Did you? Good girl." She pointed towards the temple. "Take him inside."

"Inside?" said the priest, all too aware of what would happen next. "It is our most holy place."

"And where better for the All-Father to witness this man's sedition," said Mother.

"But you don't know he's guilty of anything," said the priest.

Mother flashed that slither of a smile of hers. "Everyone is guilty, Brother. You know that. The question always is *how* guilty."

She walked past the priest into the temple, and Sarah followed. She hoped she was right about the man. Better one be put to the question than the whole village. Better one suffer than two hundred.

Better one burn than all.

It was dark inside. Quiet except for the mustached man's heavy breathing, his rising panic. Rushes covered the floor. There was a simple altar at the far end, a carved idol of Odason watching over the interior. The only light came from two windows high up near the rafters.

Memories came back to Sarah of praying in a place like it when she was a child. Her village temple had seemed so big, so overwhelming back then. Bodies packed shoulder to shoulder, the priest's voice echoing around them, the sacrifices on the alter, the tang of blood in the air, her hand so small in her father's. It was exciting and terrifying at the same time.

Now? There was comfort in the temple—but always fear too.

They pushed the mustached man to his knees in front of the alter. Two soldiers held his arms.

"Please, I've done nothing," squealed the man.

"So says the guilty man," purred Mother, walking round him. He whippes his head from side to side, trying to keep her in sight.

"I'm innocent. Innocent."

"Then why did you try to run?"

"I didn't!"

"Sister Sarah said you did," said Mother. "Are you calling one of Odason's Children a liar?"

"No," said the man. "I would never do that." His eyes met Sarah's. "She is a godly woman."

"So, you did try to run, as she said," said Mother. She stopped behind him and waited while his head flicked from side to side, trying to see her once more. "Why?" She slipped her sword and its scabbard from the hoop on her belt.

"I am a fearful man. A weak man. I was scared. I am scared. That's all."

"Ann innocent man would have nothing to fear." Mother leaned closer so her lips were near the man's ear. "Tell me what you know."

"I know no—"

Mother brought *Odason's Wrath* down on the man's collarbone. There was a crack, and the man screamed.

"Tell me," repeated Mother.

"Nothing. I—"

Crack. The scabbard struck the other shoulder.

The man screamed even louder.

"Tell me."

"My c ... cousin ..."

Mother walked in front of the man. "What about your cousin?"

"My ... cousin owns ... an inn. He said there was trouble there the other night. Three Rastaks."

"I'm not interested in any Rastaks," said Mother. She drew *Odason's Wrath*. The blade gleamed in the dark temple. "I hunt monsters."

"A man stopped the Rastaks before they could hurt anyone. My cousin ... he said ... he said the man had a Legionnaire's sword." Tears ran down the mustached man's.

Mother placed the tip of her sword into the ground and crouched down before the villager. "And did your cousin try to apprehend this Legionnaire?"

"N ... no."

"Did he report this Legionnaire to the authorities?"

"No."

Mother glanced over at Sarah and raised an eyebrow. "Well done," she mouthed.

Sarah remained still like stone.

"Where is this inn?" asked Mother. "I would like to pay it a visit."

9
———

Rane

Rane slept as well as he could remember without having a roof over his head. Fion's food had been far better than she'd suggested, and there'd been plenty to go around. Rane's cloak had been enough to keep the night chill away, and the other men had taken it in turns to watch over everyone, leaving Rane to sleep.

Rane had still woken from time to time, opening one eye to check things over before allowing himself to doze back off. Even Saphie's coughing had lessened over the night, and he was pleased to see some color back in her face as she ate some breakfast.

Fion brought him a cup of tea and some porridge. "Are you hungry?

"Thank you," said Rane, taking the bowl and cup from her. "You're very generous with your supplies."

She smiled. "It's the least we can do, dragging you all so

far from your homes. Christoph tells me we should be reaching a way station in the next couple of days where we can stock up again."

"I know the place. Prices aren't cheap, but they don't try to short-change you over anything and it's good quality—or at least it used to be."

"High prices we can cope with. As long as we can get what we need, not much else matters. I'll leave you to eat your food."

Rane watched Jak and the others ready the wagons and horses while he ate. No one needed to discuss what had to be done. They just got on with it as if they'd been working together their whole lives. It was a closeness he'd seen a lot of in the war—men and women, together all day and all night, dealing with extreme conditions, having each other's back without asking or hesitation. He wondered how long the four men had known each other. Far longer than this one trip.

"Sleep all right?" asked Jak as Rane climbed up into the driver's box.

"I did," replied Rane.

"Good because it's only going to get harder from now on. We stock up at the way station, and then straight after that, it's the Steppes and whatever is waiting for us there."

Rane said nothing as he settled into his seat. He knew only too well what an attack by Bracke was like.

"Come on then, my beauties," said Jak and snapped the reins. "Let's see what today brings."

The wagons rolled on down the northern road, with Carl and Harken once more on horseback, guarding their sides. Saphie's cough started up again, sounding just a little bit more horrible than it had the day before.

"Poor kid," muttered Jak. "Every morning, I wake up

expecting to find she's dead." The man didn't keep his voice down, and Rane hoped no one in the carriage heard him say such things.

"How long have you worked together?" asked Rane, changing the subject.

"What? Me and the lads?" That got a smile on Jak's face.

"Yes."

Jak puffed out his cheeks. "A bloody long time. Too long probably. Grew up together, we did. Even fought in the war together. Of course, there were a few more of us then. Me, Carl, Harken, of course. But then there was Jase, Lono, Das, Pier, Sal, Kidder, and a few others from our town. They're all gone now."

"Where did you fight?"

"We were in the Eastern Scouts over Liston way. Saw some bloody days back then, we did."

"I've heard of the Scouts. You had quite the reputation."

"We didn't take any shit off anyone if that's what you mean. Didn't shirk the nasty jobs either. Took more than our fair share of Rastak scalps. The rest of it is just bullshit made up to frighten people."

From what Rane remembered, the Eastern Scouts were known to be almost as bad as the Rastaks themselves. Word was they enjoyed looting and raping a bit too much—but their transgressions were overlooked in the heat of the war. 'Sometimes you fight fire with fire,' Jefferson had said. A belief he had taken to the extreme when he tried to turn the Legion into monsters. "Your son was too young to fight in the war, wasn't he?"

"Droon? Gods, you don't want to give that boy a weapon and you'd certainly not want him watching your back. You'd have as much chance of getting killed by him as by your enemy. So no, thank Odason, the boy was too young to fight.

I left him with his mother while all the nonsense was going on." Jak sighed. "Still, he's a hard-worker, does what he's told without complaint and gets on with the others well-enough."

"He was lucky to miss the war," said Rane.

"I can tell you fought," said Jak. "You get the nightmares? Jump at loud noises? Look for a knife before you shake someone's hand?"

"More times than I'd like," said Rane.

"Sometimes I can see the enemy as if they were right in front of me," said Jak. "I can see my mates die all over again, and there's nothing I can do to stop it. I thought it would get better over time — but it doesn't. Not in the slightest."

"It's not been that long since the war ended," said Rane. "Perhaps it will."

"You don't tell a man who's had his arm cut off it'll get better in time. You tell 'em that they'll adjust, get used to it —they'll learn to live with it. Same's true with us. We gotta find a way to carry on, but don't fool yourself that we'll get better. It don't work that way." Jak let out a sudden laugh, but there was no real humor in it. "Of course, we could all get eaten by bloody Bracke tomorrow so who gives a shit, eh? That's one way to put an end to the bloody nightmares."

The man had a point.

"Of course, it's only us poor folk that have to worry about all that nonsense lingering from the war," continued Jak. "The likes of him below? Rich folks didn't get called up like we did. Or they got made officers so they could stay well back from fighting while they ordered us to get killed. It's not right."

"I don't begrudge anyone being spared what we went through," said Rane. "Once, maybe. But not now. I wouldn't wish the war on anyone."

"Well, you're a better man than me. Just thinking about it gets me angry. After the blood me and mine shed, we should be living like kings now, not risking our lives for a couple of gold coins."

"Christoph and his family are good people," said Rane. "They're treating us all better than they have to."

"Oh, of course," laughed Jak. "They're great. Best employers I've ever had. I wasn't talking about *them*. It's everyone else I can't stand."

The wagons rolled on. Every now and then, Rane checked the road behind them. The Inquisition would be hunting for him. He knew they wouldn't have given up. But there was nothing to see, no one following. Maybe they'd lost his trail. Maybe he was safe. Maybe.

"Look at that," said Jak, pointing straight ahead. There was a small smudge of white against the blue sky, rising from the horizon.

"Something's burning," said Rane. He leaned forward, a knot of dread in his stomach. There was only one thing big enough to burn in the area to give off that much smoke. "How much food do we have left?"

The change in subject threw Jak for a moment. "Er ... I'm not sure about food. What we have is with my lad in his wagon. Don't think there's a lot left though. There's been too much talk about restocking at the ... way station." Jak made the connection. "Shit. You think that's what's burning?"

"Nothing else around here. It has to be."

"Shit."

"If we ration what we have, can we make it to Napolin?"

"I don't know. Maybe. But I did enough starving in the war. I've got no intention of doing it again now."

"Might not have any choice for a few days."

Jak started to say something but stopped himself.

Instead, he snorted mucus from the back of his nose and spat it off to the side of the carriage.

They trundled along in silence, moving slowly, both of them watching the smoke. Two brothers ran the way station, and Rane remembered that they looked like they could take care of themselves. But even the toughest men could be outfought by a band desperate enough. When everything was in short supply, a place that had plenty made a very tempting target.

Christoph and Fion took the news as well as could be expected when they stopped for lunch. Fion, in particular, reacted with determination, immediately adjusting the meal. A few strips of meat to quiet their stomachs and a cup of water each. Only the girls got slightly more, and Rane noticed Rache slipped her sister half of what she'd been given.

Once more, Jak and the other hired men sat together, deep in muttered conversation. All of them looked unhappy at the turn of events, and Rane couldn't help but wonder what they planned to do about it.

Even *Kibon* sensed the tension in the air. Rane could feel its excitement tingling in his mind. He hoped whoever had burned the way station was long gone, and there would be no need to use his sword.

That night, there was an argument when they set camp. Rane stopped Harken from building a fire. "We don't know who or what attacked the way station. If it was a gang of outlaws, a fire will bring them straight to us," said Rane.

"We don't even know if it is the bloody way station burning!" spat the rider. "And, so what if it is? Anyone who tries their luck with us will bloody regret it."

"It's better if we can avoid a fight," said Rane. "That way we can guarantee no one here gets hurt."

"I thought you were a tough man. You scared?"

"No," said Rane. "But a stray arrow can get past the best defenses. Doesn't matter how tough you think you are then." An image of Kara with a crossbow bolt in her breast burned raw in his mind.

"Fucking coward." For a moment, Harken's hand drifted towards one of the knives on his belt.

Kibon purred in delight.

"Please, gentleman," said Christoph, rushing over to stand between them. "Nathaniel is right. I know it means dinner will be cold, but better to be safe. We have plenty of spare blankets on the wagons to ensure everyone is relatively warm sleeping tonight. We can all manage one night of hardship, can't we?"

Harken glared at Rane for two more heartbeats then nodded. "You're the boss, Mr. Christoph." With that, he stomped off back to the others.

Christoph came over to Rane's side. "That's a relief. I thought things were going to get nasty for a moment there." He smiled. "No need for swords."

It was only then Rane realized one hand gripped *Kibon's* hilt and the other the scabbard, ready to draw the sword free. He had to force himself to let go, and he could feel the sword's disappointment. "In the morning, I'd like to take one of the horses and scout ahead. See what's happened before the rest of you get there."

"A good idea," said Christoph. "Perhaps, though, I should suggest the idea to Carl and Harken."

"That's what I was thinking."

"They *are* good men, Nathaniel. We just live in challenging times."

"The world will take a lot of adjusting to for all of us."

Dinner was a tense and quiet affair with the distance

between the two groups seeming to grow wider and more pronounced. Rane, as before, ate what little there was by himself and then spent the next hour or two walking the perimeter of the camp, watching for any threat that might be lurking.

Carl drew sentry duty for the first part of the night. Rane offered to take a shift, but the men refused. "We work better together," said Jak, before turning his back on Rane.

Carl sat on the driver's box of the wagon, his rifle cradled in his arms, looking out into the darkness. It wasn't the best position, but Rane knew better than to say anything. Even so, the man glared every time Rane passed him.

"Too scared to sleep?" he cooed. "Think there's some big bad monsters waiting to eat us all?"

Rane ignored him and kept watching the shadows. The brothers who ran the way station knew what they were doing, but, despite that, something or someone had put their home and business to the torch. So, as far as Rane was concerned, there was no such thing as being too careful or too paranoid. It was a dangerous world they found themselves in.

Carl continued to mutter sarcastic comments but Rane paid him no heed. Only fools saw caution as a sign of weakness. And rushing into a situation blinded by bravery was a good way to end up dead. Rane had learned those lessons the hard way during the war. A bit of goading now wouldn't get him to be stupid now.

Droon took the next watch, and he at least seemed to take it more seriously than Carl. He set himself up on the roof of the stagecoach, and its higher vantage point gave a much better view of the surrounding area. The others hadn't given him any weapons, but it was enough that he could warn everyone of any danger.

With him settled, it seemed a good enough time for Rane to get some sleep of his own. The comfort of the previous few nights felt long ago as he settled down near Christoph's family, but at least he had a few blankets to keep the chill away. He fell asleep with *Kibon* wrapped in his arms. He had a feeling the sword would wake him if there was any danger lurking.

The next morning, he woke tired and hungry. Fion had set a small fire to cook breakfast over and make tea for everyone, and Rane didn't argue with her. What little smoke it produced was quickly lost against the grey sky. He kept his head down and concentrated on his bowl of porridge when he heard Carl and Harken raise their voices once more to Christoph.

"I'm getting tired of this endless complaining," said Christoph in return. "You should be grateful someone else is willing to put their life at risk so the rest of us can be safe."

"Why does it have to be my bloody horse he rides?" said Carl. "Eh?"

"Because I said so!"

"If I may, Mr. Christoph," said Jak, walking over. "Let me have a word with my friends."

Christoph nodded. "Thank you, Jak." He stepped aside and let the men talk.

Rane couldn't hear what was said, but whatever it was got a chuckle from Carl, then agreement. "Fine. In that case, let him take the old mare."

"Oi, Nathaniel," called Jak. "You can have Carl's horse for your scouting. Appreciate you putting yourself at risk for us."

Rane stood up, passed his bowl over to Fion, then picked up *Kibon*. "I just want to be careful."

"You can have my bow and quiver as well if you want," said Jak. "If you know how to use one that is."

Rane smiled. "I think I do."

"Well, there you go then," said Jak, walking to rear of the stagecoach. He was back a moment later with the weapons. "Don't say we didn't do what we could to keep you safe too."

"It's appreciated," said Rane.

Rane fixed the bow and quiver to Carl's saddle and mounted the horse. It was a chestnut mare, full of strength and well-trained. Rane might not like its rider, but the man knew how to look after a horse.

"You better bring her back in one piece," said Carl.

"I'll do my best," said Rane and rode off.

It was good to be by himself again. Good to be alone. For a moment, he was tempted to just keep going, leave Christoph and the others to whatever may be, but it was only a fleeting temptation. To do so would put everyone's lives artist, and Rane couldn't do that. The Fascalians had been kind to him. Made him feel valued.

Even though a day had passed, smoke still billowed up from the way station, reminding Rane of the job he had to do. He couldn't help but wonder what he'd find, how bad it would be. He was glad to have Jak's bow and quiver full of arrows and had them slung in easy reach. A bow wasn't as effective as a pistol, but he could shoot more arrows in the time it took to reload a gun—and with more accuracy.

He took his time, riding far enough ahead to spot any trouble but always keeping the wagons in sight. If something happened to Rane, they needed to see it. Otherwise, Christoph and the others could just as easily drive into danger as well.

But there was nothing to see, nothing to fight. Just empty grass land and the column of smoke in front of him.

It was just before midday when Rane reached the way station. He pulled his horse to a stop just as the ground dipped down into a basin. A large pond, covering two acres or so, sat in the center. The ruins of the way station occupied the western shore. There were wagons and carriages too, burnt and broken, the carcasses of dead horses and cattle littered across the ground. Human bodies too. Plenty of them. Some were half in the water as if they'd run there to escape whatever had come to kill them. The station had been busy when the attack came, and no mercy had been shown. It was a heart-breaking scene of destruction.

Such a different sight from when Rane had first seen the basin as a young recruit. It had taken them five days of marching to reach it, and at the time, the pond was the most beautiful sight he'd seen in a long while. They'd all run down to the water's edge and splashed around like kids, letting off steam and playing the fool. Later, the brothers that ran the station had cooked buffalo for them over a fire pit, and everyone had sat about laughing and joking, drinking themselves sick and stuffing their stomachs.

Rane dismounted and wandered a few yards forward. He looked for movement but saw none. No people, no livestock, no horses. Nothing in the surrounding area either. Whoever had burned the place looked like they were long gone.

Rane glanced back at the wagons. They were still a good distance behind. Shame he'd not be able to keep the girls from seeing this carnage. They were too young to know such evil existed in the world. Keeping his pace nice and slow, he began to make his way down the slope. As hard as it was, he needed to get a closer look.

As he got nearer, he noticed the tang of charred pork in

the air. He'd been close to enough Rastak fires in the war to know what cooked human flesh smelled like.

Rane double-checked his weapons, happy that he had bullets for his pistols again. He glanced back at the horse and cursed himself for not bringing the bow. He hoped it wasn't a mistake that would kill him.

He circled the building, but there was little to read in the hard ground. It was all so churned up. All he knew was that whatever had happened, it hadn't been quick.

Perhaps it was *Kibon* working its magic, making him nervous, because he found his hand had drifted to the blade's hilt without realizing it. He snatched it back, cursing himself. It wasn't the time to lose focus.

Rane's eyes never stopped scanning his surroundings as he bent down to taste the water. Thank the Gods, the water was still good—crisp, fresh, cold. He scooped several handfuls into his mouth. There might not be any food for them here, but at least the convoy could replenish their water supplies.

Rane walked over to the remains of the way station, still looking for clues about the perpetrators. The four corners of the building remained standing, but everything else had either burned away or collapsed inside. He stepped over smoldering wood and clambered on crumbled brick until he reached the bodies inside. A woman's hand poked through the rubble and ashes. A child lay half-buried under a fallen beam, its skin all charred. There were at least another dozen bodies with them. They'd probably hoped they would be safe, like most people did, behind four walls and a locked door.

Some debris shifted, and Rane's head shot up, all his senses alert. He tensed, but only silence followed. Perhaps he'd imagined it. He bent down to examine what was left of the door when he heard it again. He clambered out of the ruins as the noise increased, eager to have space around him in case he needed to fight.

Rane turned in a circle, trying to see what was causing the instability. There had never been earthquakes out in the Steppes as far as he knew, but still the ground shook.

Then he saw a mound of grass move. It was only a few yards away. The grass rippled, rising like a blanket being picked up off the floor.

Something big stirred under the earth. Rane took a step back and drew a pistol as an arm appeared, as thick as a tree trunk.

Rane's heart raced and his mouth went dry as a giant body pushed itself up and then shrugged the grass off its back.

It was a Jotnar, bigger than any Rane had fought in the war. Shell encased most of its body like armor, leaving few vulnerable parts to attack. Spurs jutted out from its elbows, forearms, and knees, sharp enough to gut any man foolish enough to get close.

It looked around, and then its orange eyes fixed on Rane and it roared.

10

Rane

The Jotnar reared up to its full height. At least twelve feet of pure violence and hatred. It opened its over-sized jaw, revealing rotten fangs, and bellowed its intent, shaking a fist. Dirt and grass fell off its shoulders as it stepped out of its pit, leaving behind a half-eaten body in its lair, and came at Rane.

Up the slope, Rane's horse was off like a shot, and, if Rane had any sense, he'd be off running after the damn animal. Instead, he aimed at the Jotnar's head and fired, reaching for his other pistol before he even knew if his bullet had struck. Gun smoke obscured his vision as he brought the second weapon to bear, but he didn't need to see. The ground shook as the Jotnar charged towards him, telling him his bullet hadn't done any real damage.

The shadow fell over him, blocking out the sun as he fired a second time. At such close range, he didn't need to aim. Out of the corner of his eye, he could see an arm swinging down as the bullet struck. Black blood sprayed over him, and the Jotnar roared—but then it felt like a battering ram struck him. He flew through the air before hitting the ground hard, the impact knocking more wind out of him.

Rane spit blood and tried to stand, head spinning, lungs working to replace the stolen breath. Both guns were gone.

There was only *Kibon*. It howled along with the Jotnar, demanding to be free. And Rane knew he had no choice.

The Jotnar charged towards him as he pulled his sword off his back. Immediately, he felt his pain lessen, his head clear, even though the blade was still sealed within the scabbard. But the Jotnar was so fast, on him in an instant, swinging its massive fist. Rane dove to one side, swatting at the fist with his sword as it whistled past. He rolled, drawing *Kibon*, feeling its joy as it was free at last.

Rane hacked at the Jotnar's legs. The blade bit into the creature's shell-like skin, sending a jolt of magic though Rane, but it wasn't a deep enough cut to stop the Jotnar.

Not nearly deep enough.

The demon screamed in rage and came at Rane again. He darted this way and that, using his speed to stay one step ahead of the monster as he looked for an opening. Rane ducked under another wild swing and *slashed* Kibon across the Jotnar's face, drawing blood from chin to cheek—but again, it was only a scratch.

Rane stabbed up with the sword, but the blade skittered off the Jotnar's armor-like skin and he caught a backhanded blow for his trouble. He sprawled in the dirt, and *Kibon* flew from his hand.

His vision swam as he looked around, trying to spot his

fallen blade, feeling panic. He spat more blood, feeling his ribs grate. Where was *Kibon?*

The Jotnar raced towards him once more, shaking the ground with every step. Rane scrambled back, afraid now. A fist crunched down, pounding the earth. Rane retreated once more as he searched for his sword. If the monster drove him too far away from *Kibon*, it would all be over. Where was it?

Rane tried to circle back, but the Jotnar stood its ground and bellowed its rage. He ducked and weaved, went one way then quickly back-tracked the other. The Jotnar swiped at him, missed, then lunged, both arms coming together.

Rane dove, feeling the limbs whistle past his head. He slid in the dirt and ash, rolled, bounced back on his feet, and ran.

The demon followed, giving him no respite, shaking the ground. No wonder so many had died at the way station. How could any person stand before such a monster?

If only he could find—there! There it was. *Kibon* lay near a burned corpse. Its mottled steel glinting its promise of salvation. He just had to—

The blow knocked Rane sideways. He landed face down in the ash, banging his head on a half-buried rock, felt blood, turned, dizzy, saw the Jotnar towering over him.

He grabbed the rock and threw it with all his might.

It smashed into the monster's face, pulverizing bone and tooth. The creature staggered back, shaking black blood as it screamed and howled.

Rane moved. He had one heartbeat, maybe two, to get away, get *Kibon*. He scrambled on all fours, clawed his way through the dirt, eyes fixed on his sword. His hope.

He sensed the Jotnar give chase. Pounding the ground, howling its rage, desperate to kill.

It was a race now. Rane found his feet and ran. It was only a few yards, and yet it felt like he had to cross the whole world. A shadow fell over him as Rane threw himself forward, hand outstretched.

He slid once more in the ash and slipped his hand around *Kibon*'s hilt. Power surged through him. He twisted on the ground, *Kibon* in a reverse grip, slicing up as the Jotnar hammered a blow down.

The Jotnar's arm was covered in shell-like skin, but *Kibon* had been forged by a master sword-smith and honed to have such a fine edge that even Odason would fear it—and that was before it was powered by magic most foul. The blade sliced through the demon's limb as if it were wheat before a scythe.

The arm went flying. Black ichor drenched Rane. *Kibon* came alive in Rane's hand, full of battle frenzy as the demon's blood charged it. He attacked with a devastating swiftness, his arm nothing but a blur as he hacked and cut, chopped and sliced.

Magic ran through Rane, giving him strength, giving him fury. He drove his other fist into the Jotnar's knee, cracking shell, breaking bone, and he felt no pain of his own. He carved a chunk out of its gut as it tumbled forward, then hacked into its side as he moved around to its rear.

The creature knew it was dying. Its cries echoed in Rane's ears, but dying wasn't dead. There was no justice yet for the fallen. Rane leaped onto the Jotnar's back and thrust *Kibon* deep into its spine. A rush of magic hit Rane with a long-forgotten joy. The creature roared, tried to reach Rane with its one remaining arm. Rane lost his footing as the demon thrashed beneath him, but he held on to *Kibon*'s hilt with both hands, growing stronger as the demon struggled beneath him.

The creature slumped forward, but still it wasn't dead. It clawed at the ground with its hand and stump, trying to rise, trying to fight. Rane pulled *Kibon* free and jumped from the Jotnar's back, his mind all but overwhelmed by magic he'd absorbed. He strode around the side of the demon, spinning *Kibon* in his hand. The Jotnar growled and mewed like a pathetic thing but Rane didn't care. He stopped at its neck, took *Kibon* in both hands, raised it above his head, and slashed down.

Rane felt almost no resistance as *Kibon* decapitated the creature. Its head rolled free, its cries beautifully silenced. Another charge of magic pulsed through Rane, healing all his wounds and injuries, restoring his strength and energy.

Gods, he'd forgotten how good it felt. How right.

Yes, hissed *Kibon*. *Remember you are alive.*

Rane's body shook with the thrill of it as he stood in the middle of all that carnage and destruction, covered in black blood, dirt, and soot, feeling invincible.

His heart raced as the thrill of the kill ran through him. His head pounded with magic. And by the Gods above and below, he wanted more. He looked around for more enemies, more monsters, more anything to feed to *Kibon*.

The blood lust sang within him, and it was glorious.

But, even as the joy of *Kibon*'s magic rushed through him, there was another thought battling to be heard.

No, it said.

This is how Marcus felt. How Myri was seduced. This is the way to your damnation.

He looked down at *Kibon*. At the mottle on its steel. They were the marks on his soul. The curse at work. Killing the Jotnar had added to the stains. Even killing a demon took its toll on him.

How many lives would it need before he was lost and Tainted?

He snatched up the scabbard from the ground. *Kibon* protested, but Rane ignored it and forced the blade home once more.

The world dulled as he did so, as *Kibon* howled in protest. The magic still coursed through him, but it was manageable now. He could think. He could breathe. And he didn't want to kill.

Rane retrieved his pistols next and slipped them into his holsters. He couldn't reload them because the ammunition was with his pack. Another mistake he'd not make again. He'd spent too long running from trouble. He had to be better prepared when he found it.

He walked to the edge of the pond and knelt, washing his hands first, then splashed water over his face and neck, trying to wipe the worst of the blood and muck away. It wasn't perfect, but it would do for now. The cool water helped chill his blood as well, calming him. By the time he'd finished, he looked and felt somewhat human.

With *Kibon* on his back, Rane took his time climbing back up the slope, steadying his breathing, his heart. Halfway up, he stopped and looked back at the way station and the dead Jotnar. Even with *Kibon,* it had been a close call. Were there others like it nearby? He dared not think about what horrors a pack of such creatures could commit.

His horse—Jak's horse—was waiting a dozen yards away, watching Rane with fearful eyes. Rane couldn't blame the animal. Even after washing, he must've smelled like death. He held up both hands and approached slowly. "Easy, easy. Don't be scared. It's just me."

The horse skittered but didn't run, and that was a success as far as Rane was concerned. He continued talking to the horse as he got nearer, still moving slowly, not taking his eyes off the animal.

The horse retreated from Rane a couple of times, but finally he got his hands on the reins. "I know. I smell awful. I'm sorry." He smiled and the horse seemed to relax. Rane put his foot in the stirrup and swung himself into the saddle. Again, the horse danced around, uncomfortable with its rider, but a few pats on its neck calmed it down.

Rane turned the horse and rode back towards the coaches. They'd have to prepare the girls for the horrors they'd see at the way station, but at least now it was safe to pass. But, as Rane rode on, he saw something that frightened him as much as the Jotnar had.

The stagecoach was gone.

Only the luggage wagon waited in the distance. He touched his heels to the horse's flanks, urging it into a gallop.

What had happened to Christoph and the others while he was fighting the Jotnar?

11

Sarah

They'd arrived at the inn in the early hours, long before sunrise. Mother said it was for the best. "Catch everyone sleeping and we catch the guilty before they can run," she'd said.

And they had. Leaving the wagons behind, Odason's Children had descended on the crossroads' inn without warning. A locked door couldn't stop them from gaining entry, and it was the work of a moment to have forty-odd people in their care and on their knees in the inn's main room while soldiers prepared things outside. It took perhaps another five minutes to find out everything they could about the monster and the route he'd taken.

Mother was happy at least. Progress had been made. Information gained.

The innkeeper had given up everything he knew without the need for threats or violence. He'd been quite happy to confess all as if he'd done nothing wrong. Perhaps he was just a stupid man, not a malcontent. Perhaps he was ignorant.

Perhaps.

But everyone knew about Legionnaires and the danger they posed. Why else would the five nations give out ten thousand gold pieces for any caught dead or alive?

Sarah waited by the door, occasionally checking what was being done outside, but mainly watching Mother work. She had a manner about her that was both terrifying to those being questioned and yet inspiring to her Children.

Brother Nicolai joined her. "We have the names of the monster's accomplices and their destination. Mother said we are to leave at once."

Sarah nodded. "Where are they going?"

"Napolin," said Nicolai.

"Across the Steppes?"

"It's the only way."

"There's a good chance the monster will be dead before we reach him. Bracke roam the Steppes."

"Heras' demons do not eat their own. He'll be alive. We will find him."

"As Odason wills it."

"As Odason wills it," repeated Nicolai. "Is everything ready outside?"

Sarah pulled the door open a crack, caught the eye of one of the soldiers outside, got a nod back. "Yes."

"Good." Nicolai returned to Mother's side and whispered in her ear.

"We will leave you now," Mother announced in a loud voice. "You are all to remain here for the time being and reflect on what you could've done better to serve the All-Father." With that, Mother left the inn. Sarah followed

,and then, one by one, all of Odason's Children filed outside.

Sarah could hear the sobs of relief inside the inn as the door was shut. The fools actually thought themselves safe. "Seal them in," she said to a nearby soldier.

They went to work immediately, propping thick wooden blocks against the door so it couldn't be opened from the inside, nailing planks of wood across the windows so no one could get out. The soldiers moved at great speed, ignoring the cries of alarm their hammering provoked. It took only a few moments for the inn to be locked tight. Others placed stacks of tinder along the walls

A brother waited with a lit torch. Sarah checked with Mother, received agreement, and then pointed at the bundles of rushes by the front door.

The brother placed the torch into the heart of them, and the flames leapt quickly from one pile to another and then to the timber of the inn, climbing its walls with a hunger.

The people inside started to scream and cry for help. Some tried to break the door down, others tried to force the windows open. None succeeded.

"Are we ready to depart, Sister Sarah?" called Mother over the noise of the fire.

"We are, Mother Hilik," she replied.

"How many horses from the stables?"

"Fifteen."

"Good. Ready the horses. I want you, Brother Nicolai, and our very finest to go on ahead with them and try to catch the monster."

"As you wish."

"Then be off with you, Sister. You have the All-Father's work to do."

And so Sister Sarah rode out with fourteen of her

brothers and sisters to catch a monster. Behind them marched Mother Hilik and the rest, leaving a burning inn and forty-three people to die.

As much as Sarah tried to pretend otherwise, the All-Father's work felt a lot like murder.

12

Rane

Rane rode hard for the wagon, dreading what he'd find. The stagecoach was gone. Had they been attacked by Bracke, and the coach had driven off to save the passengers? Had the Rastaks attacked and stolen it? So many fears ran through his mind.

Then he saw Christoph standing on top of the wagon, waving at him. Then he saw Fion. Then the two girls. And he knew what had occurred while he'd been battling the Jotnar.

"By Odason, you're alive," said Christoph as Rane pulled to a halt beside the wagon. "What happened?"

"A Jotnar had destroyed the way station. It attacked me as I was checking the ruins. I killed it."

"Are you hurt?" asked Fion, rushing over.

Rane jumped down from the horse. "I'm fine. What happened here? Where are Carl and the others? Where's the stagecoach?" His own pack lay in the dirt, and he picked it up.

"They stole it," said Christoph, climbing down from the wagon. "After you left, they turned their guns on us, said they'd kill us if I didn't hand over my notes of promise."

Fion wrapped her arms around her children. "I thought they were going to murder us no matter what we did."

"Bastards," said Rane. He should've suspected them of such villainy. Jak had made little attempt to hide what motivated him. "Did you give them the notes?"

There was a moment's hesitation from Christoph, then the barest of nods. "Yes. I had no choice."

"Jax ordered us out of the coach, said he was taking it in payment for Carl's horse," said Fion. "They left us with the wagon—but took most of the food."

"I'm amazed they left you that much." Rane looked around, hoping to see the coach in the distance somewhere. "Which way did they go?"

"You can't mean to go after them?" said Christoph, his voice breaking.

"I'm not going to let them steal from you. Besides, you need that money for Saphie."

"Or do you mean to take the money for yourself?" asked Fion, with an anger Rane had not seen before. She crossed her arms as she glared at Rane, her defiance a stark contrast to Christoph's fear. "Jak said you weren't to be trusted."

"I wouldn't listen to the man who's already robbed you and abandoned you," said Rane.

"But will *you* abandon us now we can't pay you, Nathaniel?" said Fion, not backing down. "Will you pretend to go after them and abandon us?"

"I'll get you somewhere safe," said Rane. "As I promised. Somewhere you can regroup and make new plans."

"There are no new plans," said Christoph. "We have no time for new plans. We must go on." He glanced at Saphie. "Before it's too late."

"We can't cross the Steppes without the others. It was nearly an impossible mission with their help. But without it? I might as well kill us all here now and get it over with." A shiver of glee ran through Rane when he said that. *Kibon* had heard and agreed. Blood was always the answer as far as his sword as concerned.

"If we don't reach Napolin in time, you might as well," said Christoph. "Time is against us. We do not have the luxury to go around the Steppes nor to go elsewhere. We must go on."

Rane unhooked a water skin from his horse and took a long drink. "Even if we do make it to Napolin, how will you pay for your daughter's treatment now?"

"They took most of the promise notes but not all of them. We have enough for now, and my brother is in Napolin. He will lend us more if we need it."

"Will Jak and the others have to go to Napolin to cash the notes they took?"

Christoph shook his head. "There are people in every major city and most towns that will honor the notes—no questions asked."

"Did they leave you with any weapons?" asked Rane.

"No," said Fion. "They said you had their bow and that would be enough."

Rane looked from one to the other. "Can either of you use a bow?"

"No," said Christoph.

"What about pistols?" said Rane. "Do you know how to shoot and reload?"

"I do," said Christoph. He didn't sound convinced.

Rane turned to Fion. "What about you?"

"I've never fired a gun."

Rane rubbed his face, feeling a crust of dried Jotnar blood where he'd failed to wash it off. It was suicide to go on. He'd barely survived the encounter with that one demon. Who knew what else would be lurking there? He should cut his losses. Perhaps with him gone, Christoph would turn back. Then he saw Saphie watching him. Saw the plea in her eyes.

"Fine. We go on," said Rane to Christoph. "Tonight, I'll teach Fion how to reload my pistols and you can practice firing them a couple of times. I also want to you all to pack small travel bags. If we are attacked by Bracke, the horses will be the first to die. We must be able to move quickly on foot when that happens. Take only food and water. We don't need anything that won't keep us alive. Do you understand?"

"Yes," said Christoph. "We do. Thank you."

"Prepare yourselves for what you'll see at the way station. There's plenty of dead waiting there for us there, and they didn't go easy. We'll fill up on water and move on quickly. Find somewhere to camp before the Steppes."

"As you say." Christoph climbed up into the driver's box of the wagon while Fion settled the girls at the rear behind the tail gate. Only once they were comfortable did she join her husband. She sat straight-backed and touched her husband's arm, her features set with determination and dread. He cracked the reins and the horses began to move.

Rane swung himself back into his horse's saddle and followed.

When they reached the way station, Rane directed Christoph to drive down near the pool and did his best to keep them away from the dead. Even so, they were all shaken by what they saw. Fion covered her mouth with her handkerchief and asked Christoph to stop so she could climb in back with the girls.

She covered their eyes, but there was no avoiding the smell of death and the flies that had come from nowhere to feed on the corpses.

"We should bury them or cremate them," said Christoph as they carried buckets of water to fill the barrel in the back of the wagon. "It's not right leaving them."

"As you said, we haven't got time for such luxuries," said Rane. "We need to get far enough away from here and set up camp. The flies won't be the only things coming down here to feed. We don't want to be in their way when they arrive."

"All the more reason ..."

"The Bracke that roam the plains are looking for things to eat. If the dead here attract them, that's good for us. I'd rather they feed here than on us."

"I understand. It just ... it doesn't feel right."

"Not much in life does."

Christoph indicated the dead demon with a tilt of his chin. "That's a Jotnar, you say?"

"That's right."

"I've never seen one before."

"I've never seen one that big before. They were bad enough during the war, but I never had to fight any that big."

"Everything's far worse since the war ended," said Christoph. "I used to think that once we won, everything would magically go back to the way it was before. I'd tell the children to 'hold on, it won't be horrible for much longer'. But I was wrong. Things have just become worse and worse." He glanced over at his girls cuddled up next to Fion. "I worry about how bad it's going to get.'

Rane understood the man's pain. He'd experienced enough of his own. "I'll do my best to get you to Napolin."

Christoph smiled. "The last good man on earth, eh?"

"I'm far from that."

"We'll see."

Once the water barrel was full, they lingered long enough to collect some firewood from the wreckage of the way station, and then they moved on, leaving the dead behind. Rane doubted the corpses would attract the Bracke, but maybe they'd get lucky.

They drove on for another hour or two, and everyone's mood lifted once they were away from the stench of the dead. Fion sang songs with the girls, their voices mixing in a beautiful harmony. The sun shone, and the wild grass danced in the breeze. And for a brief while, all their troubles faded away. Even Saphie's cough eased in the fresh air.

For Rane, it was a joy to watch four people with such obvious love for each other, a taste of life as it should be. And he was honored to be with them, to be able to help keep their hope kindled, and he knew he would do whatever he had to do to keep them alive.

As the sky reddened, they stopped and made camp. Rane allowed them a fire. It would probably be the last they could enjoy until they crossed the Steppes, and he didn't believe there were any bandits around to worry about. The girls cooked beans while Rane taught Christoph how to use his pistols.

"You work together," he said. "One shoots while the other reloads. You have to be quick. You have to be careful. You miss or the gun misfires, it's all over. The Bracke won't give you a second chance."

Rane propped a crate up against the side of a lone tree. It

was roughly the height of a Bracke and would give Christoph something to aim at.

Christoph took three shots and missed the target each time. "Shit. I could've sworn I was better than this."

Fion placed her hand on his back. "You will be when it counts."

"Why don't you try?" suggested Rane.

"Me?" she said with surprise. "I don't know anything about guns."

Christoph offered her the pistol she'd just loaded and given to him. "You can't be any worse than I am."

"He has a point," said Rane.

Fion took the pistol, aimed, and fired. The bullet struck the center of the target.

"Do you want to try reloading, Christoph?" asked Rane, with a smile.

"I think I should," he replied, and they all laughed. It turned out that Fion was the better reloader too, but Christoph was good enough.

"Make sure you have knives with you too at all times," said Rane. "If the Bracke get too close, you won't have time to reload. Just grab your knife and stab them until they stop moving."

Both nodded grimly.

"In the morning, we'll rearrange the luggage in the wagon so the girls are in the center, away from the sides. Maybe work out a way they can be covered up as well if we get attacked."

"You sound like you think they will get past us," said Fion.

"We have to be prepared for everything," said Rane. "Hopefully if we come across any Bracke, they will be few in number, and they'll be scared off by gunfire."

Fion looked to her husband. "Are we doing the right thing?"

Tears glistened in Christoph's eyes. "What else can we do?"

Saphie coughed by the fire, and Christoph pulled his wife into an embrace.

"I think we've done enough practicing for tonight." Rane got up and left them to their hopes and fears.

The good mood returned over dinner. They only had half a bowl of beans each, but it was enough, and Christoph told tales that had everyone laughing.

Later that night, after everyone had eaten and the others had fallen asleep, Rane sat back and stared at the stars. Watching the heavens was something Rane had always enjoyed doing with Kara. Back then, it made them realize how insignificant their problems were compared to the glory of the heavens. Now? Somehow it made him feel close to Kara again, for the first time in an age. Perhaps helped by the obvious love Christoph had for Fion, reminding him of Kara.

Whatever the reason, he was grateful—for those people in that moment of that evening. For now, he wasn't the hunted—he was just Nathaniel Rane.

And it felt good.

He got up and stretched before walking away from the fire and out into the darkness, his hand on *Kibon*'s hilt.

The sword thrummed with anticipation in his hand. It knew bloody days lay ahead.

13

Sarah

Sister Sarah was no horsewoman. She'd learned how to ride years before, like all Odason's Children, but, since then, she'd walked everywhere she'd needed to go. Now, as the All-Father was her witness, she wished she was still walking.

There was nothing natural about riding a horse, especially at speed. Every part of her ached. Even her head throbbed from being thrown around as they galloped after the monster.

Brother Nicolai, of course, had no such problems. He looked like he'd been born in the saddle, sitting proud and magnificent. He looked like he could kill all the world's demons by himself. No wonder he made her head spin.

She had to admit, too, that the others traveling with them were almost as impressive as Nicolai. Hard men and women used to doing Odason's bloody work.

Not for the first time, Sarah wondered why she was in charge of them. She knew she wasn't as good a warrior as any of them, let alone have any right to lead them. Still, Mother Hilik had thought otherwise and had given her the responsibility, despite the fact that Sarah neither wanted nor had asked for it.

Her mind drifted to what would happen when they caught up with the monster. Would they be able to stop him? Surely fifteen strong hearts with fifteen swords were enough to kill the foul creature.

They had shields too, plus spears and nets. But no firearms. The church saw them as demon weapons, and they were strictly forbidden. But Odason forgive her, Sarah half-wished they had some. She'd seen the damage a pistol or a musket could do during the war. Such weapons could make all the difference against the monster.

At least they were on the right trail. They'd found long dead campfires and old campsites left behind by the monster and his companions, all pointing towards Napolin. Sarah dreaded to think what ungodly purpose the monster had in such a large city, what atrocities he planned to commit. But there was a large contingent of Odason's Children in Napolin. If the monster were to reach the city, Sarah could at least call on a small army to hunt him down.

"Sister Sarah!" called Nicolai from up ahead.

Sarah spurred her horse on and prayed she wouldn't fall off as the animal picked up speed.

Nicolai waited with the others at the top of a lip. She could tell by the look on his face that grim tidings awaited her. She saw the water first, a great pond sparkling in the afternoon sun. It was beautiful, and for one glorious moment, she thought she'd misread Nicolai's expression. Then she saw the scene of destruction along the water's edge, and Sarah's heart sank. "Odason give me strength," she whispered as she pulled her horse to a halt.

"It's a way station," said Nicolai. "The only place to get supplies for miles around."

It might have been once, but now it was a blackened ruin. "Did the monster do this?"

Nicolai nodded. "I fear so. Shall we go down?"

"Let us wait for the others. Better we go together." Was her hesitation fear? Perhaps, but it was better for all of them to have strength in numbers. Only Odason knew what waited for them down there.

Even so, looking down on all the death and destruction broke her heart. If the monster had killed the people below, their deaths were due to the Inquisition's failure to stop him. At least Harold, Roon, Jonas, and David had been punished for letting the monster go. They owed the dead that much.

Stone. She would be like stone. She couldn't cry in front of the others no matter how much she wanted. Any weakness would be reported back to Mother. She forced herself to look down at the dead while they waited for the others to catch up. She would remember this. She would avenge them all.

There was a reason why the Inquisition did what it did. They might not have asked for that responsibility nor did they want it, but Odason had given into them.

"Search carefully down below," she told the others once they were all gathered. "Perhaps the monster is among the dead, but I fear not. I think he still waits for us out on the Steppes."

The others nodded agreement, the horror and shock plain to see on their faces. Sarah knew the next hour or so would affect them all in some way. Hopefully it would temper them all like steel so they would find the strength to accomplish what needed to be done.

They rode slowly down the slope and dismounted among the dead. The bodies were everywhere. Some had been burned alive in the building, while others had been cut down by the water's edge. She saw corpses that had been ripped limb from limb, while a few of the dead looked like they had been pulverized. She could feel the anger within her change to hatred. No one deserved to die like this. And anyone who could commit such atrocities did not deserve her mercy.

"Sarah," called out Nicolai. "Over here."

She ran, hoping he'd found the monster, only to see that he'd discovered a very different kind of demon.

"A Jotnar." Beheaded in the ash. Sarah had never seen one either alive or dead before, and a tremor pulsed through her at the sight of it. It was easy to believe that the demon, with its scaled body covered in spikes, had been dragged straight out of Heras's depths. "What was that doing here?"

"Heras must've sent it to help the monster" said Nicolai. "She knows we are getting close."

"Then who cut its head off?" asked Sarah.

"One of the others before the monster killed them?"

Sarah stared at the Jotnar. It had been bad enough when they just had to worry about fighting the monster. "Do you think Heras will send other demons to help him?"

"Anything is possible," said Nicolai and, for the first time since she'd known him, there was fear on his face too.

The others crowded around, looking at the dead demon, feeding off each other's fears. Sarah felt it too. Suddenly, fifteen of Odason's Children did not seem nearly enough to charge after the monster. She wished she had Mother Hilik with her and all the rest of the Soldiers of the Inquisition.

"Sister Sarah?" Nicolai was watching her, waiting. "Do we go on?"

"Of course." Her voice was but a whisper, and that would not do. Sarah straightened her back and looked at her brothers and sisters. They needed to hear something, otherwise she could see them breaking. They would fail when it mattered most. Like Harold, Roon, Jonas, and David.

Sarah couldn't allow that. But what to say? She took a deep breath and prayed for Odason's guidance. The others watched her, wondering, doubting, worrying. And then she knew the words.

"Brothers and sisters," she said, meeting the gaze of each and every one. "What happened here is what happens when we fail in our duty. Because the monster escaped us, innocent people have died. We cannot let that happen again. That is why we have been chosen by Odason for this holy mission. We are His strongest and His most devout. Remember the people who died here, feel their pain in your very souls, and treasure it, for it will give us strength when the time comes. It will remind you why we have to do Odason's work.

"The road we ride is hard and dangerous, but better we face what lies ahead than those who have fallen here. Will you do this holy work with me, brothers and sisters? Will you hunt this monster down with me?"

"Yes," said Nicolai, as she knew he would.

"Yes," said the others.

"Good," said Sarah. "For that is as Odason wishes." She mounted her horse without care or worry and waited while the others did the same.

"We go on!" she shouted. "For Odason! For justice!"

She kicked her horse onward, feeling Odason guide her true. She heard the thunder of hooves as her brothers and sisters followed, and Sister Sarah smiled despite the horror they were leaving behind.

They found another campsite a few miles on. Another old campfire. Sarah waited on her horse while Nicolai checked the ground. He walked this way and that, bending low, then raced back to look at the way they'd come.

"What's wrong, Brother?" she asked.

"There's only one wagon now," said Nicolai. "The other wagon must've left them earlier. We ... I missed the trail."

"Two wagons. Two paths," said Sarah. "How do we know which way the monster went?"

"We don't."

"Damn."

"I can send some of the others back to find where they parted company and go after them."

"No," said Sarah. "The monster is cunning. It wants us to split our forces, weaken us. It knows we are getting closer. Calling the Jotnar, now this. We must stay together. We must stay strong."

"Then which wagon do we go after?"

Sarah stared at the ground as if that could tell her which way to go—but she was no tracker like Nicolai.

Sarah took a deep breath. Odason would guide her choice. He would not let Sarah down. "We keep going. The monster is heading to Napolin."

"As you wish," said Nicolai.

They didn't stop as they crossed into the Steppes. Mile after mile they rode, only stopping or slowing when their mounts demanded it. On they went until darkness fell and they couldn't see the tracks any more.

As the others sat and ate around the fire, Sarah

wandered by herself out into the night. The way station had changed her. She knew that now. Her doubts were gone. Her insecurities too. She could feel Odason looking down on her from his great hall, and that was all she needed. She was His servant, and she would do His will on this earth as long as she could draw breath.

She would kill the monster or die trying.

"Sarah?" Nicolai had come up behind her. "Are you all right?"

She glanced over his shoulder to the camp where the others sat. No one seemed to be paying them any attention. Even so, she kept her voice low. "I was just thinking about the duty Odason has placed on us. We must stop this monster from hurting anyone else."

Nicolai smiled. "Always so serious. No wonder Mother Hilik has shown you favor."

Sarah blushed. "I have no idea why. So many others are better suited. Others who are more deserving. Like you."

His fingers brushed hers. "No one else has your heart. I see how much it hurts you when the contaminated are purged. You want to save everybody."

Sarah stiffened. "Has anyone else noticed?"

"Probably everyone."

"Dear Odason. What if someone tells Mother?" Sarah didn't want to burn.

"She already knows. Why else has she nominated you as her successor? She doesn't want someone cold of blood sitting in judgement. It's too easy to just pronounce everyone guilty and let Odason sort out our mistakes." Nicolai's beautiful eyes met hers. "She knows you'll never take the easy path."

"I always thought I was weak."

"Another reason why you succeed. You never take anything for granted."

"You always say the right things, Nicolai. I don't know what I'd do without you."

He bit his lip. "I know what I would like to do *with* you."

Sarah's eyes drifted back to the camp, the others. "Nicolai ..."

"You can't tell me you don't want to."

"I do. More than you know. But the others ... someone will see. Someone will tell. Mother wouldn't forgive us."

Nicolai took hold of her hand and didn't let go. "We can be quick. Quiet. The night will hide us."

Sarah shook her head. "No."

His hand fell away. "A shame."

"I know."

"Do you ever think about us?"

"What do you mean?"

"You and I. Together."

"I do. Often." Sarah could feel her cheeks redden again. "Too often."

"Not like that. I mean really together. As in man and wife."

"That's not possible. We are Soldiers of the Inquisition. Odason's Children. It's forbidden."

"I know," said Nicolai. "But have you thought about it?"

Sarah's heart felt like it had stopped. She struggled to breathe. She knew what she should say. Then she saw the fear in Nicolai's eyes, and she also knew she couldn't lie to him. "Yes."

"Then leave—with me."

"But no one leaves. The Inquisition is our lives. Our calling."

Nicolai looked away. "What if our calling is to each other

instead?"

"That's blasphemy. Mother Hilik would burn us both if she heard you say that."

"She's not here. You are."

"Nicolai …" Sarah wanted him to stop talking. Needed him to be silent.

"We could run. Run so far and find a place where there was no Inquisition, no church. We could be ourselves. Together."

Sarah shook her head. "Please stop. Mother might not hear but the All-Father will. We are his children. We shouldn't even … do what we do."

"You can't tell me what we have between us is wrong. And I wouldn't believe you if you did."

She could feel tears forming. She pinched them away. It was the last thing she needed right now. "Just stop. Please. This isn't the time or the place. We have a job to do. People are counting on us. That's all that matters now."

"You're right." The passion went from his face. He let go of her hand and stepped back. It was only a single pace but it felt like a chasm had opened up between them. He looked back to the camp, then to his feet, and, finally, to her. "Don't stay out here too long. You need your rest."

"Nicolai … I …" She couldn't say the words she wanted to say.

He nodded all the same. "Me too."

She watched him walk back to the others, her heart full of regret, but knowing she'd done the right thing.

There would be other moments. Private moments when they could be themselves, out of sight of others. Away from the whispers. When they could talk.

She stared into the night. They just had to kill the monster first.

14

Rane

Christoph woke Rane shortly after sunrise. He'd spent most of the night on watch, and now Rane wished he'd had more sleep instead.

"Do we have time to cook something?" asked Christoph after he'd woken the others.

"Keep the fire small," said Rane, "and be quick."

Christoph held up some strips of meat. "The last of the bacon."

"How much food do we have left?" asked Rane.

"Some dried bread and meat, a little rice and beans. Enough to eat something over the next few days, but that's about it."

Rane stood and stretched out his back. "Maybe we'll find some buffalo to kill out on the Steppes."

Christoph smiled. "That would solve all our problems."

"Some of them at least," said Rane. "The Steppes were

famous for their buffalo. Wild herds roamed all over it. But now?" He shrugged. "They'll be good hunting for Bracke. Probably why the creatures are massing here."

Christoph's smile disappeared as quickly as it had come. "Do you think we'll find some today?"

"I don't know. I hope not. But we will cross paths with them eventually."

Christoph looked down at the strips of meat in his hand. "I'm not hungry now."

Rane gripped his shoulders. "The others will enjoy it, and you need to keep your strength up. Cook while I fix the wagon."

Rane climbed up into the back of the wagon and started shifting cases and sacks from one place to another.

"What are you doing?" asked Saphie, looking up at him.

Rane smiled. "I'm making a secret hiding spot for you and your sister."

"Can I help?"

"Sure."

The girl clambered up and started to move some of the smaller items.

"What's in all of these trunks?" asked Rane.

"Clothes mostly," said Saphie, with a cough. "Mother likes us to look smart."

"Don't strain yourself," said Rane. "I can manage by myself."

Saphie gave him a look. "Don't you start. I'm fed up with everyone treating me like I could die at any minute. I can move a few sacks, okay?"

"That's fine with me. You know what you're capable of." Rane moved another chest and finally saw the floorboards of the wagon. By the time, he'd moved another two, there was enough space cleared for both girls to sit down. He resituated some chests, creating walls. "Can you sit there so I can see how high we need to go?"

Saphie climbed into the center. Standing, the crates came up to her waist. When she sat, she disappeared from sight.

"Perfect," said Rane.

"It's not very comfortable," said Saphie.

"It'll only be for a few days."

Sophia jumped to her feet. "I know what we can do." She opened a trunk and began pulling colorful dresses from it.

"I don't think they're very practical for traveling," said Rane.

Saphie grinned. "But they'll be comfortable to sit on." She threw all the dresses into the hiding place. "Very practical, in fact."

"Your mother might not think so."

"It'll be our secret then," said Saphie, then coughed.

"That it will. Now, go and eat your breakfast," said Rane. "I'll finish here."

Rane watched the girl go, then set about making sure all the luggage wouldn't shift once they set off again. He fixed the crate side they'd used for target practice so it could be pulled over the space quickly, forming a roof of sorts, then arranged some canvas that could be dragged over everything. By the time Rane was finished, he was happy with the enclosure. Of course, whether it would help save Saphie and Rache from the Bracke was another matter.

As THEY ROLLED through the countryside, the coarse grass that had accompanied them so far on their journey began to change, becoming greener, taller, and more lush, and Rane felt his anxiety increase with it. Long grass was perfect for

Bracke. They could lie hidden from view and just wait for their prey to pass. He sat up in his saddle, searching the grass, but there was nothing he could see. Yet.

Rane signaled the wagon to stop and dismounted. The grass came up to his thigh and swayed with the wind. It looked like it went on forever. Not even a single tree varied the landscape. Only the road cut through the green, a long, brown scar heading north.

Christoph whistled. "I suppose this is the Great Steppes."

Rane nodded. "I'd forgotten how big it is."

"It's beautiful," said Fion.

"Don't let it fool you," said Rane. "Wind can get something fierce out here, freeze you to the spot before you even know it's coming. And the rain is worse than the wind."

"Wonderful," said Fion, sounding like she didn't believe it.

"Last chance to turn back," said Rane.

Christoph cracked the reins in reply.

They moved slowly, following the hard dirt road through the grass. There was no singing like the previous day, no laughing or joking. There was just the creak of the wagon wheels, the clomp of horse hooves, and Saphie's cough accompanying them.

They passed places where the grass was shorter, sometimes not even a hand high, where herds of buffalo had eaten their way across the land and trampled what was left. The flattened grass covered vast areas of the Steppes, but they had yet to see any sign of the creatures that had caused it.

"I'm going to ride ahead," said Rane. "If I should get attacked, I want you to turn this wagon around as fast as you can and drive fast back the way we came."

"And leave you?" said Christoph.

"Yes."

"I—" Christoph stopped as Fion placed her hand on his arm

"We will, Nathaniel," she said.

"Good." He spurred his horse on, gaining some distance from the others, eyes searching everywhere, looking for any movement out of place, a shape that didn't belong, a break in the sea of green.

The Bracke were out there, but where?

They made camp as the sun started to dip in a spot that was the same as any other. In many ways, it felt like they'd made no progress at all through the relentless grass sea. If it wasn't for the dirt and dust covering them and the ache in his muscles that came from a long day's ride, Rane could easily have believed they were in exactly the same spot they'd started from that morning. Everywhere, in every direction, the same view confronted them—open grasslands.

"Keep watch while I tend to the horses," said Rane to Fion and Christoph.

"I'll get the girls to cook something," said Fion.

"Only a small fire, enough to cook some rice," said Rane.

"We can do better than just rice," said Christoph. "Our stores aren't that bed yet."

"If you cook meat, the scent will carry on the wind," said Rane. "If the wrong thing smells it, we'll have unwanted guests coming to join us."

"I hadn't thought of that."

"I only know because I spent time in enemy territory during the war," said Rane. "Some of the people I fought with had to learn that lesson the hard way."

He wiped the horses down as best he could without

taking off their saddles or harnesses, then fed and watered them.

"They won't like spending the night like that," said Fion. She had Rane's holster belt tied around her waist, the pistols sitting on each hip.

"We won't have time to hitch them up if we get attacked," said Rane. "The girls must sleep in the wagon as well. You too, if you can. That way, if anything happens, we can move fast."

"I don't want to go back," said Fion. "Not if we can fight them off."

"It depends how many Bracke they are. Too many and our only chance will be to run."

Fion's shoulders sank.

"I'm just being honest with you," said Rane. "You've still got another daughter to keep alive."

Fion glanced back at the wagon. The girls were stacking a small pile of firewood underneath the cooking pot. "Rache needs to get to Napolin just as much as Saphie."

"She has the disease as well?"

Fion nodded.

"I didn't know."

"Nor does she. But I've been through this ... experience twice now. I know the signs, what to look for. She has it too, like her sister and her brother before her."

"I'm sorry."

She smiled. "That's why we can't go back."

The mood was subdued while they ate, and once the meal was finished, Rane insisted the fire be put out. Even so, the smell of smoke drifted out into the night, and he only hoped it wasn't enough to attract predators. The girls grumbled, but Fion made them climb up into the wagon. Rane left them to it and wandered away from camp.

"Would you like me to take first watch?" asked Christoph, coming to join him.

"You get some rest first. It'll help everyone else settle down," replied Rane.

"You need rest too."

Rane touched *Kibon*'s hilt. "I'm not tired."

Christoph went to say something, then stopped himself. "Goodnight. Wake me when you're ready."

"I will." Little pulses of energy ran from *Kibon* up through Rane's fingers. It could sense the danger they were all in, and, what was worse, the sword welcomed it.

Rane knew the sword could be the difference between life and death for them all, but killing Bracke would corrupt *Kibon* . Not as much as taking human lives did but it would all add up.

He breathed in deeply, steadied himself and let go of the sword. Instead, he went to his horse and removed the bow and quiver from his saddle. The horse snorted at him as he did so, unhappy to still be tacked up. "Better safe than dead," whispered Rane as he stroked her face.

Rane slung the quiver over his shoulder and then strung the bow. He tested the tension on the string, pulling it back to his cheek several times, getting a sense of its power. One arrow might not be enough to kill a Bracke, but it would know it was hurt.

As everyone settled in, a beautiful night fell over the camp with a near full moon and a sky full of stars, bathing everything in a silver wash. Rane stared into the night, bow in hand, looking for danger. The temperature dropped, but, for Rane, that was a good thing. The chill kept him alert as the hours passed, and he continued to keep watch.

Something else worried him too. Something else far off in the distance, back the way they'd come.

A fire, maybe two, burned on the road behind them. A red glow in the darkness. Someone was on the road behind them, and Rane couldn't help but wonder who they could be and why they, too, were on the road through the Steppes. He couldn't think of any good reasons for anyone to be there.

RANE HAD all of two hours sleep at most by the time morning came. It was his own fault yet again. He'd stayed on watch longer than he should've, until he was nodding off and a danger to everyone. Only then did he wake Christoph. Truth was he didn't quite trust the man to do a good job of keeping watch even though he'd done nothing to make Rane doubt him.

At least they'd made it through the first night without being attacked.

Mist swirled around them as they got ready. No one spoke. The horses grumbled and snorted. Breakfast was cold and meager. But they hadn't been attacked. They were alive. For Rane, that was as good as they could hope for.

They continued as they had the day before: Rane leading the way, and Fion and Christoph driving the wagon. They followed the road, chasing the horizon. Always moving but never seeming to go anywhere.

Rane found it harder going that day. The sight of endless grass irritated his tired eyes, and his anxiety grew with each step they took. He didn't believe they'd make it across the Steppes without being attacked. It was just a question of when and how bad the assault would be when it came. Accepting that truth meant he couldn't relax in any way. And danger could come from any direction. He had to check their rear as much as he had to watch their front and flanks. Demons could just as easily creep up from behind them. Bracke were cunning creatures, after all.

It was late afternoon when something caught Rane's eye. A break in the green. A small dark bump on the horizon line. Rane couldn't make out what it was, but he called the wagons to a halt all the same. Better safe than sorry. Better alive than dead.

"What's wrong?" asked Fion.

"There's something over there." Rane pointed, and the family looked the way he indicated.

"Is that a Bracke?" asked Christoph.

"It's too big for that." Rane loosened *Kibon* in its scabbard. "Wait here. Keep your eyes open. I'm going to take a closer look."

It felt strange leaving the road and riding his horse out into the grass as if he was crossing a boundary from somewhere safe to somewhere dangerous. But it was just grass and he could see nothing else moving.

As he got closer, he could see that the shape was a fallen buffalo. Closer still and he could smell the rot of its flesh.

He dismounted ten yards from the animal and went the rest of the way on foot, his hand on *Kibon's* hilt. Just holding the sword made his senses flare and his exhaustion disappear.

Rane paused every few steps, looking for danger, expecting a trap, but he was alone. The only life he could sense was back at the wagon.

The buffalo was maybe eleven feet snout to tail, and its horns were nocked and chipped—a big beast that knew how to look after itself. Bbut it had been taken down and killed. As Rane circled it, he already knew what had killed it. Sure enough, there were claw marks and gashes across its flank. A hind leg had been severed. Its throat ripped out. Its stomach feasted on.

And it had only happened a couple of days ago.

Rane backed away, mounted his horse, and returned to the others.

"Dead buffalo," he said as he pulled his horse level with the wagon.

"Do I want to know how it died?" asked Christoph.

"It looks like it was killed by a Bracke."

"Shit."

Christoph's family all started to look around them, and Fion had a pistol in her hand, as if expecting to see demons coming out of the grass at them that very instant.

"What do we do?" asked Fion.

"Nothing's changed," said Rane. "We knew they were out here. The buffalo has been dead for a few days at least, so we're in no immediate danger as far as I can tell. We keep moving. We keep our eyes open. When there's a problem, we'll deal with it." Another twist in his gut told him that might not be the case, reminded him that he need *Kibon*, needed its power. The Bracke were out there, waiting for him.

No. Rane breathed in slowly, counted to five, exhaled slowly. That was the sword talking, trying to work its darkness on him. He didn't need the blade. Not yet. But the time was fast approaching when he'd have no choice but to use it.

He turned his horse to face the road ahead. "Let's go."

"What about the buffalo? Could we eat its meat?" asked Christoph.

"It's been dead too long, and the Bracke have feasted well on its corpse. Better we go hungry than eat what's left," said Rane.

They continued for the rest of the day, alone with the

wind and the grass. The clump of horse hooves, the creak of wagon and wheel, and Saphie's cough once again the only sounds. In the vastness of the steppes nothing ever seemed to change.

They stopped as the sun set, in a spot like any other, like their camp site of the previous night.

"If I didn't know any better," said Christoph, "I'd think we'd just gone around in one big circle."

"It's like we're the only people in the world," said Saphie.

"Alone is good," said Rane. "Alone is safe."

"Can we have a fire?" asked Rache.

"No," said Rane. "No fires until we're out of the Steppes."

"Then how are we going cook?" asked Saphie. "We can't eat dried bread every day."

"We have three days to go. Better to be careful," said Rane.

Saphie turned to Fion, but her mother shook her head. "Nathaniel is right. I don't want any of us to end up like the buffalo."

They ate in silence, and the girls went to sleep in the wagon without being asked. The days of singing and laughter already seemed like someone else's memory.

Once more, Rane stood watch, his bow ready. But everything was like the night before, the wind and the grass and the shadows and nothing else.

Only the camp fire in the distance was different. Closer. Rane even thought he could smell their fire on the wind. Someone followed and didn't seem to care about Bracke attacking them.

"Who are you?" Rane asked the night.

15

Rane

Rane woke to the sound of Saphie having a coughing fit. Her parents rushed to their daughter's side as Rane threw off his blankets and stood up.

The cough sounded worse than ever, thick, wet, and violent, and Rane's heart went out to the girl as another fit racked her body.

Fion held her daughter as she tried to get Saphie to drink from a water skin. "Take your time," she cooed. "Calm yourself and drink."

Christoph rubbed Saphie's back while Rache looked on with alarm.

"Can I do anything to help?" asked Rane.

"I have medicine in my bag, but we need some hot water for it to work," said Fion.

"I'll get a fire going."

"Thank you," said Christoph.

Rane set about stacking a small pile of twigs and kindling, then used his flint to strike a spark. Once that caught, he blew on it, feeding it into a flame. Only then did he start adding bigger twigs and larger sticks. Hopefully the smoke wouldn't drift too far and bring Bracke looking. Then again, Saphie's coughing was enough to wake the dead.

He filled a small kettle with water and set it over the fire.

While he waited for the water to boil, Rane stretched and looked around, aware that it would be just their luck for Bracke to attack while everyone was concentrating on Saphie.

Rache ran over with a small pouch in her hand. "Mother said to put a handful of these leaves into the pot."

Rane took the pouch. The leaves were dry and dark with a bitter scent, but he duly added them to the water as directed. "How long do they need to boil?"

"Not long," said Rache. She looked over her shoulder, towards her sister. "Too long."

"She'll be fine," said Rane.

"No, she won't," replied Rache. "If we don't die getting to Napolin, we'll die soon after. There's no cure for what we have."

"We?"

The girl nodded. "Mother and Father think I don't know, but I've heard their whispers, seen their looks. I'm not stupid—no matter what they think."

"No one thinks that."

"Really?" She looked up, a blaze of anger in her eyes. "Mother and Father do. They think I'm fooled by their fake smiles and fake promises."

"They just want to protect you. That's all."

"Maybe they should trust me more."

Rane didn't know what to say. He wasn't a father. He was a warrior and an outlaw. "Perhaps you should speak to them. Let them know that you—"

"Is the water ready?" Fion called out.

"They have enough to worry about," said Rache. "And don't you say anything."

"I won't." Rane filled a cup with the medicine and gave it to Rache. Once she took it, he kicked dirt over the fire, smothering it.

By the time he'd checked the horses and the wagon, Saphie's coughing had subsided, and she looked well enough to continue.

"Thank you for your help, Nathaniel," said Christoph, climbing into the box seat of the wagon.

"Stop thanking me, please," he replied. "We all do what we can."

"Even so ..." The Fascalian smiled. "Ready for another day of never changing scenery?"

"If that's all we have today, I'll be very happy."

"Here's to boredom then," said Christoph. He gestured towards the road. "Lead on, my friend."

For a while it was as they both hoped. Mile after mile of boring grassland and slow, steady progress. They had to be at least halfway across the Steppes. Closer to Napolin than anywhere they'd been before.

Of course, their luck didn't last.

They stopped to stretch their legs and rest the horses at a spot where the grass was no more than fresh stubble coming out of the ground. They all felt the tremor in the earth. It was barely noticeable at first, but it grew in strength with each passing second. Even the horses started to get nervous, prancing about and neighing.

"Is it an earthquake?" asked Fion.

"Not out here," said Rane. He clambered into the back of the wagon, found his pack, and pulled out his old, battered telescope, given to him back when he was something in the world. He extended it and started scanning the grasslands. There was a small trail of dust in the direction they'd just come, but whoever was creating it was still too far away for Rane to see who they were. The people with the campfires most probably—but they weren't the cause of the ground tremors. He carried on looking, moving his gaze to the west and then to the northwest. Christoph climbed up next to him, but Rane ignored him because something had caught his eye—a large dust cloud with black shapes at the heart of it. Lots of black shapes, and they were coming straight towards their wagon.

"Buffalo," he said. "Stampeding." He passed Christoph the telescope.

"Shit," said Christoph, looking for himself. "What do we do?"

"What's happening?" asked Saphie, her arms wrapped tight around herself.

"Buffalo," said Rane again. "A lot of them on the move and heading our way."

"That's good isn't it?" Said Fion. "We can shoot one. That'll solve our food problems."

Rane shook his head. "A stampeding herd of buffalo would trample us into the ground if we get in its way."

"Why are they running?" asked Christoph.

"Who knows?" said Rane, not wanting to worry anyone any more than necessary. "Get everyone in the wagon. With any luck, they won't come in our direction or they'll slow down before they get to us. If they don't, get going as fast as you can out of their way."

"What are you going to do?"

Rane took the telescope back and looked one last time. There was only one thing he could think of that could help. "I'll head out towards them. Maybe I can encourage them in a different direction or take out what's scaring them."

"No, Nathaniel. You could get killed," said Christoph. "Stay with us. We'll just get out of their way, as you said."

Rane placed the telescope back in his pack and stowed it. "It's too risky. At least this way, we have a better chance."

Christoph shook his head. "You'll get yourself killed."

"I hope not." He patted the Fascalian on the shoulder. "Keep the others safe."

"I will."

Rane jumped down and ran to his horse.

Once in the saddle, he headed towards the swirling dust at a trot. He couldn't go any faster. He couldn't risk tiring the horse—it would need all its energy once they reached the buffalo; especially if it was a Bracke chasing them. Truth was, though, he was glad to take his time. Give himself a chance to find his courage.

He loosed *Kibon* in its scabbard. If it came to it and he had to use the sword, he didn't want the blade sticking. A thrill ran through him the moment he touched the hilt, and his fears vanished. Nothing could stand before *Kibon's* might.

Even so, he checked the bow slung on the side of the saddle and the quiver full of arrows next to it. Finally, he touched Kara's locket, rubbing it between his thumb and forefinger, hoping she'd bring him luck, knowing that she would've killed him for doing something so stupid. He wouldn't have blamed her.

The rumble of buffalo hooves sounded like rolling thunder as the cloud of dust filled the sky as far as he could see. He could see the buffalo clearly now, running for their lives, coming straight for him. Straight for the wagon.

Rane spurred the horse then, aimed for the eastern flank of the stampede. He could see the buffalo clearer with every yard that disappeared beneath his horse. By the Gods, there were so many of them. Charging with their heads down, horns out, with all the weight of their massive bodies coming on behind them. Anything in their way didn't stand a chance. And there wasn't anything he could do to alter their course. He might as well have tried to stop the world from turning.

The ground felt like it was about to break apart, and Rane's horse tried to turn away to safety, but Rane forced it onwards. He raced around the flank, looking for the cause of the herd's fear, not wanting to find it.

Suddenly a buffalo went down, tumbling into others. Even over the thunder, Rane could hear its cry. He peered into the dust and dirt, craning his neck to see past the other buffalo. He caught a glimpse of something perched on the buffalo's back. He raised himself up off the saddle, fear gnawing at his gut, because even without a clear view, Rane knew what it was.

A Bracke.

Then there was a gap and Rane saw the demon, hooked onto the buffalo with its hind claws, while it hacked and slashed and ripped and bit.

The buffalo was dead in seconds. Immediately, the Bracke was back on its feet and running for its next target. And it wasn't alone. Amid the dust and blood, he could see three other Bracke hunted the buffalo as well. He watched the Bracke hurl themselves amongst their prey in a killing frenzy, no longer interested in food for themselves, just wanting to destroy, utterly blood crazed.

Gripping the horse with his thighs, Rane unhooked the bow, selected an arrow from the quiver, and nocked it. He chose the Bracke nearest to him, raised the bow, straightened his left arm and aimed. He drew back on the string, until his right hand rested against his cheek, the tip of the arrow aimed at the Bracke's head.

The Bracke buried its teeth in the neck of a buffalo and tore the flesh open, spraying blood everywhere as Rane released the arrow. It struck the demon in the eye and sent it sprawling in the dust.

One down, three to go. He reached for another arrow as he looked for his next target, only to find the other Bracke had already spotted him. The buffalo were forgotten as the creatures ran towards him.

The Bracke were a hundred and fifty yards away and closing fast. Rane slipped from the saddle with bow in one hand, quiver in the other. Riderless, the horse deserted Rane as quickly as it could.

He ignored the urge to run himself. He ignored the urge to draw his sword. Instead, he selected another arrow, nocked it, drew back the bow string, and aimed at the head of the foremost Bracke. He slowed his breathing down, grateful that he was no longer being thrown about on horseback. His hand was steady despite the fear coursing through him.

The Bracke were just over a hundred yards away when he released the arrow. It flew swift and sure, striking the right eye. It died instantly, carried forward only by its momentum for a few more yards before collapsing in the dirt.

He picked another arrow as the remaining two Bracke closed the gap. He'd never get used to how fast they could run despite their size, never get used how easily they could kill.

They were eighty yards away when he nocked another arrow. Seventy-five yards away as he drew back the bow string. Seventy as he aimed, sixty-five, sixty. He released the arrow. Missed.

The Bracke were fifty yards away as he repeated the process, thirty-five yards away as he aimed, thirty, twenty. He released the arrow when the devil dogs were fifteen feet away. From such close range, he couldn't miss. The arrow took one of the beasts in the throat and it tumbled down dead.

The last Bracke leaped, mouth roaring, all claw and fang. Rane dropped the bow, and drew *Kibon*. Time slowed. He threw himself backwards as the Bracke lunged. Claws pierced his flesh as he thrust the sword into the creature. There was a rush of magic, but then the creature fell on him, teeth filling his vision. He seized the Bracke under the muzzle, straining every muscle to keep its snapping jaws away from his face. Blood dripped from its fangs as Rane dodged his head from side to side. He could feel warm blood leaking all over his chest as the Bracke's claws slashed at him. He thrust *Kibon* deeper into the creature, twisted the blade, jerked it up, desperate to kill it.

Slowly, ever so slowly, the fight faded from the creature. Its jaws snapped out of reflex rather than intent and its slashing claws grew feeble. Finally, the hatred in its eyes, its terrifying eyes, dimmed.

Rane heaved the corpse off and rolled clear, wincing in pain. His clothes were shredded and his body a mass of cuts both shallow and deep, and he was soaked in blood. A lot was the Bracke's. A lot was his.

"Lucky, lucky fool," he whispered to himself as the

strength went out of his legs. He held onto *Kibon,* needing its magic if he was to survive his wounds.

Through dimming eyes, he could see the buffalo slowing down and moving south, away from the wagon. He'd done it.

He attempted to wave to the others, hoping they'd seen what he had done and would come to help him, but the effort was too much for him. Even with the sword's power, he wasn't healing quickly enough.

The horse watched him from a safe distance. In one of its saddlebags, Rane knew there was a cloak he could use as dressing for his wounds. He just had to get to it.

With *Kibon* in his hand, Rane tried to climb back onto his feet but failed. Blood ran down his chest chased by sharp, rapid pain. By the Gods, it hurt. He crawled towards the horse, one painful inch after another, dripping blood.

Why wasn't *Kibon* healing him? Was it because he'd not fed it human lives for so long? Hadn't killing the Jotnar and the Bracke done anything to replenish its power?

He dragged himself a few more steps, clutching at one of the deeper wounds just below his ribs, trying to stem the bleeding, but still blood found its way through his fingers and down his side. How much blood did he have to lose?

Faces came to him of comrades long forgotten, growing pale on the battlefield with similar injuries, waiting for Odason to take them to His great halls.

Such a fate wouldn't happen to him.

"Come on," he croaked to the horse. "Don't let me do all the work."

The animal turned its head to one side but still didn't move.

Rane shuffled forward another few feet. A welcome

breeze kicked up, and he closed his eyes for a moment, enjoying its caress on his face.

If only he wasn't so tired. Maybe he'd feel better after a rest, give the others a chance to catch up with him. Opening his eyes was like lifting a mountain, and still that blasted horse watched him.

Rane tried to stand once more, but his right leg crumbled under him, and he went down hard, knocking the wind out of himself. He sucked in air through gritted teeth as he did his best to block out the pain. Failed miserably at that as well.

Once more he pushed himself up, took one step, then one more. The ground wasn't helping, rolling like a ship in a storm, but he fixed his eye on the horse and walked on.

Maybe it was the loss of blood but for one mad moment, Rane thought he got a reaction from the animal. He wasn't sure if it took a step towards him, wasn't sure of anything truth be told, but amidst all the pain, he felt a glimmer of hope. He staggered on—and found himself spread-eagled on the ground again, grass in his face. The world went black.

He blinked, not sure how much time had passed, feeling like he had all the weight pressing down on him. He swung his arm forward, dragged himself along with that, moved the other arm, scrapping *Kibon* through the grass, dragged himself some more. The darkness pulled at him as he nodded in and out of consciousness, aware of the fading pain. He shivered with a sudden chill, recognizing the signs of a dying man from a million battlefields. It was easy to imagine the trail of blood he was leaving. He could see his life dripping away.

He gripped *Kibon*, willing it to stop the bleeding. He—

Somewhere close by, a creature growled.

16

Sarah

The people in the wagon didn't even notice Sister Sarah and the other Soldiers of the Inquisition until it was too late. They'd ridden in at speed to catch the monster off guard, but here was only a man and woman and their two children.

The buffalo stampede had helped, drawing the family's attention and drowning out any noise the Inquisition's horses made. In the end, one of the children saw them approach and screamed, but by the time her parents reacted, Sarah and the others had the wagon surrounded.

The mother went to draw a pistol, but Brother Situs had a spear at her throat before the weapon could leave the holster.

"There's no need for anyone to get hurt," called out Sarah. "We only want the monster."

"What monster?" said the bearded man.

"The ... Legionnaire you've been traveling with," said Sarah. "Where is it?"

The whole family looked confused. "Legionnaire?" said the woman. "Do you mean Nathaniel?"

Sarah gritted her teeth. "If that is his name. Where is he?"

"He's gone to drive off the buffalo." The man pointed towards the dust storm. "He didn't want them to run over us."

"Don't lie to me," said Sarah. "Why would he do that?"

"To save our lives," said the woman, jutting her chin forward in a false display of courage.

"Because you are his servants," said Nicolai. His lip curled in disgust. "We should burn you where you stand."

"No," cried the man, holding up both hands. "We are no one's servants. My daughter is ill, and we just need to get to Napolin. We've done nothing wrong. Nathaniel was just riding with us. We didn't know he was a Legionnaire."

"Did you not see his sword?" scoffed Nicolai.

No one in the family spoke. A sure sign of their guilt.

"Tie them up," said Sarah. "We'll judge them later." She didn't bother to watch her orders carried out. Instead, she dismounted and walked to where she could get a good view of the stampede. It was still hard to tell what was going on. The buffalo were a good mile away and kicking up a lot of dust and dirt. A wave of fear passed over her when she thought about the buffalo charging towards them, but she knew Odason would protect them. He would not allow harm to befall His Children.

She tried to spot the monster and his horse, but it was impossible. All was chaos.

Nicolai appeared beside her. "Shall we put the heretics to the flame?"

Sarah glanced back over her shoulder. The family were tied up in their wagon. All four glared at her with hate in their eyes. "Get the firewood in their wagon but don't light it yet. They are the monster's servants. Perhaps he feels something for them if he has gone to stop the buffalo. If they are alive, he'll have a reason to come back. If they're not, he won't."

"As you wish."

"Have torches ready though," said Sarah. "The moment we see him, I want that wagon aflame."

That put a smile on Nicolai's face. "As you wish."

Sarah returned her attention to the buffalo. Something was happening, but she couldn't see what exactly. She sensed rather than saw the center of the stampede had turned away and was now heading more to the west. The buffalo seemed to be slowing down too, as if whatever was scaring them was no longer there. What had the monster done?

As the buffalo calmed, Sarah became aware of the noise behind her—her own horses' disquiet, the sobbing of the mother, the coughing of one of the children, the pleas of the father. Once it would have affected her. Made her doubt. But now? She knew the truth. Heretics were all the same. They would say anything to hide their guilt.

So where was the monster?

Sarah watched, and she waited. Clouds rolled across the sky, smothering much of the late afternoon light. It would be night soon enough. Sarah tried not to let that thought make her feel uncomfortable. She had fourteen Soldiers of the Inquisition with her, good steel in their hands and Odason in their hearts. The dark could not harm them.

The monster would not harm them.

The pleading and the cries from the heretics grew

worse as her brothers and sisters threw luggage from the wagon and stacked firewood around them. They protested their innocence, begged for their children, cried to be freed. They even called on Odason for mercy, despite the fact it was Odason who had sent the Inquisition to judge them.

Good. Let it draw the monster to them.

And still the night drew in. Shadows crept across the grasslands. More clouds filled the sky. There'd not even be any stars to cast light later.

"Make sure we have people watching all the approaches," she told the brother next to her. "Who knows which way the monster will come."

"As you wish," he replied.

Sarah smiled. No one questioned her anymore with look or with word. They all could feel Odason's hand guiding her.

Ten brothers and sisters moved to stand in a circle around the wagon and their horses while four remained to guard the prisoners. Let the monster try his luck.

Time passed. Even the prisoners quietened as they all waited for any sign of the monster. Where was he? By Odason, he better not have escaped. Had Sarah made a mistake baiting a trap? Why would a monster care about anyone or anything?

She shook the thoughts from her head. They were doubts when she needed patience. The All-Father wouldn't let her fail.

As the sky darkened, she saw movement. "Keep alert," she called out, drawing her sword. "Something's coming towards us." She heard the hiss of steel leaving leather scabbards as the other brothers and sisters did the same. They all knew there would be fighting. The monster would not give up easily. But he would meet his match in the Soldiers of the Inquisition. Her soldiers.

She rolled her neck from side to side as her heart began to race. She felt Odason's strength flood through her. Sarah had never been the best fighter, but she had no fear now, no doubts. They were chosen.

"Shall I torch the wagon?" called out Nicolai.

"Wait until we see the monster," replied Sarah.

She peered straight ahead in the failing light, trying to see what had caught her eye. It was a man's height ... but the way it moved ... had the monster changed its appearance ... or was this another of Heras's creatures? Sarah tightened her grip on her sword, cursing the darkness.

"It's a horse," called one of the brothers.

And so it was. A chestnut horse with an empty saddle ran towards them. "Let it in," said Sarah. She sheathed her sword as they stepped aside to let the animal race in. Two brothers caught its reins and pulled it to a stop. It was agitated and fought to be free as they tried to calm it. Its alarm scared the other horses in camp as well, and soon all were complaining and shifting their feet. If they hadn't been tied up and hobbled, some would have run. "Quiet them," she barked. Noisy animals were the last thing she needed.

"Something's frightened this one something bad," said Brother Lucius, as he stroked the riderless horse's nose. There was blood on its flanks and legs.

"Is this the monster's horse?" Sarah demanded of the family.

They all stared back at her, mouths firmly shut.

"I haven't got time for this," said Sarah. "Would you rather burn?"

"You're going to do that anyway," said the man. "Even though we've done nothing wrong."

"You have aided and abetted a monster to escape the Inquisition. You called this monster friend," replied Sarah. "None of which are the actions of the pure, the godly, and the righteous. Now, is that the monster's horse?"

The woman nodded then looked away.

"Thank you." Sarah walked back over to Nicolai. They both looked out into the early evening gloom. "What do you think?"

Nicolai frowned. "Maybe the monster's dead. Maybe the horse is a distraction. But something out there frightened it."

"Not the buffalo."

"No."

"Send two people out to see if they can find a body," said Sarah. "Or see what else might be lurking."

"Two people won't be enough if he's alive."

"To send more would weaken us here if the horse is a trick. Just tell whoever you send not to engage with the monster if he is alive. Tell them to come back here as fast as they can."

"They could still die."

"So could we all—if that is Odason's will." But Sarah did not believe it would be so. The All-Father would not allow it. "Send two. No more. No fewer."

"As you wish."

Brothers Maxim and Arland were given the honor of searching for the monster. They walked from the camp with swords in one hand and torches in the other. Soon, only their torches could be seen.

Sarah watched them, barely breathing, wondering whether she should draw her sword again. To do so and not use it for a second time would make her look uncertain. Scared even.

The torches started to move apart. One going left, the other right.

"Why are you doing that?" Sarah whispered. "Stay together. Stay together."

But still Maxim and Arland moved farther away from each other and the camp.

"Shall I call them back in?" asked Nicolai.

"They should've stayed together," said Sarah.

"I know. Maybe one of them—"

Howling drowned out anything Nicolai had to say. The torches stopped moving at the sound.

"Is that a dog?" asked Sarah once it stopped.

Before Nicolai could answer, something crashed into Maxim. His torch sailed through the air as the brother screamed. The torch hit the ground in a splutter of sparks, then lay there burning and untouched. Maxim shrieked as something howled and barked.

Arland ran to help, but something crashed into him too. A second later, he was screaming as well.

All Sarah and the others could do was watch the darkness, listening to the agonized shrieks of pain, the sounds of flesh being torn, of biting and growling, for one heartbeat, two heartbeats, three ... then silence fell. There was no sound from either predator or prey. Was it the monster? She'd heard tales of what the Tainted could do, the atrocities they'd commit. Feasting on human flesh was not uncommon.

"Draw your swords," said Sarah, trying to keep her voice calm. "Shields ready." She realized that she didn't have a shield of her own and hoped she wouldn't regret that fact. Odason would have to protect her.

More howling came from out of the darkness. This time farther to the east. Then another howl from the west, then another, still more distant. It wasn't just the monster. He wasn't alone.

She peered out into the darkness. All she could see were Maxim and Arland's torches as they continued to burn on the ground. Two flickering lights against a wall of black.

"By Odason, what's out there?" said Sarah. "Can anyone see anything?" The howls grated at her, making it hard to even think. They seemed to come from everywhere all at the same time. Surrounding them.

The children started to cry. The horses pulled evermore at their reins and tried to free their hooves.

"Sarah, what shall we do?" As Nicolai said the words, a creature stepped into the light given off by the discarded torches. Its eyes gleamed red, and it bared bloody fangs.

"Bracke!" shouted Lucius.

"Stand your ground." Sarah had only seen dead Bracke before, back during the war, but that hadn't prepared her for what she saw now. Suddenly her sword seemed so inadequate in her hand, her chainmail so light. What could stand before such a creature's fury? "Odason will protect us. The monster has called demons to his aid."

The Bracke's head suddenly snapped to its left. It growled and leapt. There was a flash of steel and then a thud as something heavy hit the ground.

"What happened?" asked Sarah, through gritted teeth.

"Wait," said Nicolai. "Look."

A shadow appeared out of the darkness, a long, curved, single-edged sword in his hand—a Legionnaire's sword covered in blood. He walked slowly, purposefully. As he got closer, Sarah could see his clothes were in shreds, and ragged cuts and wounds covered his torso, arms, and legs. No human could live with injuries like that. And yet, this man was on his feet and coming towards them.

He was the monster.

"To me! Everyone to me," called Sarah. "Form a circle on me." There were thirteen of them with swords, spears, shields, and Odason. Even with Bracke, the monster would not win.

Her brothers and sisters obeyed her order instantly, standing shoulder to shoulder.

"What about the horses?" asked Brother Situs. "The prisoners?"

"Torch the prisoners," said Sarah, "and be quick about it."

"You fools," cried the monster. "Bracke are everywhere." He marched towards them, eyes full of hate and evil magic.

"We do not fear your servants," shouted Nicolai. "Send all of Heras's creatures against us and we will kill them all."

"For Odason!" screamed Sarah, thrusting her sword in the air. "For justice!"

"Odason!" shouted the others, banging their weapons against their shields.

The monster ran towards them.

17

Rane

The fools. The bloody fools. The Soldiers of the Inquisition were so busy shouting to Odason and rattling their swords at Rane, they weren't looking for the real danger.

The Bracke were everywhere.

Rane didn't know if it was the slaughter of the buffalo or the smell of his own blood that had attracted the creatures. Maybe it was the soldiers and all their damn noise. Maybe the devil dogs had just been nearby all along.

In the end though, it didn't matter. There were too many of the damn things, and chances were everyone was going to be dead sooner rather than later.

One had gone for Rane when he'd collapsed earlier. Sheer luck alone had saved his life. The Bracke had tried to leap on him and landed on *Kibon* instead. Killing the creature sent a pulse of magic through Rane that had healed him enough to get him back on his feet. It wasn't as powerful as the charge he got from killing a human, but Rane was grateful for that. He couldn't afford to lose his head to the sword's magic-induced battle madness and hopefully the price against his soul would be equally limited.

And now he had to save a load of fools who wanted him dead. Rane moved quicker, pushing his battered body, desperate to get to the wagon before the demon dogs attacked. If he could protect Christoph's family, they might have a chance.

Of course, the Inquisition were lined up to meet him.

"Monster!" called out a woman. "Come and meet your end! Odason demands your death."

"You fools," cried Rane. "Bracke are everywhere."

"We do not fear your servants," shouted one of the zealots. "Send all of Heras's creatures against us and we will kill them all."

"For Odason!" screamed the woman, thrusting her sword in the air. "For justice!"

"Odason!" shouted the others, banging their weapons against their shields.

They were all mad, making enough noise to bring every Bracke from miles around to feast on them.

"Kill him!" howled the woman.

Rane heard the whistle of a spear in flight and ducked, felt the weapon pass an inch over his shoulder.

The bloody fools.

A Bracke appeared out of the darkness and leaped at Rane. He had a half-second to swing *Kibon*. Demon met steel, and steel won. More magic ran through Rane as the two halves of the Bracke hit the ground.

Another spear sailed towards him, but he swatted it

from the air. "Protect the family! Protect the children." He started to run once more towards the wagon. "Protect the children."

But the Bracke were running too. Rane could see them now, coming out of the long grass, coming from every direction. He didn't know how many there were in the dark—too many—and they were a damn sight faster than him. Two crashed into the zealot's shield wall, sending it into disarray in an instant. Some soldiers went down, Bracke on their shields, slashing with their claws. The other Soldiers of the Inquisition tried to help, stabbing at the demon dogs with their swords and spears, but they turned their back on the night in doing so.

It was all the invitation the other Bracke needed.

Three more Bracke pounced, hooking their claws into the backs of soldiers, bearing them to the ground. With no shield between them and the demons, they died in seconds as the Bracke eviscerated their bodies. More Bracke appeared, throwing themselves at the horses, who pulled at their reins. Hobbled as they were, there was no escape. Only Rane's horse broke free and ran. With other, easier prey, the Bracke let her go.

The camp was in chaos. Every man and woman fighting for their lives—and Rane was still ten yards away. A soldier ran towards the wagon, a torch in hand, but a Bracke smashed into him, and he was lost in the dirt and dust as the creature savaged him.

He saw Christoph's family duck down in the wagon, keeping low and out of sight of the demons as best they could, but it wasn't going to be enough.

Those still on their feet were fighting hard, using shield, spear, and sword to fend the devil dogs off when Rane arrived in their midst, *Kibon* already in motion.

He hacked the head off a Bracke, stabbed another through the side, and kicked a third off a soldier before cleaving it in half. Each kill gave him another pulse of magic, another boost to his power. And always *Kibon* was hungry for more.

He heard Saphie scream and spun to see a Bracke perched on the edge of the wagon. He grabbed a dropped spear and hurled it with all his might. It struck the creature in the side, but it wasn't a killing blow.

It didn't matter. Rane had closed the gap and jumped onto the back of the wagon, slicing the Bracke in half as he did so. Blood splattered Christoph and the others, but they were alive for now. Rane pulled a knife from his belt and passed it to Christoph. "Cut your bonds but stay here."

The Fascalian nodded. Rane hauled the makeshift cover over their hiding hole. It wasn't much, but it was better than nothing. Then he turned back to the carnage.

Only four of the zealots still stood, back to back, hiding behind their shields, covered in wounds. The rest were dead, as were all the horses. There were at least a dozen Bracke, but more converged on the zealots.

They poked and jabbed at the Bracke with their swords, but there was no real threat in their actions. The Bracke knew this as they circled the survivors, testing their defenses, looking for openings, happy to tire the humans out.

Rane leaped from the wagon, *Kibon* a blur. His arm crackled with energy as he struck. Two Bracke were felled in an instant. Another turned to face him and lost its head. He ducked under the lunge of a fourth and dragged *Kibon* across its stomach, opening the creature from hip to hip.

Two Bracke remained.

They backed off, growling, wary of Rane's sword, but

Rane wasn't going to let a single one live to hunt another day.

"Die!" One of the zealots broke from the shield wall and lunged at Rane.

He reacted without thinking. *Kibon* shot out, its edge gleaming and eager. The man's sword arm tumbled away with a jettison of blood, then his head followed. It was as easy as that. Whatever magic Rane got from killing the Bracke was nothing compared to the charge that rushed through him then.

"Murderer!" screamed the woman, and she, too, attacked. But she might as well have been moving in slow motion.

Rane blocked her sword with Kibon and punched her with his free hand. She went sprawling in the dirt, sword tumbling from her hand. Rane stepped forward, enraged.

Taking advantage of his distraction, the Bracke attacked.

One hundred and fifty pounds of fury slammed into Rane, claws already sinking deep into his flesh. The demon's jaws snapped at his head, and he only just got his arm up in time. Rane tried to follow with *Kibon*, but the demon had learned and hooked a clawed hand on his arm, forcing it to the ground.

Rane tried to shake the creature off, but even with his enhanced strength, he was trapped.

The other Bracke slashed at the remaining zealots as they tried to protect the red-haired woman with their shields.

Blood oozed out of Rane's arm as his Bracke bit down harder, trying to rip the limb off so it could get to Rane's face. He shifted his legs, hoping to get them under the demon dog and throw it off somehow, but the Bracke's back claws were lodged into his sides. His only hope was to use

Kibon, but the creature wasn't going to let go of his sword arm any time soon. If it wasn't for the magic he'd only just absorbed, Rane knew he'd already be dead.

A man screamed, and something smacked into the side of the Bracke. The demon shuddered, then fell on Rane unmoving. Rane blinked and saw his knife jutting out the creature's head, then saw Christoph standing over the Bracke, panting, his eyes wide.

A crack of gunpowder followed.

Rane threw the dead Bracke off himself and saw Fion holding both his pistols. She'd shot the other Bracke at close range, killing it instantly. Now she had the other, loaded pistol pointed at the Inquisition.

"Don't move." Fion's voice was low and harsh and full of authority.

"Are you okay?" asked Christoph as he helped Rane stand.

"I will be," replied Rane. He gripped *Kibon,* needing the sword's magic. Already the wounds on his chest and arms were closing. Soon they would just be more scars to add to his body. Still, as he looked at the slaughter around him, he was lucky to be alive. "Thank you for saving me."

Christoph tried to smile, but it didn't last. Instead, tears came, and he started to shake. "I thought you were going to die. I thought we were all going to die."

"It's okay," said Rane. "We're alive now, and that's all that matters. Go get the girls. They need you."

Christoph sniffed and wiped his eye. "Yes. Of course." He looked to the wagon where the girls watched, and this time the smile stayed. "We're alive."

Rane turned back to the others. Fion's pistol was unwavering. "What do we do with them?" she asked.

"I should've burned you when I had the chance," hissed

the red-haired woman, her face full of hate. Blood covered her face and neck, only some of which came from her own cuts. The other two soldiers with her were in an even worse state. The man to her left had a dark red stain on one shoulder and the arm beneath it hung limp. His face was pale from loss of blood, and Rane had to wonder how he was still on his feet. The man to the woman's right was doing better, but he'd still lost an eye in the attack.

"You'd be dead if you had," said Fion bluntly. "We just saved your lives."

The woman shot forward to attack Rane, but Fion moved the pistol so it pointed straight at her forehead. That was enough to halt her in her tracks.

"I'm not your enemy here," said Rane. He looked around at the dark plains. "The real demons are still out there. More Bracke will come. We haven't got time to fight amongst ourselves."

"They come because you are here," spat the woman. "They come to help you as Heras commands them to."

Rane shook his head. "Look at me. Do you not see the wounds all over my body? They want me dead as much as you."

"I see wounds that heal with magic," said the woman. "I see a man with my friend's blood on his sword. I see a monster."

Kill her, said *Kibon. End her nonsense.*

Rane tightened his grip on *Kibon*. The sword was right. The Soldiers of the Inquisition would never see him any differently. He stepped towards them.

"Don't," said Christoph, putting his hand on Rane's chest. One word—but it was enough.

Rane stopped, turned his gaze from the zealots to Christoph. The girls were standing next to their father. Both had been crying, but Rane couldn't see any wounds on them. "You're not hurt?"

Saphie and Rache both shook their heads.

"No thanks to them," said Saphie, stabbing a finger towards the Soldiers of the Inquisition. "They were going to burn us."

"But they didn't," said Christoph, both to his daughter and to Rane. "We're all alive, and we need to stay that way."

Howls from the darkness told them all how difficult that was going to be. More Bracke were coming.

18

Rane

The Bracke howled from all around them, but none seemed too close just yet. Rane turned back to the zealots. "Do you hear that? We can carry on arguing, and we'll all end up dead—or we can work together, and maybe we'll survive this."

"I don't want you to survive," said the red-haired woman. "I want you dead."

"And what about your friends?" said Rane. He nodded at the man to her right. "If we don't bandage that arm and his other wounds, he'll be dead before morning."

The woman glanced at her comrade. "If that's the All-Father's will, so be it."

The other man put his hand on her back. "Sister Sarah, I'm in no condition to fight the monster. Nor is Brother Situs. If the Bracke attack, we will die, and he could escape."

Sarah glanced over her shoulder at the man with his

bloody eye and gashed tunic, then at Rane. Only then did she lower her weapon. "You're safe for now, monster, from us."

Kill them now, urged *Kibon. Kill them!*

Rane took a deep breath and forced himself to sheathe *Kibon.* "Fion, find the powder and bullets and reload. We'll need those guns soon enough."

Fion nodded.

"Sister Sarah is it?" Rane asked the woman.

"Yes." She forced the word out through gritted teeth.

"See to your comrades. The girls will help. You might need some of their clothes as bandages."

"I'm not helping them," shouted Saphie. "They wanted to burn me."

"Nathaniel is right," said Christoph. "We will need everyone working together if we are to make it through this night alive." He leaned in close to his daughter. "Prove they were wrong about us."

Saphie glared at the zealots but nodded. "Fine."

"What are we going to do?" Christoph asked Rane.

"Get the travel packs for you and the family. Make sure we've got full water skins too. Now, we've lost the horses, so we're walking. Anything we don't need to survive is going up in flames. I plan to surround us with fire and hopefully that'll keep the Bracke away."

Christoph went wide-eyed. "That's everything we have."

"Your children are all you need."

For a moment, Rane thought the man was going to break under the pressure of the situation. His lips quivered and Christoph grasped his shaking hands tightly together. Then, he saw his family watching, their eyes on him and something changed in the man. He took a deep breath and nodded. "Agreed," he replied, his voice cracking with the effort.

"We can do this," said Rane, even if he wasn't convinced himself that they had any hope.

As Christoph organized the travel packs, Rane began hauling the dead into one big pile. Men, women, and Bracke went on top of the horses.

"What are you doing?" shouted Sarah. "Those are Odason's Children. Keep them way from those fouls creatures."

"They're lumps of meat now that can burn with the rest of them," said Rane.

"I will not let you—"

"Sister," said the one-eyed man, stopping her from rising. "Better they burn than feed the creatures out there."

"It's not right," said the red-haired woman.

"None of this is," said the one-eyed man.

The man wasn't wrong. Rane resumed working. He moved everything the Inquisition had bundled together to burn Christoph and his family, creating a fire line from the bodies to the wagon on one side and then from the wagon back to the bodies on the other. It left them with a fighting space behind it of about twenty feet in diameter.

All the while, the howling grew louder and closer.

"How many are there?" said Christoph. The man looked petrified, but he kept working, helping Rane build the barricades.

"Too many," replied Rane. "Help me overturn the wagon."

"We won't be able to do that on our own."

"We will."

The wagon was empty, but even still, it weighed a hell of a lot. Rane gripped the undercarriage and braced his legs.

Christoph took up a position next to him, but Rane knew he'd have to take most of the weight.

"Ready?" he asked.

"As I'll ever be," said Christoph.

With a deep breath, Rane lifted up the wagon. The wheels rose an inch or two off the ground and then Christoph joined in, grunting with the effort. It helped but not by much. Still, Rane didn't give up. The wagon rose another inch and then another.

Someone moved to stand on Rane's other side—the zealot who'd lost his eye. A bandage covered half his face. "Let me help."

Between the three of them, the wagon rose, and Rane was able to get under it enough for it to topple onto its side with a crash. The impact collapsed half the wagon, but that wasn't a problem. It was all firewood.

"Get the torches," said Rane. "Set everything alight."

There were enough of the Inquisition torches still burning for that to be an easy job. Rane threw three onto the pile of corpses, then moved to the fire line. He was halfway along when he sensed movement, looking up just as a Bracke leaped at him. He threw himself backwards and rammed the torch into its gut as it flew over his head. Its fur caught as Rane hit the ground and rolled, *Kibon* already in his hand. Rane cut it down with a single stroke and threw the corpse onto the pile with the rest of the dead.

The smell of roasting flesh and burning fur soured the air already thick with smoke.

"Stay with the packs," Rane told Saphie and Rache. "Keep low beneath the smoke. Everyone else form up around them. Fion, shoot anything that gets close enough. Christoph, reload the pistols like we practiced." Rane paused when he got to the zealots. Situs had been bandaged up, but there was no fight in him. He lay next to the packs, covered with a blanket. The other two though, Sarah and the one-eyed man, were on their feet and holding swords.

"I don't know what's going to happen next," said Rane, "but you're going to have plenty of chances to stick a sword in my back. That might kill me. It might not. And if it doesn't and some harm comes to these children because of it, I'll feed you to the Bracke myself."

"You're safe from us, monster," said Sarah, "for now."

"I'd prefer you called me Nathaniel," said Rane.

Sarah spat at him in response.

"My name is Brother Nicolai," said the one-eyed man.

"We've got company," called Fion.

Rane turned his attention back on the perimeter. The Bracke were coming out of the darkness in ones and twos, growling at the humans behind the fire lines. They prowled around, looking for weak spots, looking for a way in.

A Bracke seized a horse's leg that wasn't burning yet and started to drag it from the pile. Another joined it, adding its strength, and they all saw the pile of corpses shift.

Fion stepped forward, aimed, and fired. Her first shot hit one of the demon dogs in the eye, felling it instantly. Her second hit the other Bracke in the side. It wasn't a fatal injury, but it was enough to dissuade it from trying to dislodge the horse further.

Another Bracke jumped through the fire. Sarah and Nicolai reacted quickly, lunging at it with their swords, striking it from opposite sides.

Another jumped the fire line near Rane. It landed, its fur alight, looking for an easy target, finding *Kibon* sweeping down. But still more came, eager to chance the flames.

Fion fired again and again. Christoph somehow calmly kept reloading the weapons despite the chaos around him.

The night wore on. Sweat ran down Rane's face as he fought, eyes stinging from the heat and the smoke, ears ringing from the pistol fire and the howls. Even with his magic-enhanced strength, Rane felt the ache in his muscles from the relentless fight. He had to admire the stamina of the others, but he could see they weren't going to be able to keep it up for much longer. Even the space they had to fight was growing smaller as they killed one Bracke after another.

Nicolai was dragging a Bracke corpse to throw onto the fire when another bounded through some spluttering flames. It was on his back in an instant, and he screamed as it forced him to the ground. Fion shot the creature at point blank range, and Christoph hauled the fallen man towards the center, leaving a trail of too much blood behind.

"Nicolai!" shouted Sarah. "Is he alive?"

"Give me some bandages," said Christoph to the girls. "Quick!"

"Is he alive?" repeated Sarah, turning her back on the fire lines.

"Keep your eyes on the demons," snapped Rane. He had a torch in one hand and *Kibon* in the other as he roamed his half of the perimeter. "Christoph, let the girls deal with Nikolai. We need you reloading the guns."

"But ... he'll die." Christoph looked up, his hands all bloody.

"Then he dies," said Rane. "So might we all—but until we do, we fight."

"Monster," spat Sarah, but she resumed her position.

"How many of these creatures are there?" said Fion, her face covered in sweat-streaked soot and ash.

"I don't know," said Rane. "Fewer than there were." He looked out over the Steppes. Morning wasn't far off, and the sky was brightening, letting him see well past the light thrown off by the fires. He counted at least a dozen shadows prowling through the grass still, their eyes shining red as they watched Rane and the others, inching closer, waiting for their moment.

Not many compared to earlier, but more than enough if they attacked at once. The fire lines were failing. They were already too many gaps in the lines or places where the fire barely burned.

If the dozen Bracke attacked them now from all sides, Rane and the others would be overwhelmed. He had to do something. Give them something else to attack.

With torch in one hand and *Kibon* in the other, Rane stepped over the fire line and marched out into the killing ground.

19

Sarah

"Odason protect me. Odason protect me. Odason protect me." Sarah whispered the words over and over and over again throughout the night. She was covered in cuts and scrapes and had a few wounds that some hastily applied bandages were stopping from being fatal for now. Her sword had grown heavier in her hand—now it felt like lifting a mountain.

And still the Bracke came at them.

Had she not seen them with her own eyes, she would've thought it impossible for so many foul creatures to exist in the world. Even during the war, the Bracke had been a rare thing, used by the Rastaks to attack on the front lines. They should've all been destroyed when the Legion set fire to the enemy forces out in what had become the Dead Lands, but now they were everywhere.

She glanced down at Nicolai, her only friend, her love.

The demons had savaged him in the last attack. A god-fearing man, a holy man, and yet Odason hadn't saved him from the Bracke's fury.

Sarah wasn't convinced He was going to save her either.

She'd hoped that, by some miracle, Mother Hilik would arrive with the rest of Odason's Children in the nick of time and put the last of the demons to the sword. But Mother was at least a day, if not more, away from reaching them.

Her eyes scanned the ground past the dwindling fires. They were too many of the Bracke left even with daybreak so close. The next attack would be the last.

Then the monster stepped over the fire line and strode out towards the remaining demons.

"What are you doing?" cried the woman.

"Nathaniel! Come back!" shouted her husband.

They all stared as the demons rushed towards the monster. It would've been a suicidal thing to do for any human but not for the monster. He struck with lightning speed, his sword darting everywhere, cutting down Bracke as he marched farther into their midst.

He used the torch as well as his blade, burning some while fending off others. Bracke were hacked, chopped, and decapitated. The demons were fearsome, but the monster was death incarnate.

In the end, the last couple of Bracke ran from him, howling into the night.

"Odason protect me," whispered Sarah again as she watched the monster surrounded by the dead, blood dripping of his sword and covering his face, arms, and hands, looking for something else to kill.

He roared in victory at the sky, and Sarah was more scared than she had been all night. How could she stop such a monster when even Heras's own creatures fled?

The faces of Harold, Roon, Jonas, and David flashed through her mind. She understood why they'd failed and felt new guilt at the memory of their purging. Even with Odason in their hearts, they had been doomed to failure from the moment they had stepped out to face him. Instead of the holy fires, their courage should've been rewarded.

As it was, her own was failing. She nearly dropped her sword when the monster returned. She could see the magic burning in his eyes. She could see his power. Wounds on his body healed while she watched until there wasn't a scratch on him. By Odason, he truly was a demon in the flesh.

He went over to the Fascalians. "Are any of you hurt?"

"Some scratches," said the man. "Nothing that won't mend."

Then the monster looked at Sarah. "What about you and your men?"

"I ... I ..." Sarah didn't know. She hadn't checked on her brothers. She'd been transfixed on the monster. She looked down. Situs was covered in a cloak stained red with his blood, already dead. But where was ... Nicolai was on one knee while one of the girls bandaged a gash across his chest. "Nicolai."

Sara could feel her heart shatter. She ran to him, pushing the girl to one side. "How bad are your wounds?"

Nicolai tried to smile, showing bloody teeth. "S ... Sar ... ah."

"It's going to be okay," she whispered into his ear. "Help will be here soon. Hold on. Mother will know how to fix you."

"I'm fine," he said, his voice a whisper.

"Can you move?" said the monster. "We need to go. The Bracke will be back if we stay."

"We're not going anywhere," said Sarah, climbing to her

feet. "Not until Odason's Children get here. You all must be judged." She pointed her sword at the monster. "You must be purged."

He shook his head, his bloody sword still in his hand. "That's not going to happen."

The Fascalian held up his hands. "Please, there is no need to fight. Not after what we have been through. We've survived. By working together, we survived."

The monster didn't move. He just stared at Sarah. Blood dripped off his sword.

She didn't know what to do. She couldn't beat the monster in a fight. She knew that. She couldn't let him go either. Mother would burn her alive.

"Sarah," said Nicolai. "He's right. They're all right. None of us will survive on our own." He struggled to his feet and staggered to her. He placed a bloody hand on her shoulder and leaned closer. "We go with them. It's the only option. If we do that, we can wait for another opportunity to capture or kill him. Perhaps that's why Odason spared us and not the others."

Sarah lowered her sword. She looked over at the monster. "A truce, then."

The monster's eyes never left hers. His head tilted slightly as if he were reading her thoughts. Did he have that power? Then he nodded. He stepped back and flicked the blood off his sword before sheathing the weapon. "Get your travel bags. We carry whatever food and water we have."

The family all jumped at his words, slinging bags and water skins over their shoulders. No one resisted him, and Sarah could only be horrified at the control the monster had over them.

The monster ripped off his ruined shirt and retrieved a new one from a small pack. Before he put it on, he wiped the blood from his body as best he could with the rags of the old one. Sarah couldn't see a single cut or wound left on him. She spat on the ground at such unholy magic. "Demon."

The monster ignored her. He picked up Nicolai's sword and returned it. "Keep this. You might need it."

"Thank you." Nicolai struggled to sheathe the weapon, and Sarah couldn't help but wonder how much longer her love had to live. It wasn't right that the monster was unharmed and someone as righteous as Nicolai was on the brink of death.

She had to trust in Odason. He had placed her in this awful situation for a reason. She was alive for a reason. So was Nicolai—for now. They still had a chance.

Well, let them enjoy their brief respite from justice. Sarah would see all of them burn for their sins.

Then, one of the girls broke out into a coughing fit, and both parents rushed over. They helped the girl sit down and gave her water, but it seemed to make no difference.

"What's wrong with her?" asked Sarah.

The father looked up. "She's ill."

"I can see that," said Sarah.

"She has a sickness in her lungs," said the mother, stroking her daughter's brow. "That's why we're going to Napolin—to get treatment for her."

Sarah nodded. No doubt Odason had made their daughter ill to punish the parents' transgressions.

"Can Saphie walk?" asked the monster. There was a surprising gentleness to his voice—as if he actually cared about his servants' well-being.

"Let her rest a bit longer," said her father.

"I'm fine," said the girl. She took another sip of water.

"I'm fine." She stood up, looking far from it, but there was a determination about her.

"Give me her pack," said the monster. "I'll carry it."

The father gratefully handed over the girl's small bag, then helped his other daughter sling hers over her shoulder "Are you ready?" he asked her.

The girl nodded.

"We follow the road north," said the monster. "Sister Sarah will lead with Nicolai. Then Christoph. The girls will be in the middle, followed by Fion. I'll take the rear. If anyone sees anything, speak up. I'd rather stop for a false alarm than die because you thought you were mistaken. Understand?"

Everyone nodded. Again, Sarah had to give begrudging respect to the monster. She'd have thought and, indeed had hoped, that he would want to lead. If he had done that, she could've stabbed him in the back.

She just had to be patient. She glanced back the way they'd come. How far was Mother Hilik behind them? She squinted, hoping to see some sort of sign, but the horizon shimmered with heat and nothing else.

They set off soon after. Sarah set a slow pace, helping Nicolai, glad that they were giving Mother a chance to catch up with every step. She also kept her eyes open and her hand close to her sword. Bracke cared not whether they attacked in daylight or darkness, but all she could see was grass in every direction.

No one spoke. Only the sick girl made noise—a small cough every few steps. Sarah knew people who'd had the lung sickness. She knew, too, that there was no cure. It would be a mercy to kill her now and end her suffering.

"We're doing the right thing," said Nicolai.

"Killing them is the right thing," she hissed back.

"Maybe Odason is telling us otherwise."

"How can you say that? If Mother heard you ..."

"She's not here, thankfully. It's just you and me, my love."

"Don't say that."

Nicolai laughed and then wiped blood from his lips. "You are, and I don't care who hears. I'm dying, so there's nothing anyone can do to hurt me more."

"You're not dying. You just need to hold on until we get help."

"I'll do my best ... my love."

Sarah had to smile despite herself. Even in the worst moments, Nicolai made it better.

The monster called for stops often, but even so, it was obvious the sick child was weakening as much as Nicolai. The others fussed over the child while the monster stood watch. They left Sarah to look after Nicolai and change his bandages. Bandages that were always soaked through with blood.

She exchanged looks with Nicolai. He shrugged. "It is what it is."

"I'll ask if we can rest longer," said Sarah.

"It'll make no difference," replied Nicolai and climbed to his feet.

They set off again. Sarah thought about leaving signs for Mother Hilik, but the monster and the others weren't making any effort to hide their tracks, and they stuck to the main road through the Steppes. A blind man could follow them.

It was late afternoon when Sarah saw something out of place. "Monster," she called out. "Something's over to the northwest."

They all stopped.

"What is it?" said the Fascalian.

"It's too big to be a Bracke," replied the monster. He walked forwards a few yards into the grass and shaded his eyes with his hand. "It can't be …"

"Another one of your demons?" Sarah thought she heard him chuckle in reply.

"It's no demon. It's my horse, I think," said the monster. "Wait here. I'll be back in a minute."

Sarah smiled. The moment his back was turned, she'd kill the Fascalians and then use the woman's pistols on the monster.

The monster stopped suddenly. He didn't look back, just called out. "Fion, if Sister Sarah so much as moves an inch towards any of you, shoot her."

The woman drew a pistol, pointed it at Sarah, and pulled back the hammer. "My pleasure."

Sarah just stared at the monster as he set off towards the animal, mouth open. How had he known what she was thinking? Or was he just smart? She kept her sword in her scabbard while the monster retrieved his horse.

For a moment, Sarah hoped he'd get on his horse and ride off, leaving them, but immediately felt guilty for the thought. The monster was her problem. And she knew now, the monster wouldn't leave the Fascalians. There was a bond between them that wasn't natural.

He rode back a few minutes later, looking very pleased with himself. He held up a long bow. "This was still attached to the saddle, along with the quiver." He jumped down and lead the horse over to the others. "Maybe our luck is changing."

The man stroked the horse on the nose. "I always liked you."

"Saphie and Nicolai can ride her," said the monster. "It'll allow us to move quicker."

Sarah half-expected Nicolai to refuse, but instead he allowed the monster to help him into the saddle. They placed the sick girl behind him and told her to hold on. Sarah stood to one side, confused. She was glad that Nicolai was no longer walking, but the horse helped the monster and the others more. How could Odason allow this? How could they be gifted with such aid? Was this Heras at work? The Bracke were her creatures, yet they'd tried to kill the monster and the others, not help him. None of it made sense.

Once Nicolai and the girl, Saphie, were settled, the monster turned to Sarah. "There's no excuse to dawdle now."

"What do you mean?" replied Sarah, trying to hide her shock.

"Just pick up the pace." His gaze lingered on her a moment longer, then he went back to the rear of the procession.

As Sarah set off, she realized that she'd been underestimating the monster all this time. He wasn't a mindless beast like some Legionnaires she'd faced. He was clever, calculating, and steps ahead of her. She would need to be smarter if she was going to get the better of him.

There was no fire that night when they made camp and little food to eat. The family huddled together for warmth while the monster stood watch. He was ten yards away from them, a dark shadow against the blue night. Sarah sat next to Nicolai, his head on her shoulder, on the opposite side of the fire.

The girl with the cough caught her eye. "Why do you want to kill us?"

"Shush," said the mother.

"Why?" said the girl. "She was going to burn us alive. I want to know why."

"She doesn't like us," said her father. "She thinks we're unclean."

"But we're not. We're good people," said the girl, then coughed. She looked over at Sarah again. "You can see that now, can't you?"

Sarah didn't reply. She was aware, too, that the monster had stopped walking. He had his back to them all, but she had no doubt he was listening.

"So, why do you hate us?" asked the other girl.

The whole family watched her now, eyes gleaming in the darkness.

"Tell them," said Nicolai.

Sarah shivered. She could feel Odason watching too. She straightened her back. "I don't hate you. I feel sorry for you."

"Sorry for us?" repeated the girl with the cough.

"You do seem good people," said Sarah. "A loving family."

"We are," said the man.

"Perhaps you didn't know the man you travel with is a monster. Perhaps you did. It doesn't matter. You've been corrupted by his presence as he has been corrupted by the foul magic that keeps him alive." Sarah lifted her chin. "The only path for your souls' salvation is through purification."

"Burning us, you mean," said the mother. "Killing us."

"You have brought this on yourself." Sarah smiled. "Unless you wish to prove that you are not his thralls. Then, perhaps, the All-Father will see you in a different light."

"How would we do that?" scoffed the man.

"Join with me and kill the monster." Sarah enjoyed

seeing the shock ripple through them. Even the monster turned to stare at her.

"You're mad," said the girl with the cough. "Nathaniel's no monster."

"No?" said Sarah. "You say that when you've seen his magic at work? What more proof do I need that you are lost to him?"

"Nathaniel has saved our lives numerous times already," said the man. "We'd be dead without him."

"You'll be dead *because* of him," said Sarah.

"Then why are you even traveling with us?" said the girl with the cough. "If Nathaniel's a monster and we're all unclean, why not leave us?"

"She's waiting for a chance to kill me," said the monster from the darkness.

"Then why give her the chance?" said the girl. "Why don't we kill her before she can hurt us?"

The monster stepped closer, his face forming out of the shadows. "Because that is what a monster would do."

Sarah stared at the man. Was this some game he was playing? Was he hoping to corrupt her and Nicolai as he had done the others? Dear Odason, that couldn't be it, could it?

Nicolai sank against her, and she put her arm around him, pulling him tight.

"I'm cold," he said.

"All-Father, protect us," she whispered as she rubbed Nicolai's hands, but Odason felt very far away.

20

Rane

Rane stayed five yards or so behind the others as they made their way through the Steppes, watching for sign of more Bracke. As each hour passed and with each mile travelled, he felt a small glimmer of hope building. Perhaps they were over the worst of it.

Finding the horse had been a blessing. Walking at a pace that suited Saphie and the soldier was never going to get them anywhere quickly, but now the two were riding, they had a chance. Even so, he could see Saphie's cough was getting worse. He honestly didn't know if they would get to Napolin in time to save her.

And it was a miracle that the soldier was still alive. The man was surviving on will power alone.

It was hard to work out how much farther they had to travel. Two days' journey remained when the Bracke had attacked. They were now on the second day of walking, but with no landmarks to judge distance, all they could do was keep walking and hope they were making good progress.

Maybe, if they were lucky, they would reach Napolin in two more days.

Two more days if the Bracke stayed away.

But the demon dogs weren't their only problem. The Inquisition was closing in on them too.

When they stopped for a rest, Rane would take his telescope and check their rear for any sign of Odason's Children. He knew Sarah was looking too. Her disappointment matched his joy at seeing no trace of them. Still, they both knew they were out there.

As they were walking, Christoph passed the reins of the horse to Fion and dropped back until he was beside Rane.

"How are you?" he asked. The man looked and sounded exhausted.

"Fine," replied Rane. "You?"

"Feet a bit sore. I'm not used to all this walking."

Rane smiled. "You're doing fine. How's Saphie?"

"Her cough's not good, but she's not complaining. She's tough like her mother."

"You've got two good girls there."

"I know."

"Something you wanted to talk to me about?"

"I was just thinking about last night."

"And?"

"I don't think you're a monster."

"That's good."

"But I am worried about my family."

"I'm not going to kill them. I promise you that."

"I've heard terrible things about the Legion since the war. Granted, a lot of that has come from the Inquisition but, even so ... Last night ... I mean, you saved us but ... you looked terrifying. Almost more so than the Bracke."

"Is there anything you wouldn't do to save Saphie? Or Rache?" asked Rane.

"No."

"Are you sure?"

"Of course, they're my daughters. I mean, I've left our home, my business, to seek out a cure. I'm even putting all our lives at risk right now."

"What about magic? Would you use it?"

"Magic is outlawed."

"I know. But what if the doctors in Napolin can't help Saphie and someone came along and said they could save her—but only with magic? Would you agree?"

"Without hesitation."

"Even if you damned your soul in the process?"

"It would be a small price to pay."

"Then you understand the choice the Legion made when the war was all but lost. The only way we could change the fate for not just ourselves but for everyone in the five kingdoms was to resort to magic. Our souls were fused with our swords by a mage named Babayon to give us unnatural powers.

"What misgivings I had were nothing compared to the good I thought we could do." Rane's eyes roamed the plains, looking for trouble, while his thoughts drifted back over the years. "And we won the war, saving who knows how many lives in the process. We felt superhuman—stronger, faster, and almost impossible to kill. It was—it is—a wonderful feeling."

"You were all heroes," said Christoph. "I remember the excitement of listening to the tales of your exploits."

"What we didn't know was that our souls were being

corrupted with each life we took with our swords. Kill enough people and it turns us in a monster."

"I thought that was just something the Inquisition were saying to turn people against the Legion."

"I wish that was the case, but the Inquisition and Sister Sarah are right in many ways. Once the corruption is complete, the Legionnaire has to be killed, or they will murder everyone around them."

"I ... I'm sorry, but how do you know ... how do you know how close you are to ... to ..."

"Becoming a monster? The corruption taints the Legionnaire's sword, leaving blemishes across the steel. When it turns black, the Legionnaire is lost."

"I see. Is there a cure?"

"I'm going to find Babayon. When I do, I'll get him to undo what he did to us."

"Do you have any idea where he is?"

"No."

"Ah."

"I just hope I find him before the Inquisition does, or it'll be too late to fix things."

"Can I ask ... your sword ... I've seen the marks on it. How much time do you have left?"

"Enough, I hope."

"I'm sorry, my friend," said Christoph. "I really am."

"Don't be. I've had a lot of time to think about it, and, if the choice was offered to me again and I knew all the facts and consequences, I'd still let Babayon work his magic. The lives we saved outweigh the cost to me."

"What will you do about the two of them?" Christoph nodded towards Sarah and Nicolai.

Rane's gaze shifted to Sarah at the front of their little procession. "I don't know."

"She'll betray us all the first moment she can."

"She probably will, but I meant it when I said I'm not a monster. I certainly can't kill her in cold blood."

"So, we wait and see?"

Rane nodded. "We wait and see—but I promise you this: I won't let any harm befall your family. Not from her. Not from the Inquisition."

Christoph smiled. "You are a good man."

"I swore an oath once to protect those weaker than myself. It's an oath I mean to keep as long as I can."

They walked on in silence. A cool breeze took some of the heat out of the day, weaving through the grass and dragging the odd cloud across the blue sky. In many ways, it was beautiful out on the Steppes. Peaceful even. If it wasn't for Saphie's coughing and the sight of a Soldier of the Inquisition leading them, Rane would've said it was almost enjoyable.

They saw a herd of buffalo grazing in the distance, and even that gave them all some comfort, for the animals wouldn't have been so calm if there were Bracke nearby.

Undisturbed, they made good progress that day, only stopping as night fell. Saphie's coughing had gotten worse, so Rane allowed a small fire to make her medicinal drink.

There wasn't enough firewood for more than that though. Christoph and Rache spent some time pulling grass from the ground and built a small pile of it near the fire. Every now and then, someone would throw another handful onto the flames to keep it burning. It was enough to keep the chill away for a while. Christoph's family sat on one side of the fire, while Sarah and Nicolai were on the other just like the previous night. Nicolai was already asleep, his head in Sarah's lap.

Rane stood to one side, checking the horse. At least she was happy with plenty to eat all around her.

"Where are you from, Sarah?" asked Christoph out of the blue.

The sister looked up, surprised at the question. "Why do you ask?"

"Just curious. I like to get to know people."

Sarah looked at Christoph for a moment as if she was trying to work out what other reason he could have for asking questions. "My order is based in Chandra, but it's been a while since we've been there."

Christoph nodded. "What about before that? Where were you born?"

"A small village near the coast. It was called Chobham."

"I haven't heard of it," said Christoph.

"It doesn't exist anymore," said Sarah.

"No?"

"No."

"What happened?" asked Christoph, his voice full of genuine curiosity.

"It was purged."

"Ah. Sorry. I ... I ... didn't mean to bring up unhappy memories." Christoph looked around, looking for help from someone else, and eventually caught Rane's eye.

"I used to live in the south," said the Legionnaire. "Near a town called Eshtery."

Sarah nodded. "I remember it. Famous for its stone quarries. It was about a day's ride from Chobham. My father would work there sometimes to earn extra money."

"It's a beautiful part of the country," said Rane. "I had a cottage by a small stream. It was peaceful, especially after the war. I wish I was there now."

"What made you leave?" asked Christoph.

"Bounty hunters came to kill me, ended up killing my wife and unborn child instead."

The Fascalian winced. "Shit. I'm going to shut up. Sorry. Both of you. Sorry."

"Will we reach Napolin tomorrow?" asked Saphie with overenthusiastic brightness, obviously trying to change the subject. The medicine had done her good, and her coughing had eased once more.

"Perhaps, if we're lucky," said Rane. "But if not tomorrow, we'll be there by the following morning."

"I can't wait to sleep in my own bed again," said Rache. "Uncle's house in—"

"Rache!" snapped Fion. "Some details are better kept to ourselves." She nodded towards the Soldiers of the Inquisition. Sarah glared back.

Rache winced. "Sorry. I wasn't thinking."

An even more uneasy silence fell over the group. Christoph's family huddled closer, their eyes on the sister. She, in returned, had her hand on the hilt of her sword. Her eyes drifted from the Fascalians to Rane and back again, as if she were mulling over terrible choices.

It was a look Rane had seen plenty of times in the war, normally on the faces of soldiers trying to find some courage before an attack, knowing that whatever they did would probably result in their death.

Out here, it wasn't hard to work out what Sarah might be planning.

"Can I show you something, Sister?" said Rane.

The question threw them all for a moment, but none more so than Sarah. She visibly shook off whatever thoughts had been going through her mind. "What is it?"

Rane went over to his pack and delved inside for the

newsletter he picked up at the inn a few days before. He held it up. "This."

"A news sheet?" She took it off him. "What of it?"

"It came from Napolin. I picked it up a few days ago. There was a story in it that I found interesting."

Sarah unfolded it and angled it towards the fire. "What story?"

"The one about the murders."

Sarah scanned the sheet until she found the article. She read it quickly. "There's a killer in the city—so?"

"Mutilated bodies found in rooms behind locked doors. No sign of entry, forced or otherwise."

She shrugged. "I'm sure the law keepers will catch whoever is responsible."

"And if they do, they'll probably die too," said Rane.

Sarah squinted at Rane. "Why do you say that?"

"Because I think this is the work of a Legionnaire. Someone lost to the taint. A monster."

"One of you." Sarah spat on the ground.

"Once, yes. But now they're a monster so they are now my enemy. I'm going to Napolin to hunt whoever it is and stop them."

"Why would you do that?"

"Because I don't want innocent people dying," said Rane. "It's as simple as that."

"Why are you telling me this?" said Sarah.

"Because you should be hunting this monster too."

"You want me to go after the Tainted in Napolin and forget about you? Is that it? You'd betray your own kind?"

"I'm protecting my own kind—ordinary people. Whoever is doing the killing is no longer human and needs stopping. It's only Legionnaires like me who haven't changed yet who have my absolute loyalty."

"And you want me to help you? Is that it?"

Rane shook his head. "No. Not at all. But when we get to Napolin, perhaps instead of wasting time persecuting a family who are, as you said yesterday, good people, you should mobilize the Inquisition to find *this* monster."

"And forget about you too?" Sarah sneered.

"No. You can hunt me too. I don't care. I can look after myself." Rane pointed to Christoph and his family. "I just want you to forget about them."

"I can't do that. Odason demands—"

"Odason demands nothing," said Rane, cutting her off. "He's not appeared, issuing decrees, demanding them dead. It's people that make demands. The heads of your church make these demands, Mother Singosta, Mother Hilik, and the rest. Humans."

"Odason speaks through them," said Sarah. "They act on his will."

"Do they? Or do they just like seeing people burn?"

21

Sarah

As Sarah led everyone off the next day, she had a million thoughts rushing around her head. The same thoughts that had kept her up most of the night as they played over and over again in her mind, making her doubt everything she'd ever believed.

She just couldn't shake off the monster's words.

It didn't help that the monster—Nathaniel—was not what she'd been expecting. He wasn't some sort of frenzied animal, killing all before him. She remembered him willingly going out alone to face the Bracke in order to save everyone else. When he spoke, he did so with calm intelligence, and he genuinely seemed to care about the Fascalians.

Over the last two days in their company, she'd watched and listened to what was said and done in the hope she would work out his purpose and how and why he controlled the others—but she'd found nothing.

They appeared to be a loving family with a sick daughter, and all Nathaniel wanted to do was get them to Napolin safely.

Even when Nathaniel had told Sarah his suspicions about the Tainted in Napolin, he'd not done so out of any self-interest. He'd not tried bargaining for his own life in any way. Far from it. He'd only asked that she let the Fascalians go. Something she was already tempted to do.

What was worse, his words about Mother Singosta and Mother Hilik rang true too. She'd seen first-hand the zeal Mother Hilik had for interrogating suspects, how readily she could order a town or village to be purged. By all accounts, Mother Singosta—the head of their order—was even more unforgiving in her dealings with any she saw as corrupted or tainted.

Sarah also knew a wrong word or action on her part could just as easily send her to a pyre. She'd spent most of her life being careful not to give anyone reason to inform on her. Odason Himself knew that if she and Nicolai failed to kill Nathaniel, Mother would burn them both. She would say that Nathaniel had either corrupted them both or that they were not a true believer in the All-Father.

But was this Nathaniel's way of corrupting her? With sweet words masquerading lies as truth? Was his charm just a demon's way of seducing her? Was he testing her faith in Odason, in Mother and the order?

And what of Nicolai? Had the All-Father failed to protect him because of their love? Had He heard Nicolai suggest they run from the order and made him pay for it? But, if that was the case, why hadn't He punished Sarah too? Because even now, she wished she'd taken Nicolai up on the offer.

They would've had a chance at a normal life. Now, all she could do was watch him die.

She'd prayed on the matter before they'd left their camp site, hoping that Odason would answer her questions but He was as silent as He ever was. And why shouldn't He be? What made her struggle so important? She had been given a task that she should see through, no matter what words were whispered in her ear, no matter what feelings were in her heart.

She glanced back. Christoph led the horse with his daughter, Rache, beside him, while Fion followed behind, and Nathaniel himself was at the rear as normal, bow in hand. He caught her looking, of course, and gave her a nod before she turned away. He'd not mentioned the conversation of the previous night, let alone pressed her for an answer as to what she would do when they reached Napolin. But what more was there to be said? His words were in her head, and she couldn't shake them free.

Her hand drifted to her sword hilt. Sarah should just turn around and try to kill him now, before they took another step towards Napolin. She could pretend she wanted to speak to him, perhaps about the other Tainted, and then draw her sword when she was close enough. If Odason willed it, she would be successful.

If He didn't, she'd be dead.

If He didn't, what did Odason want? Had Mother Singosta led the order down the wrong path?

Sarah's head spun with it all.

She didn't attack Nathaniel. She just walked, putting one foot in front of the other, and hoped for some sign that would help her see the right way forward.

She didn't have to wait too long for it to arrive.

"We need to pick up the pace," called Nathaniel, around mid-morning.

They all turned to see why he sounded worried.

In the distance, there were black shapes spread out along the horizon.

"Buffalo?" asked Christoph.

"No," said Nathaniel. He looked straight at Sarah. "It's the Soldiers of the Inquisition."

Sarah's stomach lurched as she peered into the distance. It was hard to tell what the shapes were, but she knew instinctively that Nathaniel was right. "Mother Hilik."

"Dear Gods," said Fion. "How far behind us are they?"

"Maybe half a day," said Nathaniel.

"We need to stop," said Sarah. "Wait for them. Odason has sent them to help me."

"We're not waiting," said Nathaniel. "You can come with us or you can stay here on your own. Choice is yours."

Ten yards separated them. If Sarah attacked, he had plenty of time to draw his sword and strike her down. Even if she got lucky, any wound would heal before it would slow him down or incapacitate him. She needed all of Odason's Children if she was going to win a fight with him.

She drew her sword.

"What are you doing?" said Christoph. "There's no point to this."

"There's every point." Sarah moved into a fighting stance. Every second she delayed them allowed Mother to get closer.

Nathaniel didn't move. He stood watching her, bow in one hand. "Fighting is only going to end up one way. No one wants that. Come with us to Napolin. Help stop the Tainted there."

"Just shut up! I've had enough of your words," shouted

Sarah. "All you try and do is confuse me. My job is to stop you—or die trying."

The horse snorted, reared up, and almost pulled away from Christoph's hands. The girls squealed as they held on desperately.

"Easy, easy," said Christoph, but the animal didn't want to listen. The horse continued to breathe rapidly, hooves skittering on the road. She didn't want to be near whatever had spooked it.

Then Nathaniel was moving; raising his bow, pulling an arrow from his quiver, nocking it onto the bowstring, drawing it back to his cheek, aiming, firing. It happened so fast, Sarah could only follow the arrow's flight and heard a squeal as it hit something, then the thud as the target fell to the ground.

"Bracke!" shouted Nathaniel, fitting another arrow to his bowstring.

"Where?" screamed Sarah, but he'd already fired the second arrow. She followed its flight, saw it strike another Bracke that had been running parallel to the travelers. The demon stumbled but didn't fall. It reared up, howling in fury, then ran straight towards them.

Sarah charged out to meet it without thinking. "For Odason!"

The Bracke leaped as she swung. She struck its ribs, her sword sinking deep, as she felt claws rake across her gut. She fell back, the demon on top of her, snapping jaws going for her face. She stabbed wildly with her sword, screaming for her life, her god.

A shadow moved past her and struck the Bracke. Hot blood gushed over her, and she screamed again. The shadow hauled the creature off her.

Sarah lay there, panting. She reached down, felt where

the claws had struck her stomach and the broken links on her chainmail beneath her slashed robes, but the claws hadn't gone through the iron links. She wasn't wounded. She had to look, to double-check, but thank Odason, her armor had held. She wheezed air back into her lungs, her heart racing, shocked but grateful she was still alive.

Hands grabbed her, pulled her back and up onto her feet. She looked up, saw Nicolai, deathly white, leaning on a bloody sword. "Are you all right?"

"Yes," she said, but she wasn't sure.

"Come on. You need to get out of here."

"But Mother ..."

Nicolai smiled. "Mother isn't the answer. You know that."

Fion fired a pistol, scaring the horse some more. The girls screamed. Nathaniel shot another arrow, then another.

"Come on," said Nicolai, dragging her back to the others. Sarah stumbled along with him, covered in Bracke blood, still in shock, her sword heavy in her hand.

"How many are there?" shouted Fion. She all but threw her spent pistol into her husband's hands.

"I can't see any more, but they could be hiding in the long grass," said Nathaniel. He moved in a circle, his arrow nocked and ready. He looked over to the girls. "Both of you get down. I need the horse."

They did as they were told, and the Legionnaire climbed up. The horse seemed happier with him in the saddle, and he turned her, searching the long grass, slowly at first then quicker a second time. "Shit."

"What is it?" asked Christoph. "What do you see?"

"We're surrounded. There's at least a dozen of them closing in." Rane drew back his bow, fired another arrow into the long grass and reached for another arrow.

Sarah turned to Christoph. "How many bullets do you have left?"

"Four."

Sarah raised her sword and tried not to think about how she'd nearly died facing one Bracke.

Rane loosed another arrow, then another, while Sarah cursed the long grass for hiding the creatures.

"You need to move," said Nicolai. "Get away from here. Give me your bow, and I'll hold them off. Give you time."

"Nicolai, no," said Sarah. "We'll all wait for Mother."

"She'll burn you with them. This is the only way."

The Legionnaire shot arrow after arrow into the grass while Sarah stared at Nicolai. "I can't leave you."

"You must. I need you to live," said Nicolai. "I'm already dead."

"We need to go now," said Nathaniel.

A Bracke howled to the south.

Nicolai took the bow off the Legionnaire.

"May Odason protect you," said Nathaniel.

Nicolai laughed. "Go."

Nathaniel dismounted and put Rache and Saphie back up on the horse, and then they were all off, leaving Sarah behind.

There was movement in the grass. Another Bracke raced towards them. Nicolai shot it with an arrow. There were only five arrows left in his quiver. He drew another, nocked it, took aim, and loosed. "Please go," he said without looking at her.

"Nicolai, I ..." Sarah couldn't move. She couldn't leave him to die. Not alone.

"Go!" he shouted.

More Bracke howled around them. She could hear the demons rushing through the grass. Nicolai shot another one while Sarah tightened her grip on her sword, mouth dry, and waited for the creatures to explode from the long grass.

"Please, Sarah." Nicolai's voice was full of emotion. "Don't die. Not for me, not for Mother, not for Odason. Please." He fired another arrow, then looked at her, eyes full of tears, blood on his chin. "Please."

Sarah nodded, took a step backwards. "I love y—"

A Bracke leapt out the grass and snatched Nicolai away.

For a moment, Sarah stared at the empty space where he'd been, then her brain kicked into action. She could hear Nicolai's screams, and the snarls of the demons. She went after him, knowing she'd be too late but she had to try. She had to—

Another Bracke appeared, stopping her in her tracks, and this demon wanted her. Sarah screamed as it jumped and thrust her sword deep into its chest. It sank into the creature more by accident than design but its momentum still bore Sarah to the ground. She pushed the dead weight off her and scrambled to her feet. By the time she'd retrieved her sword, Nicolai had stopped screaming.

Instead, she heard the growling of more Bracke in the long grass.

Sarah ran as fast as she could, after Nathaniel and the others, away from the deadly creatures, away from Mother, tears streaming down her face, trying hard not to think of Nicolai.

When she caught up with the others, they continued to move quickly. Barely stopping, pushing all their limits to exhaustion. Sarah kept looking back, but she couldn't see any more Bracke. They'd escaped.

Gradually, the land around them began to change once more. Rocks appeared out of the grass like stone giants watching over the Steppes, and the ground itself began to slope up towards the roll of a hill breaking up the horizon in front of them. The scent of the sea was in the air.

They all noticed. Little smiles spread from one face to the next, and it made Sarah happy to see them, despite the pain in her own heart.

On they walked, stopping only to eat the last of their food halfway up the hill. Sarah looked back the way they'd come, but there was no sign of Mother.

"They'll catch up soon enough," said Nathaniel, coming to join her. "If there's one thing I've learned, the Inquisition keeps on coming."

"The Bracke will kill many of them," replied Sarah.

"There's always more." He smiled. It was nothing like Mother Hilik's smile. It felt warm and genuine. "I'm sorry about your friend. He was a fine and brave man."

"He was the best."

"They always seem the first to fall."

"Why is that?"

"If I had the answer to that ..." Nathaniel shook his head. Then he looked at Sarah, all humor gone. "I need your word that you will not pursue Christoph and his family once we get to Napolin."

"I will leave him be. I can see they're not your thralls." She glanced over at the others. "They're good people."

"Swear it before the All-Father."

Sarah swallowed. This was no mere promise the Legionnaire sought. Once again, she was reminded that Nathaniel was no fool. "I swear before Odason that I will not harm Christoph or his family, nor will I renounce them before the Soldiers of the Inquisition."

Nathaniel nodded. "Thank you."

She turned to leave, but Nathaniel caught her by the arm. "Yes?"

His eyes were like flint. "If you break that vow, I will find out, and I'll come after you."

"As you wish."

The travelers moved on, leaving the grass of the Steppes behind. The first tree they saw was gnarled and twisted by the wind but, after the endless green, it was a welcome sight. More followed, appearing here and there in ones and twos, witness to their passing. The ground became rockier, the salt in the air more pronounced.

Then, when they crested the hill, they saw it—Napolin. The city was no more than a smudge in the distance, the ocean on either side, but it was there.

"Thank Odason," said Christoph. "We've made it."

Sarah watched them clap and cheer, a mix of relief and joy on all their faces, but she couldn't help but think their ordeal was far from over.

The Inquisition were in Napolin already, and no matter Sarah's promises, they would want to see them all burn.

22

Rane

Rane and the others carried on through the night, following the road to Napolin. With the city in sight, no one wanted to stop for longer than necessary. They were all exhausted, but the city drew them on.

Rane's gaze kept drifting to Sister Sarah as she marched along in her blood-stained gown. Her oath had given him some comfort, but he couldn't help wondering if trusting her was a bad decision.

Kibon murmured in his ear. As ever, it knew only one way to deal with the issue. *Kill her*, it whispered. *It's the only way to be sure.*

On and on it went. Playing on his fears. It knew he was tired. Worn out. Weak.

It took all he had to ignore the damned thing, to remind

himself that to give in was to become the monster the Inquisition believed he was.

He was no cold-blooded killer. He was a Legionnaire who fought to protect others and for justice.

Kibon just laughed. *I know what you are.*

As they climbed up the side of yet another hill, they all heard the crash of waves and the squawk of seagulls. There was a moment when they all exchanged looks with each other as if to question what they had heard, then Christoph ran to the top of the hill, leading the girls on the horse. They whooped when they reached the top—and with good reason.

When Rane, Sarah, and Fion caught up with them, they, too, saw what the excitement was all about. They had reached the end of Ascalonia. Half a mile away, cliffs fell away to the ocean a hundred feet below with only a lone, stone bridge crossing over to the city of Napolin and the country of Fascaly on the other side of the channel. Guards protected the bridge, and a knot of travelers waited to get across.

The city itself was made up of white stone buildings topped with spires flying colorful flags, all nestled amongst lush green vegetation. At the water's edge, smaller dwellings stretching on stilts stood over the green water streaked with white surf. Even at that early hour, fishing boats darted this way and that while seagulls rode the warm breeze, occasionally diving into the ocean to snap up their breakfast. After all Rane and the others had been through, it looked like the promised land.

Looking down on the city, memories came flooding back of Rane's first visit to the city as a new recruit to the Legion. If the soldiers had relaxed their discipline out at the way station, they lost their minds in Napolin. He remembered nights filled with beautiful food, plenty of wine, and the city's lax moral attitude to all things young soldiers love. It was the last time he could remember just laughing and laughing without a care in the world until he met Kara.

Happy memories. Painful memories. He shut his eyes. So many of the Legionnaires had been lost in the war. And of those who survived, how many had been lost to the Taint?

"We made it. We bloody well made it," said Christoph, slipping his arm around Fion. They both helped their children down from the horse and embraced each other. "We made it!"

"It's beautiful," said Fion, wiping away a tear.

Rane turned away. He needed time to get his feelings back under control. He needed to concentrate on the job at hand.

There were enemies after him after all. People who wanted him dead. Rane gazed back across the land they'd just walked, wondering how far away Mother Hilik was.

"She'll be here before the end of the day," said Sarah beside him.

"That she will," said Rane.

"Your friends will need to get in the city long before then."

"I know."

They rejoined Christoph and his family. Rane watched the Fascalians' faces bloom with hope as they gazed down on Napolin and felt happy for them. He'd kept them safe though it all and resisted every urge from *Kibon*. That alone was something to be proud of.

"You best be going," said Rane to Christoph. "I think it's time to go our separate ways for now."

"What do you mean?" said Christoph. "I thought you had to go to Napolin as well."

"I do, but not with you. A Fascalian family should get past those guards without a problem. A former Legionnaire with a forbidden sword? Not so much. I'll make my own way into the city."

"What about you?" Fiona asked Sarah.

"She's going to wait with me until you're in the city," said Rane before Sarah could answer.

"Fair enough." Fion unbuckled the gun belt. "You better take these back."

Rane held up a hand. "Look after them for me for now. Stick them in a bag and carry them through. I'll get them off you tomorrow."

Christoph nodded. "It'll be our pleasure."

Rane walked over to the girls and bent down to their eye level. "You two take care."

Saphie hugged him. "Thank you for everything."

"The doctors will get you better in no time," said Rane.

"I hope so," said Saphie.

"Look after your Mum and Dad for me," said Rane as he put his arm around Rache.

"I promise," she replied.

He stood up, and Fion wrapped her arms around Rane's neck. "May the Gods bless you, Nathaniel."

"I hope they do. I could do with some help." Rane gave Fion a quick squeeze around her shoulders before stepping back.

Fia looked at him with raised eyebrows. "You're a good man. Never forget that no matter what happens, no matter what others might say."

"I'll do my best to remember that," said Rane.

"Where shall I meet you tomorrow?" asked Christoph.

Rane guided the Fascalian to one side, out of earshot of Sarah. "From what I remember, there's a good tea house on

Twelfth Street. I'll aim to be there when it opens in the morning. If you could meet me there and return my guns to me, I'd be grateful."

"I know it."

"Take care, my friend. Thank you for believing in me."

Christoph hugged him. "Thank you for saving us."

They rejoined the others. The girls climbed back onto the horse, and then Sarah and he watched Christoph and Fion lead them down to join the others trying to get into the city.

"You didn't trust me enough to go with them," said Sarah once they were alone.

"It's not a question of trust," said Rane. "I just thought traveling with a Soldier of the Inquisition would lead to too many questions—especially with you covered in blood."

Sarah smiled. "Good point."

Rane found a rock that offered a view of both the city and the road back into the Steppes and sat down. Sarah joined him.

"So how long do we wait?"

"Give them an hour, then you can go."

"You're not going to come with me either?"

"No. I don't think that's a good idea."

"You know I'm going to have to tell them what you told me—about the Tainted in the city."

"I know."

"The Inquisition will come out in force, and when Mother Hilik gets here, it will get even worse until we catch them—or you."

"I know. Hopefully, that will draw the Tainted out. Maybe make them do something stupid."

"I don't know what to make of you, Nathaniel," said Sarah. "I really don't."

"I'm just trying to do the best I can," replied Rane.

"That's not easy when the world wants you dead."

"Who I am doesn't come into that. They want Legionnaires dead. They want the Tainted dead. They want magic users dead. They want monsters dead." Rane shrugged. "Easy to hate a label. But you know me as a person now. You know I lost my wife and child. You know I'm not some blood-sucking killer, that I actually care about others. Not so easy to hate me now, out here when it's just the two of us. But once you cross that bridge, I'm going to be just another Legionnaire to you, another monster to be hunted."

"No, you won't."

Rane smiled sadly. "Yes, I will."

"I can talk to Mother Hilik, explain things to her ..."

"You'll end up burning with me if you do."

Sarah didn't try to argue with the truth of his words. "I wish it wasn't like this."

"But it is," said Rane. "And I've got a feeling things are going to get a hell of a lot worse too."

"Why do you say that?"

"Everyone's so busy hunting Legionnaires, they're not looking at the bigger problems—like why are there so many demons on the loose now? All the Bracke and the Jotnars and the Valkryn haven't just appeared out of nowhere."

"Heras released them from—"

Rane held up a finger to silence her. "Heras is like Odason. She doesn't care what we get up to in the world. Someone's behind this. Someone who wants us weak and too preoccupied to defend ourselves when the time comes."

"The Rastaks? Mogai?"

"Maybe. I've heard rumors that he's trying to build a new army, but if it's not him, it's someone, and until we discover who that is, these demons will keep on coming. Farming will suffer. Trade will suffer. Our lives will suffer."

"Everyone blames the Gods."

Rane nodded. "That's why it's so clever. Each city, each town is becoming more isolated—even great Napolin, the heart of trade, closes its gates to some—when we should be joining forces, becoming stronger together. When we did that during the war, it wasn't enough, but it helped us survive. Now? When whoever is behind all this does attack, it'll be too late to stop them."

"Odason won't allow it," said Sarah.

"No?"

Sarah remained silent.

Rane looked down at the bridge. There was no sign of Christoph or his family. "The others have gone. It's your turn now."

Sarah followed his gaze. "So they have."

"You'll remember your oath?"

"I will."

"May Odason watch over you, Sarah."

"And you too, Nathaniel."

Sarah took her time standing up, then adjusted her belt and sword and straightened the front of her gown. Then she smiled when she realized what she was doing. "It's beyond a few creases."

Rane returned the smile. "You might need a new one."

"Try not to get yourself killed, Nathaniel."

"I'll be seeing you, Sarah."

Rane watched Sarah head down to the bridge for as long as he dared, then headed back over the crest of the hill and out of sight. It wasn't worth risking his life based on whatever rapport he thought he'd built with Sarah. All she had to do was tell the guards at the bridge he was a Legionnaire, and they wouldn't hesitate to try to capture him. That would mean a fight and a chance he'd have to use *Kibon*. And if he used *Kibon*, there would be more deaths to corrupt his soul. He couldn't risk that.

Keeping low, he ran off to the east, moving far from the main road. Weaving his way among outcrops of rock and through depressions in the ground, he headed for the cliff edge. It was strange being on his own again and not having to worry about anyone's safety but his own. They'd all been through so much on the road together, he'd become used to having everyone around. He hoped Saphie would get the help she needed.

He kept moving until the sun was high in the sky and Napolin was far behind him. Even though there had been no sign or sound of any pursuit, Rane wasn't going to take any chances. Then he spotted a place that looked perfect. A large rock jutted out of the grass. It looked curled by the wind as it tilted to one side, creating a pool of shadow beneath it.

He ran over and crawled under the leaning rock so he was facing Napolin. It was a tight fit with only an inch or so to spare above his head, but it would hide him well. More importantly, if anyone came looking for him, he'd see them long before they got close.

Sheltered from the wind and the sun, Rane began to relax. He rolled his neck, trying to get rid of some of the aches and pains from the trek across the Steppes, but there was no shaking off how tired he was.

His thoughts drifted to Sarah. Doubt nagged at him. He must've been mad to trust her. She was a Soldier of the Inquisition after all. One of Odason's Children. How many Legionnaires had she hunted down and killed? What was her oath to him compared to the one she'd made to her order?

What a fool he was.

Kibon agreed. It pulsed as it lay next to him. It knew what to do if he saw Sister Sarah again. *There's only one way to deal with people like her.*

No. Rane wasn't going to listen to his sword. He closed his eyes and concentrated on his breathing instead, emptying his mind of all thoughts. The world disappeared as he meditated. He felt the air fill his lungs, then breathed out slowly, carefully. In and out. In and out. That was all that mattered. Tiredness seeped through his body, and Rane didn't fight it. He needed the rest. He needed to sleep.

When he reopened his eyes, the sun was long gone, leaving behind a star-filled sky with a near-full moon nestled among them. It was time to go. He slipped his pack and *Kibon* onto his back and started to make his way back to Napolin.

He took his time, looking for any surprises. He felt better for the rest, but anything could've happened while he slept. Mother Hilik would've arrived with all her soldiers and they would've had plenty of time to prepare a welcome for him.

A thought that was confirmed the moment Napolin came into view. The city itself was lit up with torchlight, shining bright in the darkness. Guards lined the bridge and even more were scattered over the approach roads and surrounding area. Rane couldn't tell if they were city guards or Soldiers of the Inquisition, but it didn't matter either way; he wasn't going to be able to get within half a mile of Napolin without being surrounded.

Good thing he had no intention of using the bridge the traditional way.

Leaving his pack hidden under the rock, Rane ran in a

crouch to the cliff edge, dropping to his stomach to crawl the last few yards. Once there, he peered over the side. It was a vertical drop to the sea below. Waves crashed against the base of the cliffs, creating a churn among the jutting rocks. A breeze tugged at his hair as he gazed down at the swirling surf. A fall from the cliff would be fatal, even for him. Still, climbing the cliff face seemed a safer option than trying to fight his way across the bridge.

Of course, he could've just as easily walked away, left Napolin to deal with its own problems and look after himself. "I must be mad," he whispered to himself.

Spotting some decent foot and hand holds, he swung his body sideways so his right leg dropped over the side. Once he had a good nub of rock to rest his foot on, he brought his other leg down. The moment he'd committed himself and was perched on the side of the cliff, the breeze turned into a more purposeful wind, weaving past him on its way west. The expanse around him grew ever threatening, and gravity reminded him that he didn't belong so high up. Still, there was no going back.

He felt his way along the rock, climbing down and across. Every time some small rock dislodged under his fingers or under foot, his heart leaped into his mouth. Up on top of the cliff, the moon and stars had provided more than enough light, but now he seemed lost in shadow, feeling his way sideways along the rock face. It was slow going, but the hand and footholds were plentiful, and Rane slowly relaxed into the climb. He'd enjoyed climbing since he was a small boy, spending time with his father scrambling around the local hills and mountains. The secret to climbing was to use the legs more than the arms, to find secure footholds and then push on, using the hands only to guide and steady the rest of the body.

Still, the surf continued to grumble against the cliff face below him, reminding him what could happen if he were to slip, and he had a long way to go.

Slowly, he inched along the cliff. Voices drifted down from above. Guards complained about being on duty all night, while others prayed to Odason or jumped at shadows. There were traveler's too, locked out of the city until the next morning, talking amongst themselves about monsters being on the loose or making plans for when they were let into the city. Aromas from their campfires wafted down to Rane too, piquing his hunger and making his mouth water.

He moved on, hand by hand, foot by foot. Sweat trickled down his back despite the cold wind dancing around him. Rane could feel the strain starting to build in his fingers as he wedged them into tiny crevices. He still had the bridge to cross. Maybe this really wasn't one of his best plans.

Then he was under the bridge and lost in its shadow. He paused for a moment on a crack of a ledge, drawing air into his lungs and, one hand at a time, he shook the cramps out of his fingers. As rested as he could be, Rane started to climb up once more. Ten feet up, the cliff face merged with the stone bridge, and he moved from one to the other, angling back out and onto the side of the bridge. This was the most dangerous part of it all—and not just because he was going to be a hundred feet in the air, clinging to ancient stone. All it would take was one person to look at the side of the bridge and they'd see him dangling there. Rane would have no escape except to fall to the sea and the rocks below, and that would be the end of it.

The blocks used to build the bridge gave Rane a very different challenge. Old and worn, he had regular foot and hand holds to traverse, but the lips of each were almost nonexistent in places, and the stone was cracking and crumbling in other parts.

The wind seemed to sense his unease, plucking at his clothes, rattling his sword and biting his skin. The drop pulled at him too, eager to have him fall, but Rane inched on, concentrating only on making it to the next stone. He refused to look at the other side of the bridge, fearing that the reality of how far he had to go would sap what little remained of his strength. Traversing the side of the bridge would have tested him at the best of times, and he was only too aware how far from the best he really was.

He flexed his right hand, trying to stave off cramp again. His fingers bled from cuts and ripped fingernails. Decades old grit fell into his eyes, but still he inched along.

His muscles quivered under the strain as his whole world became the few feet of chiseled stone in front of his eyes.

He reached across to the next stone, squeezed his fingers around its edge before he slid his foot along. With that settled, he shifted his weight from his left foot to his right side and pulled his body over. His left foot followed, feeling for a new position to rest it but finding none. Each time he thought he had purchase, his foot slipped. Each slip threatened to dislodge him. The emptiness below pawed at him, eager to drag him from the wall. Panic flared inside with a rush of blood that did nothing to help the situation. The quivers in his right arm and leg became shakes as already tired muscles were put under even more strain. His grip began to slip.

Rane forced himself to be calm, filled his lungs with air and very deliberately brought his left leg up and felt for a new foot hold. It was there somewhere, he'd already used it for his other foot. He closed his eyes, resisting the urge to try for another handhold, fighting the panic telling him he was going to die. And, just when he thought he was lost, his foot slotted into place, resting on top of the lip of a stone.

Rane took a few moments to steady himself and allow his heartbeat to drop back down.

"Bloody hell, I'll be glad when we're off duty." The man's voice cut through the night. It came from a few yards above and to the right of Rane's position. He looked up just as some phlegm was hawked over the edge.

"Only Odason knows when that will be," said another voice. "It's been too long already."

Two guards leaned on the top of the wall, looking out over the ocean, unaware that Rane was clinging to the rock a foot below them.

"And back again at dawn for the same shit," said the one nearest Rane, so close they could almost touch. It would only a slight turn of the head to see the man hanging off the side of the bridge.

"At least we're not out patrolling the streets," said his friend. He snorted and spat again out into the night. "The Inquisition's got everyone out banging on doors."

"Did you see the state of that one that turned up all covered in blood? Like something out of a nightmare, she was."

"Yeah, I did. The ones that followed weren't much better. They had carts of dead bodies with them. Got attacked by Bracke out on the Steppes."

"Those bloody thing are only getting worse."

"Not as bad as having a Legionnaire loose in the city."

"You think that's who's doing the killings?"

"Makes sense doesn't it? No normal person would go around mutilating people like that."

"Bloody Legion. I can't wait till they're all dead."

"I hear they had women in their ranks. The worst of the lot. Cut your balls off as soon as look at you."

"Sounds like every woman I've ever met."

The two men laughed.

But while they joked, Rane could feel his strength fade, unable to move for fear of making a sound, praying they wouldn't look his way. He could feel his fingers slipping as old stone flecks shifted under his grip. He glanced along the bridge. Only a quarter of it remained. He would never make it. His hand slipped.

23

Rane

Rane clung from the side of the bridge, only too aware of the hundred-foot drop to the rock-filled sea below, waiting for the guards above to move on. He readjusted his grip and footing as his whole body shook with the effort.

"You two!" A third voice called out as footsteps approached.

Rane heard the shuffling of feet as the guards straightened up. "Yes, Sergeant."

"Stop gossiping like a pair of old fish wives and go home. For some reason, the boss thinks you've done enough hard work for the day."

"Yes, Sergeant. Thank you, Sergeant."

"Don't thank me. I know you're a pair of lazy bastards. Now clear off before I decide you need to do an all-nighter."

"Yes, Sergeant."

Rane heard the sergeant leave, his arms trembling. He didn't know how much longer he could hold on.

Kill them, whispered *Kibon*. Its answer to every problem.

"Come on," said the first guard after what seemed like an eternity. "Let's get some beer down us. Tomorrow will be with us soon enough."

His friend laughed. "Just the one. I'm not spending all day standing out in the sun tomorrow with a thumping headache."

"One day, you'll learn to hold your alcohol..." The voices drifted away with the rest of the traffic traveling along the bridge, and Rane breathed a sigh of relief.

He didn't waste any more time and resumed traversing along the side of the bridge. He went as fast as he could, racing against his weakening muscles, eyes now focused on the end of the bridge and the rock face.

His hands cramped up, and his legs weighed a ton. Sweat stung his eyes as he tried to rasp air in through his dry throat. The wind whipped around him, desperate now to pull him off the stone bridge. Gravel crumbled away under his fingers and feet as the roar of the wave called up to him from below.

Ten yards. Five yards. He was so close he was almost tempted to jump. He could see a ledge he could stand on. So close, he could almost touch it. Rane slid his foot along the last stone section, moved his hand along, feeling his way across the lip. He licked dry lips, exhausted from the blood rushing through him. Another step. Another inch. He was so tired. Every part of him shook with the strain.

Shouting from above him. Angry voices. Rane thought he'd been spotted, tensed, waiting for the alarm to ring or a spear to come flying at him.

But none came, and Rane forced himself on. He reached

out, touched the cliff face, and stepped over to the ledge. He stood there, fingers hooked into crevices, panting, and listened to Soldiers of the Inquisition bark their orders above as they argued with the city watch over what to do, happy that their disagreement wasn't about him. He looked back at the bridge at what now seemed an impossible distance to traverse. "Madness."

He stood there, lost in the shadows, until the shaking stopped and his breathing returned to normal.

Above him, leading off the main road and the bridge, were the primary trading areas of Napolin, where the merchants lived and worked and where the Inquisition waited. Rane had another destination in mind. He started to climb down the cliff face, towards the water and where the poorer residents of Napolin lived.

The city had grown out into the ocean over the years. Fishermen's housing sat on stilts above the water at the bottom of the cliffs. The buildings were lashed together and stretched out some hundred feet into the sea, with a myriad of boats bobbing away tied to piers and walkways. Washing hung on poles or ropes strung between buildings, and, despite the late hour, neighbors shouted conversations from one open window to another, accompanied by the barking of dogs and the laughter of children.

Climbing down seemed like child's play as he stepped from one outcropping to another. A thousand different aromas wafted up towards him, full of spice and salt, of food frying and grilling. Napolin was famous for its street food, and the smells brought back many a happy memory of Rane's time in the city when he was younger. There'd been a stupid competition between the recruits on who could eat the most chilies, quickly followed by who could drink the most ale. Rane wasn't the only one to be ill after that.

Such innocent days even with a war brewing.

Rane stepped from the rocks onto a railing and then jumped on to a wobbling wharf. No one seemed bothered at his sudden appearance, as if someone climbing down the cliff was a frequent occurrence. Even so, he walked quickly towards firm land, his head down, losing himself in the hustle and bustle around him. Despite the late hour, the streets were packed. Some were on the way home after a hard night's work, others were heading out to their boats for a new day's fishing, while a good few seemed happy to sit around laughing and joking over steaming bowls of noodles and prawns.

Rane kept his eyes open for the Inquisition and the city guard, but, for now, there were none to be seen. He knew they'd work their way down to the docks soon enough, but he had some breathing space.

Tired and hungry, Rane sat down at a small table outside a noodle shop in an alley just off a busy road, and placed his sword out of sight at his feet. There were another half dozen tables in front of the shop, all full, but Rane didn't mind. His table was at the back and there were plenty of shadows to offer privacy. Even so, he snuffed out the candle on his table. With his back to the wall, he had a good view of the main street in both directions

The owner came over, smearing his hands down an already dirty apron. Sweat glistened on his bald head. "What do you want?"

"Whatever's good," said Rane.

"It's all good," said the man, his eyes already wandering around other tables.

"Some prawn noodles. Thank you."

The man sniffed. "Prawn noodles it is."

Rane didn't have to wait long for the food. The owner

plonked down a large bowl of thick noodles with sliced chilies floating on top of the broth. The prawns were fat and juicy, probably only caught that morning.

Rane watched the world go by as he ate, taking his time with the meal.

Slowly, he could see the mood change. Whispers about the Inquisition started to make their way from stall to stall. He could see nervous glances on scared faces. A few of the stalls started closing up, putting away tables and pulling down shutters.

A man came over and spoke to the owner of the noodle shop, before moving onto another stall. The owner watched him go, all color gone from his cheeks, then he began going around the tables, speaking to his customers. One by one, they all got up left, all but running down the street.

Rane was the last customer.

"Time to finish up and get home. The Inquisition are arresting anyone they find on the street," said the owner.

"Do they do that often?" asked Rane.

The owner looked at Rane as if seeing him for the first time. "Where are you from?"

"Up north, from Milaze. I escorted a trader down with some cloth he's hoping to sell. Got here this morning."

"You got somewhere to stay?"

"Not yet. I was going to ask around. Wanted to try everything Napolin's famous for." Rane pointed to his empty bowl. "Then I thought I'd find some company."

"You picked the wrong night for that, my friend."

"What about an inn where I could get a bath and a bed? I don't need anywhere fancy."

The owner leaned out and checked the street again. It was emptying quickly, and there was already an uncomfortable silence falling over the area.

"Go two streets down," he said. "There's a building with three red lanterns hanging outside its door. If they've not locked up for the night, you can get a room there."

"It's not near any of these murders I've heard about?"

"Nah. Whoever's been doing that has been sticking to the western quarter, on the other side of the big park, where all the rich live."

"Thank you for the food," said Rane, standing up. He dropped some coins on the table.

The owner scooped the coins up and slipped them into his apron. "Be quick or those Inquisition bastards will put you up for the night in one of their cells. That happens, there's a good chance they'll have you on the rack or a pyre by morning."

Rane picked up his sword. "Thank you again."

"Bloody hell," said the owner, staring at the sword in Rane's hand, the sword he'd not covered up. The distinctive Legionnaire's sword. "You're one of them."

"No," said Rane, already backing towards the street. "No, I'm not."

"Legionnaire!" bellowed the man. "Legionnaire!"

Rane turned onto the street and started walking. He didn't care in what direction.

"Legionnaire! Legionnaire!" The noodle shop owner continued to shout. "Legionnaire!"

A window opened up above him somewhere. "Legionnaire!" screamed a woman. "Legionnaire!"

Another woman, further along the street, took up the cry. "Legionnaire!"

Ran ran down the deserted street, chased by the cries.

"Legionnaire!"

"Legionnaire!"

"Legionnaire!"

He turned right, down a narrower street, hoping to get lost somehow, and skidded to a halt.

Soldiers of the Inquisition was at the other end of the street. They drew their swords as they saw Rane.

24

Sarah

Sister Sarah knelt before Mother Hilik, her forehead pressed against the stone floor of the temple.

"Rise, child," said Mother, her voice even colder than normal. "You've been through so much."

Sarah sat up. "I'm glad to see you here unharmed, Mother," said Sarah. "I was so worried. After what happened ..."

"What happened to me—to your fellow brothers and sisters—is of no importance. It is your story that interests me. Tell me again what happened." There was a glint in Mother's eyes that quite unsettled Sarah.

They were in Odason's temple in the heart of Napolin. It was a spectacular temple, one of the most beautiful Sarah had ever been in. Lit by tall candles stretching all the way down the prayer hall and filled with pews facing the central alter. Marble pillars towered on both sides, reaching up to a domed ceiling, covered in paintings of the great halls amongst the stars. A tapestry covered the left wall from one end to the other, intricately sewn with the First Commands —Odason's directions for living a righteous life uttered on the day the world was born.

Mother sat on a chair on the dais at the end of the hall. Her sword, *Odason's Wrath*, lay across her lap. A statue of the All-Father towered behind her. Carved out of stone, he wore his warrior's garb with spear in one hand and a crow perched on his shoulder, whispering wisdom into his ear.

"We followed the monster into the Steppes," said Sarah. It was the fifth time she'd told the story since she'd arrived in the city and the second time Mother had heard it. "As you ordered."

"I do recall that detail."

"We discovered the burnt remains of his coach when we were halfway across the grasslands. As we were examining it, we were attacked by Bracke. Only Brother Nikolai and I survived that assault. We continued our pursuit of the monster, despite our wounds. More Bracke attacked us, and Brother Nicolai ... he ... died the next day from his injuries. I ... carried on and pursued the monster here. On arrival, I alerted the city guard and the local Inquisition. They have been searching the city ever since."

"Odason has obviously blessed you, Sarah," said Mother. "To be the lone survivor of such an ordeal."

"Yes, Mother."

Mother leaned forward, her elbows on her sword. "We too were attacked by Bracke on the Steppes. They didn't seem to care that I had over three hundred god-fearing Soldiers of the Inquisition with me."

Sarah bowed again. "Thank Odason for His protection."

"What of the people the monster was traveling with? What happened to them?"

Sarah straightened once more. "I presume they too died out on the Steppes—either killed by the monster or by Bracke."

"You did not see any bodies?"

"We didn't have time to look before we were attacked."

"What of the monster? You said you pursued 'him'. Do you know it was a man?"

Sarah took a deep breath. "I only ever saw the monster in the distance. I presumed it was a man by the shape of its body."

"I can only commend your determination and diligence, Sarah. To keep in pursuit after all your brothers and sisters died, under constant threat of attack by the Bracke. Odason truly loves you, child." There was something about the way Mother was looking at her that made Sarah very uncomfortable and quite scared. The gleam in her eyes reminds her of how the Bracke had looked when it had tried to bite her face.

"I did only what any of us would do, Mother."

"But you're sure the monster was alone when you saw him in the distance?"

"Yes, Mother."

"There wasn't anyone at all with him?"

"No, Mother."

There was a pause, then Mother glanced over her shoulder and indicated with her finger that someone should approach. A brother emerged from the shadows at the rear of the temple. He didn't look at Sarah as he approached Mother, nor when he stopped by her side.

Again, Mother smiled, and the fear within Sarah rose another notch. "You remember Brother Finn?"

She did. She remembered his whispered words of compassion before Harold, Roon, Jonas, and David were burned at the stake. She had wondered then whether he was testing her. Now she was certain. "I do. It is an honor to see you again, Brother."

Brother Finn stayed silent, staring straight over the top of Sister Sarah's head.

"Brother Finn is an excellent tracker," said Mother. "It was he who led your brothers and sisters across the Steppes in your wake."

The breath caught in Sarah's throat.

"Brother Finn seemed to think that your ... experience didn't quite match what he saw in the tracks he followed."

"It didn't?" Sarah hoped she'd conveyed just the right amount of surprise in her voice and not panic.

Mother glanced up at Finn. "Brother?"

"After we came across the site of the burnt wagon and the bodies of Sister Sarah's search party, we followed the tracks of a small group traveling together. Initially, it consisted of four adults and two children. They then came across a horse and children's footprints disappeared, presumably because they were riding the horse, until reappearing at a camp site. We then came across Brother Nicolai's ravaged body. I had assumed that he had been one of the adult footprints we followed, except we continued to see the tracks of four adults walking in single file and a horse. This led me to believe that Brother Nicolai had, up to the point where his body was discarded, been carried by one of the adults."

Anger flared in Sarah. "Brother Nicolai was not 'discarded'. He ... gave his life so I could ... go on with my mission."

"Did he?" Mother arched an eyebrow. "Did he really?"

"Yes!"

Mother stared at her in shock. "Did you just raise your voice to me in Odason's very house?"

Sarah's anger vanished in a heartbeat, leaving only fear. She bowed. "Forgive me Mother. I am not myself. I have been through an ordeal and survived only by Odason's blessing."

"Of that one fact, we are in agreement, child," said Mother. "Sit up."

Sarah did as she was ordered, though she couldn't meet Mother's eye.

"Now, Brother Finn believes you traveled with the monster and his familiars to Napolin," said mother. "If he is correct in this assumption, that would also mean you are lying to me and to the All-Father." She glanced over her shoulder to the statue.

"I would never do that," said Sarah.

"Then is Brother Finn lying?"

"No," said Sarah. "Merely mistaken."

"I do not make mistakes," said Brother Finn.

"And yet you suggested I offer mercy to four condemned men by soaking the wood for their pyre," said Sarah. "Against Mother and the All-Father's commands."

Mother smiled. "I asked him to do that. A little test to make sure I wasn't wrong about you."

"In that case, I passed it."

"You did — and that's part of the reason why you're still alive. I hate being wrong, especially about someone for whom I had such high hopes."

"Thank you."

"Still ... I hate being made a fool of more. You will be assigned a cell to pray in. You will remain there until we've caught the monster and interrogated it. We're also searching for his familiars."

"They're dead," said Sarah. "I told you that."

"If you lie about one thing, you've lied about everything.

The city watch gave us the details of everyone who entered the city before you. They'll all be put to the question, and the truth will come out."

Sarah's blood ran cold. Christoph's family would be tortured. Guilty or not, if they entered the temple, they wouldn't be leaving. And Sarah would die with them.

"Take her away," said Mother.

Brother Finn didn't need to be asked twice. He hauled her to her feet, his fingers digging into her arm in an attempt to make her cry out.

Sarah didn't give him the satisfaction.

They walked in silence through the temple and down the stairs into the crypt until they reached the cells. Originally designed for those who tended to the temple to have somewhere to sleep, the order used them more often than not now for the faithless and fallen.

Finn opened an iron door with a grate at head height and pushed Sarah through. The only light came from the torch in the corridor outside. There was a simple cot with no blankets in one corner and a bucket with water in the other. When Finn slammed the door, Sarah found herself in near darkness.

She stood, not moving and listened to Finn's footsteps disappear down the corridor. Only then did she sit on the cot and let the tears come.

25

Rane

Rane stared at the six men at the other end of the narrow alley. Warning cries of 'Legionnaire!' echoed across the rooftops. If he let himself get trapped here, give the Inquisition time to get reinforcements, it would be all over.

Kibon hummed with glee. Six men. Six lives to take. His sword knew it would be easy if only he drew it.

Six lives to take though. What would they do to his tally? Would they turn his sword black? Would he become a monster like Marcus and Myri and so many others?

He couldn't allow that.

"Legionnaire," hissed the first soldier, and then they all charged at Rane.

There was nothing he could do but charge to meet them.

The first soldier swung his sword down at Rane in a wild blow. Rane ducked in, blocked the man's sword arm with his left, and drove *Kibon's* hilt up into his chin. The soldier's head snapped back, and he started to fall, but Rane was already moving, swiveling around the second soldier's sword thrust. As Rane turned, he smashed his elbow into the back of the man's head.

The third man was close, too close for either of them to use their swords, and Rane had no choice but to grab him and throw him against the wall.

The fourth man swung at Rane then, not caring if he killed his comrade in the process, but Rane blocked him with *Kibon's* scabbard. He kicked down on the soldier's knee, the crack of broken bone loud in the narrow alley. He turned back to the third man, kneed him once, twice, three times in the gut, then threw him to the ground.

A sword whistled towards him, aimed at his neck. Rane ducked down under the attack, and the two men turned together. *Kibon* screamed to be unleashed and the sword's anguish threw Rane's concentration. He only just got his scabbard up in time to parry the blow, but the soldier kicked out and caught Rane in the chest. It was his turn to fall back against the wall, and the soldier pressed the attack, thrusting his sword at Rane's heart.

Rane lurched out of the way, and the sword hit the wall. He slashed down with *Kibon,* and its metal scabbard struck the man's leg, sweeping him off his feet. Rane kicked the man as he went down, and that just left ...

A body clattered into him—the sixth soldier. The impact knocked Rane off his feet, and he hit the ground hard. *Kibon* clattered from his hand.

The soldier was on top of Rane, straddling him, sword grasped in both hands, tip pointing at Rane's head.

The blade came down, and Rane jerked to the side, felt the blade cut his cheek. He swung a punch up, connected with the soldier's nose, and felt some of the weight lift. Rane shifted his body and pushed the man to one side. They both rolled clear of each other and bounced up onto their feet. Rane moved faster as the other tried to bring his sword around, darting in, thrusting his stiffened fingers into the man's throat. Rane heard him choke, and then punched him with the other hand, shattering his nose. The soldier bent over double, clutching his face, and Rane brought his knee up to meet him.

The last man fell to the ground.

Rane looked around, saw *Kibon* and snatched it up. The blade cursed him, demanding blood, bur Rane ran from the alley, leaving six broken and bleeding men—but they were all very much alive.

He ran down the narrow streets, not paying any heed to the direction, just eager to get away from the shouts and the cries. He came to some stairs, going down, back towards the water, and he took them two at a time, then headed east. He snatched a cloak off a washing line, threw it over his shoulders and tucked his sword out of sight.

Rane forced himself to walk then, keeping his head down. A man running always attracted attention, after all, always looked guilty. He carried on, weaving his way through the narrow streets, grateful for the darkness, until he felt he was far enough away from where he'd fought the Inquisition. Rane took the next set of stairs he found, taking his time climbing to the higher levels of the city.

The Inquisition were still everywhere though, forcing him to hide on more than one occasion. Then he saw a ladder leaning against a wall, in a small path between buildings.

The ladder was tall enough to let him reach a window ledge, and, from there, he clambered up to the roof. Rane moved from building to building, jumping the small gaps between each. He felt safer high up, away from Odason's Children as they trawled the streets. Safe enough to find a spot where one roof overlapped the next to settle down and rest.

He pulled the cloak tight around him, and with *Kibon* resting in the nook of his arm, fell asleep a heartbeat later.

THE SQUAWK of seagulls woke him a few hours later as the sun creeped out over the horizon, chasing the night away, leaving blood-red streaks across the water and sky.

Rane smiled to himself, enjoying the warmth of the sun on his face. The world would keep turning no matter what happened. Even when man and demon alike ceased to exist, the sun would rise and the night would fall.

Rane edged over the roof until he could get a good view of the streets below. Plenty of people were out and about, hustling this way and that. He couldn't see any Soldiers of the Inquisition, but that didn't mean they weren't out there.

He took his time climbing down from the roof, careful not to disturb anyone from their slumbers or make someone look up. Rane didn't need another mob riled up.

He paused for a moment at the edge of the path between the buildings and checked the comings and goings around him. The first thing he noticed was that there were no Soldiers of the Inquisition in sight. That in itself brought Rane a massive sense of relief, but he was no idiot either— he knew they'd be on guard throughout Napolin. Everyone else were just average Fascalians going about their business. There weren't many smiles on display though. Nearly everyone was in a hurry, with grim set mouths and furrowed brows, moving at a pace with no time for chit chat. It was so different from what he'd experienced when he'd first come to the city, but he wasn't going to complain now. It was easier to move about undetected if no one was trying to notice anyone else.

Once back on the street, he hunched his head and shoulders like everyone around him and set off with *Kibon* hidden under his cloak. He headed north, towards the tea house on Twelfth Street, where he'd arranged to meet Christoph. He only hoped his friend's time in Napolin had been less eventful than his own.

He bought a news sheet off a stall on a street corner and saw two stories taking up the front page: another murder on the westside and the on-going hunt of a suspected Legionnaire. The description of the Legionnaire couldn't have been more vague—tall, male, dark hair—but the story reminded everyone to check for scars on the right hands of anyone new they met and watch out for Legionnaires' swords.

Whenever he saw the Inquisition, he changed his route to give them a wide berth. He wasn't the only one doing that either. Odason's Children had everyone scared.

He found the tea shop easily enough. Yet to fill up with the day's business, it overlooked a quiet square with a fountain and an olive tree at its center. He settled down at a table tucked away in a corner outside, ordered a pot of green tea, and read the paper while he waited for Christoph. The murder was the third in five days—a money lender walking home after working late, to be with his wife and family. His body was found shortly after midnight, both ears missing.

According to the paper, the murders had accelerated from one every few months to one every few days. The more Rane read, the more convinced he became that it was the work of a Tainted Legionnaire, lost to madness and an insatiable urge to kill.

Once he had met Christoph, Rane planned to head over to the Western District and walk around the various murder sites. Perhaps he'd notice something the guards and the Inquisition had missed.

Rane glanced around. The square was starting to get busier. Some children had appeared, intent on chasing each other around the olive tree, laughing and shouting amongst themselves while their mothers chatted nearby. A few people had settled down at other tables outside the tea shop, but no one looked his way, and the owner seemed happy to leave Rane alone.

Still, Christoph should've been there by then. The fact that he was late was unsettling.

Rane kept the news sheet up, hiding his face, while he scanned the street over the top of it. He tensed as two Soldiers of the Inquisition wandered into the square on the far side, but if he moved suddenly, it would draw their attention. There was nothing he could do except sit and drink his tea.

Then he saw a girl approaching, clutching a bag to her chest, eyes darting everywhere, a worried look on her face. It was Rache.

Rane lowered the news sheet so she could see his face and waved her over. She half-ran the last few yards, tears springing up in her eyes.

"What's wrong?" he asked, rising to his feet.

Rache fell into his arms sobbing. He held her for a moment, but people were starting to turn their way, wondering what the fuss was about. He helped her sit and took the bag off her, only realizing then that it held his pistols.

"Rache, take a deep breath. Whatever it is, you can tell me and I can help, but you've got to stop crying if you can," said Rane, keeping his voice low. "People are watching, and there are Soldiers of the Inquisition nearby."

The girl nodded and rubbed her eyes. "Sorry." She looked around too, shaking with fear. "The Inquisition ... They came to the house this morning."

The breath caught in Rane's throat. "They did what?"

"I was asleep—we were all asleep—when they smashed their way in. There were dozens of them. Mother lowered me out of a window and gave me that bag. She told me to find you—tell you what had happened."

"Did they take the others?"

"Yes. Mother, father, Saphie—and my uncle and his family. They had wagons outside the house. Wagons with cages on the back."

"How long ago was this?"

"Not long. Just before dawn. I came straight here as fast as I could." Rache gulped as if trying to stop more tears.

Rane squeezed her hand. "You did well to find me." He glanced around again, aware now that too many people were trying hard not to pay them any attention. "We need to move from here."

"Where are we going?" asked Rache as they stood up.

"Just away from here to start with." Rane stood up and placed some coins on the table—more than enough for what he'd had but not too much to raise questions. "Better we walk."

They set off, Rane holding Rache's hand, the bag with his guns slung over one shoulder and *Kibon* hidden beneath his cloak. He led her back the way she'd come, keeping a good distance from the soldiers in the square.

"Can you show me where you were staying?" he asked after a few minutes.

"But the Inquisition ..."

"Should be long gone by now."

"But why there?"

"They'll have taken your family to Odason's temple," said Rane. "I'll go there and try to get them out, but I can't do that with you by my side. It's too dangerous. If your uncle's house is empty, you can stay there while I do whatever needs to be done."

"What if you ..." Rache put her hand over her mouth, unable to finish the sentence.

"What if I fail? What if I die?" said Rane. "Let's hope it doesn't come to that. But I promise you, I'll give everything I have to get them free."

They walked on through the busy streets, retracing Rache's steps to the house. Rane soon realized they were heading to the Western District, where the murders had occurred.

The area was very different from the rest of the city. Streets grew wider and buildings larger. Gradually, the stores and stalls faded away, and soon there were only homes for the very affluent lining the roads. Trees offered shade from the sun, and flowers added color to the buildings.

People walked around in bright clothes as if they had no care in the world, more often than not followed by servants waiting to answer their employers' every whim.

After the wilds of the Steppes and months on the run, it felt like Rane had stepped into an alien world. No one in the Western District had to worry about where their next meal was coming from or how they would get through the day. He felt his anger rise at the sight of all that affluence when so much of the world was suffering.

It was as if the war hadn't happened nor any of the horrors since. No Bracke were raiding in their city. No

Jotnars steeling their flocks. Instead, there was a bubble of wealth that protected the people who lived there from everything.

Perhaps that was why the Tainted had targeted the area? Perhaps, in some twisted way, that was how they were justifying their actions? Whatever their reasons, it didn't make murder and mutilation right. He had to stop them somehow —after he had freed Christoph and his family.

"Nathaniel." Rache squeezed his hand. "It's the house on the corner."

Her uncle's house wasn't the largest house in the street, but nor was it the smallest. Spread over two stories, the white stone walls gleamed in the sunlight. A row of three olive trees stood watch over the street while red and gold flags fluttered from the dome in the center of the rooftop.

It looked beautiful—if not for the smashed front door and the two Soldiers of the Inquisition that stood outside it.

"Where's the window you escaped from?" asked Rane.

"Around the back," replied Rache.

"Show me."

Rache took a small side street half a block from her uncle's house. They passed walled gardens at the rear of the houses before coming to a small pathway.

"This is for servants to come and go," said Rache.

"So, they don't have to use the main entrance," said Rane with a sharpness he'd not intended.

Rache caught his tone and looked up. "My uncle only has two people helping him. They've been with the family all my life."

"I didn't mean any criticism," he replied as he led her down the alley. "I'm sure your uncle is as nice a person as your father. It's just ... My mother worked for a wealthy family for most of her life, and they certainly appreciated what she did for them—but they also wanted her to be invisible. That way they could pretend everything in their house happened as if by magic. She said they only spoke to her directly three times in fifteen years."

"I'm sorry."

"Nothing to be sorry about. My mother worked hard and earned money for the family. She certainly never complained—I just never liked having to hide on the occasions she had to bring me with her. I'd never seen a house like theirs, and I wanted to play in it, not hide under a table."

Rache stopped by a small gate in a wall. "This takes us to the back of the house."

"Let me go first." Rane eased the gate open and peered through. There was a small path that led through a well-tended garden to the main house. It looked deserted as far as Rane could see but *Kibon* buzzed with excitement at the prospect of violence.

Rane tried not to think of what the consequences of saving Christoph would be. How many lives would he have to take? By the Gods, his very soul was at stake.

He moved quickly down the path, Rache at his back. The house loomed up ahead. Dark windows watched him approach. He could see no movement in any of them, but that didn't make him feel any better.

The back door was locked, but it gave way under a slight push from Rane. He paused by the door, waiting to see if there was any reaction to the noise, but the house was silent.

They stepped into the kitchen. A half-prepared breakfast lay scattered over tables. Flour covered the floor, marred by scuffed footprints.

Rane picked up a carving knife as he made his way into the main house. There was a heavy silence all around them, occupying the space where life should be. He saw broken vases and overturned tables, knocked down chairs and discarded clothes. There was blood too. The scarlet easy to spot on the white tiled floor.

Rache let out a sob but quickly covered her mouth. Rane pointed to the stairs and Rache nodded back.

The second level was as much a mess as the downstairs. Rane could feel his anger coming back. The Inquisition had just stormed in and dragged good people away.

"Where's your room?" he asked Rache.

"This way." She led him down the corridor to the last door on the right. It was a small room with a bed covered in colorful sheets and a two-seater chair by the window over-looking the garden. A wardrobe held some clothes, half of which were scattered across the floor. "I had to grab what I could," said Rache in way of an explanation. "I got dressed in the garden."

"You did very well," said Rane. "Now, can you stay here until I get back?"

Rache nodded. "Yes."

"Good. You should be safe enough up here. I'll bring you up some food before I go."

"What about the soldiers in the street?"

"They won't be there much longer," said Rane.

"What are you going to do?" asked Rache.

He smiled. "I'm going to cause some mayhem across the city, and then I'm going to get your mother and father."

26

Sarah

Sarah knelt on the floor of the cell with her head bowed in prayer. She had no idea what time it was or how long she'd been there. A sister had brought her water and bread, but she'd refused to speak to Sarah. In fact, she'd not even had the courage to look Sarah in the eye. Other than that, Sarah had been left alone.

Mother was obviously still of two minds about what to do with her. The fact that she'd not been tortured and was, in fact, still alive was testament to that. Mother, after all, had never been shy of putting any of her own on a pyre.

And yet, there was no doubt either that Mother wasn't satisfied with Sarah's account of what happened on the Steppes. That's why Sarah was in the cells.

"Odason, All-Father, guide me to the right path forwards," she whispered. "Grant me the wisdom to under-

stand what you want me to do. Give me the strength to with-
stand what challenges I will face."

Had she been wrong to vow to help Nathaniel and the
others? Had she been fooled by his powers? Was he truly
evil and she'd just not seen it?

The questions ran through her mind over and over
again. But, where once she'd had doubts, now there was
only certainty. Rane had never tried to hurt her or any of the
others except when he'd been directly attacked. Christoph
and his family were not in his thrall. They were just a
normal family trying to look after each other. Only circum-
stance had brought Nathaniel into contact with them, and
the Legionnaire had saved their lives at great risk to his own.

The truth, she understood, was that the world wasn't as
black and white as the order made out. It wasn't right to
sentence people to death just because they crossed paths
with a Legionnaire, Tainted or not. The order began to
protect all of Odason's children in the world and guide them
in His ways but what had it become now? An organization
that struck terror in the hearts of the very people it was
supposed to look after? It was wrong. So wrong.

But what could Sarah do about it? Chances were she'd
be dead before nightfall.

Unless there was a way out.

There was a way, of course. She could confess her lies,
tell the truth, give up Christoph and his family and give her
brothers and sisters precise details about Nathaniel's
appearance. As a plan, it had its risks, not least that she'd be
relying on Mother's mercy, and, in a lifetime of service,
Sarah had seen little evidence that mercy even existed, but
still there was no getting past the fact that the truth could
set her free.

But even as she thought of it, Sarah knew she couldn't

give up the others, and Mother's mercy would be a swift strike from *Odason's Wrath* rather than a slow burn on a pyre.

There had to be another way.

Footsteps interrupted her thoughts. Sarah got to her feet and turned to face the door.

Brother Finn's face appeared at the grate, then the door bolts were pulled to one side. "Mother wants you," he said, pushing the door open.

The words took the air out of Sarah for a moment. A summons could only mean one thing—death. The sword or the flame. She forced a breath first and then focused on her legs. She got them to move. One step, then another. Odason had to be helping her, for she managed to move out of the cell and into the corridor.

She glanced up at Brother Finn's face, trying to read something in his features—find some clue as to her fate— but his features was as impassive as she hoped hers were. Sarah set her eyes on the floor and began to walk down the corridor to the stairs, then up to the temple.

She saw the back of the throne first. Mother was sitting in it. Her hand was near *Odason's Wrath* as it leaned against the side of her seat, its naked blade for all to see.

Sarah kept walking, but then she saw who was also in the temple, on their knees before Mother, as terrified as can be, and Sarah's legs wobbled. Christoph, Fion, and their daughter Saphie watched Sarah approach. There was another couple with them Sarah didn't recognize, with two young children of their own. Perhaps they were relations of Christoph's snatched up when the others were seized.

Sarah concentrated on keeping her own face still. Mother would be watching for any sign of innocence or guilt, looking for an opportunity to condemn her or perhaps even save her.

She turned so she faced the throne and bowed. "Greetings, Mother."

"How are you, child?" asked the high priestess, that gods-awful smile on her lips.

"I have benefited from having time to pray, mother," replied Sarah.

"And has the All-Father heard your prayers?"

"I would hope so, Mother, but with all that is happening in the world that demands His attention? I would not be so vain to presume He has."

"Well said, child. In the end, we can only live our lives by His values and follow His teachings. In doing so, we can become His voice on this earth."

"So you have taught me, Mother," replied Sarah. She had no idea how she kept her voice steady, how her legs didn't give way on her. There was strength in her where there should've been none—for her life truly was on a precipice.

Mother nodded as if sensing her thoughts. "Now, child, tell me—have you seen these people before?"

Sarah turned and looked on Christoph and the others as if seeing them for the very first time. "No, Mother. What have they done?"

"All we know is that this man," Mother pointed at Christoph, "arrived at the city bridge with his family an hour or so before you. He claimed to have traveled up the coast from Estenberg, but the guards believed he crossed the Steppes instead."

Christoph looked up, eyes pleading. "We've done nothing wr—"

"SILENCE!" roared Mother, loud enough for even

Odason to hear. "You will speak only when questioned. Brother Finn, if this man pollutes the All-Father's temple again, cut his throat."

Finn bowed. "Yes, Mother."

That quieted the room.

"Sarah," said Mother, her voice as sharp as *Odason's Wrath*, "I ask you again—have you seen these people before?" She held up a finger and pointed to the statue of Odason behind her. "Remember, you are in His house and He will know if you are lying."

Sarah's eyes flicked from the statue to Mother, and suddenly she saw the world in a new light. There was a gleam of excitement in Mother's eyes, brought on by the prospect of blood and pain. Her sickening smile only came alive when death waited in a room. She had no care for anyone's innocence. She only wanted fuel for the pyre. What was said in that room would have no bearing on the verdict she would deliver. It was all just a game to her. A show of power.

Mother was a monster as evil as any of the Tainted. As the statue of Odason looked down on her, Sarah knew she had to stop Mother somehow. This path the Inquisition was on wasn't right.

"Well?" said Mother, her hand resting on the hilt of her sword.

Sarah straightened her back and set her chin, locking eyes with Mother. "I've never seen them before—not even from afar. If they had traveled across the Steppes a mere hour ahead of me, I would've seen them."

"And that's your final word?"

"Yes, as Odason is my witness."

"Brave words," said Mother.

"Honesty requires no courage," replied Sarah.

Mother laughed. "My dear naive child, to speak the truth often requires the greatest strength of all." She waved Finn over. "Take the man downstairs and put him to the question. We'll see if his truth is as unwavering as Sister Sarah's."

Finn didn't need asking twice. With two other brothers to help him, he snatched up Christoph. Fion screamed and tried to stop them, but the back of Finn's hand sent her sprawling to the ground.

"I'm innocent," cried Christoph as they took him to the stairs. "I'm innocent."

Dear Odason. Sarah liked the man, but she had no doubt his strength would fade quickly under Brother Finn's work.

Fion stared at Sarah with tear filled eyes, but Sarah couldn't react to the horror around her. Mother would be watching. But unless something happened soon, it would be over for all of them.

27

Rane

After Rane had made breakfast for Rache and himself, he went to a bedroom and took some time cleaning himself from a bucket of water. With his dirty hair and grimy skin and stolen cloak, he looked too out of place in the city to move around without drawing unwanted attention, and for what he had planned, he needed to be able to disappear in plain sight.

So he scrubbed and scrubbed until his skin lost its grime and his hair no longer hung in clumps around his face. Then he looked in the wardrobe to see if Rache's uncle had clothes that would fit him. He found a pair of grey trousers with a black pin stripe that looked the right length. When he tried them on, the waist was fitted for a larger man, but it wasn't anything a tight belt couldn't fix. There was plenty of room in the shirt as well, but Rane didn't mind—it was better than something that would restrict his movements.

Delving deeper into the cupboard, Rane smiled as he pulled out a long coat. Exactly what he needed.

He placed it on the bed and then retrieved his guns and holsters from the bag Rache had brought him. Ran checked the pistols. Fion had looked after them. She'd cleaned them thoroughly at some point, and they gleamed from her work. He quickly set to work loading both of them, only too aware that he only had four bullets. After that, he slipped them into their holsters and fixed them to his belt.

Rane put on the long coat. It fell just past his knees and covered his weapons perfectly. The kitchen knife went into a pocket. All that was left was *Kibon*.

He strapped the scabbard to his belt. Again, the coat covered most of it, except for a small part that poked out the back, but it was good enough. Whatever happened next, he needed the weapon close to hand.

Kibon tingled with glee, eager to take lives and drink blood. Rane shuddered at the prospect. He wished he knew how many souls would turn his blade black, how long he had before he turned into a monster. He drew *Kibon* half out of the scabbard and stared at the speckled blade. Like the rot, black stained the blade in patches. Irreversible.

It would be the death of him—or worse. Unless he found Babayon, the mage responsible for the curse.

Rane shook the thoughts from his head. He had to rescue Christoph and the others first. He could worry about everything else after that.

He looked in on Rache before he left. She lay curled up on the bed. "Are you going to be all right?"

"I'm scared," she said, looking up. "What if you can't rescue them? What if you're too late?"

"I won't be. I'll bring them home. I promise."

"Thank you, Nathaniel."

"Be brave," said Rane with a wink. "I'll see you tonight."

He left the house then, back through the garden, and took the path to the alley. He retraced his steps until he was on the main street, half a block from the house. The two Soldiers of the Inquisition still stood guard outside, unaware their quarry had been in the building behind them for the last couple of hours.

He saw a boy walking past, trailing a stick against the cobblestones. "Would you like to earn some money?" asked Rane, holding up a coin.

The boy looked at him, confused. "How?"

Rane bent down so he was eye level with the boy. "Can you tell those soldiers something for me?"

The boy looked over at the two guards. "They're Inqui ... Inker ..."

"Inquisition," said Rane. "I know. But don't worry. They won't mind. They'll be happy in fact."

"What do you want me to tell them?"

"Just that you saw a strange man with a sword and point to me."

Now the boy was scared. No one spoke to the Inquisition willingly. "Why?"

Rane smiled. "It's just a game we're playing." He held the coin out, and the boy snatched it from his hand.

The boy sprinted off and ran straight to the soldiers. Rane watched as he said something to the men and then pointed at Rane. Both men looked his way, mouths open.

Rane waved at them and then he ran in the opposite direction. He didn't go too fast, just enough to make them think he was trying to escape.

"Stop him!" One of them shouted from behind.

"Legionnaire!" shouted the other. That made people

scatter from around Rane and he was happy about that too. He didn't want any innocents to get hurt.

Rane ran into a smaller side street, dark with shadow. He carried on until he was halfway down and then stopped. He turned to face the pursuing soldiers and unhooked his scabbard from his belt.

Kibon growled at not being unleashed, but Rane had to admit it felt good having the weapon in his grasp. The hilt was smooth with age, shaped around his fingers. Its weight was perfectly balanced. The sword was a part of him, as much loved as loathed. It would be the death of him as it had been his savior.

The two Soldiers of the Inquisition skidded into the narrow street. Their white robes stood out in the dark shadows, and their swords rasped out of their sheaths.

"On your knees, monster," said the soldier on the left. He was older than the other, perhaps by ten years or more. The second followed a few steps behind, eyes just a little bit wider, sword a little bit shaky.

"Make me," said Rane.

The older man ran at him, hollering with rage, sword high in a two-handed grip. The younger soldier hesitated for a moment and then followed with a cry of his own.

Ran waited, letting them do all the charging. The older man stared to swing his sword a few steps from Rane, and still Rane waited. He watched the sword get closer, arcing down towards his head, then side-stepped out of the way at the last instant.

The sword whistled past his nose. The soldier had a second to realize he'd missed before Rane struck, chopping *Kibon* into his gut. If the sword had been unsheathed, it would've cleaved the man in two. As it was, the steel scabbard slammed into him, knocking him off his feet.

The younger soldier tried to halt his own momentum as he saw his comrade fall, but Rane was already moving. *Kibon* struck his sword arm, breaking the wrist. The man's weapon tumbled from his hand as he screamed in pain. Then Rane hacked down with *Kibon*, straight into the man's knee.

He collapsed, howling.

The older man was trying to get back to his feet, wheezing for air, fumbling for his sword.

Rane smashed *Kibon*'s scabbard across his jaw. The man spun in a perfect circle, spitting teeth and blood before falling to the ground unconscious.

The younger soldier watched Rane, panting with fear, tears streaming down his face, no doubt wondering if he was about to die.

Rane fixed his sword back on his belt. "Tell your friends I'm coming for them. All of them. Odason's Children won't be safe anywhere in this city."

Rane left the two men, heading back into the street, walking quickly until he found a crowd to get lost in. Now, all he had to do was find some more brothers and sisters of the Inquisition to hurt.

Luckily enough, they were everywhere. From down by the wharves to up in the merchant districts, Rane roamed through the city leaving Odason's Children broken and bleeding. He kept *Kibon* leashed in its scabbard at all times and used it to batter the Inquisition every which way he could. Everywhere he went, he left to screams of "Legion-naire!" and "Monster!"

People ran in every direction, soldiers to wherever he had last struck, citizens fleeing the blood and pain he'd left behind. It was easy to get lost in it all. He looked like everyone else, and there were plenty of shadows offering shelter when he needed it.

All the while, the sun crossed the sky as alarm bells rang over the city. Rane wanted it to be dark when he entered the temple. He wanted the place full of injured soldiers taking up too much of everyone's attention. He wanted their nerves frazzled. He wanted them to know what it was like to be the hunted.

Of course, he had to stay one step ahead until nightfall. He had to live long enough to free Christoph and the others.

Rane turned a corner and found himself facing a squad of city guardsmen. Unlike the Inquisition, they didn't have a problem using guns.

"Legionnaire!" roared one while another raised a rifle to his shoulder. The man pulled the trigger and a boom split the air as the flint struck the powder in the mizzen.

Rane jerked his head back, on instinct more than anything else, and felt the lead ball whizz past. A second guard fired. Rane grunted as the bullet clipped his shoulder, then charged the guards. Two came to meet him, swords in hand.

Rane had *Kibon* in his hand, happy the blade was sealed within its scabbard still.

A guard swung his sword at Rane's waist. He blocked it with *Kibon* and stepped in close, driving his left elbow into the side of the guard's face. The fourth guard shouted some battle-cry as he chopped down with his sword, but all Rane had to do was step back one pace to allow it to whistle past and hit the ground with a chunk. Reversing *Kibon*, he drove the pommel of the sword into the guard's mouth, then ducked as another shot was fired.

He slashed to the side, catching the first rifleman in the

side of the head, then reversed the blow to sweep the other off his legs

More guards raced towards him. He threw himself into a roll as one brought a rifle up to bear, and then sprang up, driving *Kibon* into the man's stomach, lifting the guard off the ground. He spun, kicked the legs out from under another before clubbing *Kibon* around a third man's head. With some space around him, he sprinted off down the street, just wanting to get away. With *Kibon* in hand, he could feel the power surging through his legs. Guns fired behind him, but he didn't worry—he was too far for the bullets to have any hope of hitting him.

He sprinted down a narrow road, past people cowering in doorways, frightened by the gunfire, then turned another corner into another, equally deserted street. Bells rang out over the city, echoing off the buildings. No one watched from windows or tried to add their voice to the cries. Most of Napolin seemed to have worked out that it was best to stay out of whatever was going on in the city.

Rane slowed at the end of the road, straightened his jacket, and took the next right.

A squad of six city guards, all carrying rifles, were running down the street towards him—rather, towards the chaos he'd left behind.

"Quick!" shouted Rane, pointing back the way he'd come. "There's some sort of fight going on back there. Hurry!"

They picked up their pace, sprinting past Rane. He allowed himself a smile as he walked on, head down, and found an alley to disappear into. He kept walking, turning this way and that, watching the sky darken. Soon it would be time.

But there were fewer and fewer civilians on the streets

and more city guards and Soldiers of the Inquisition. They moved in larger groups, seeking safety in numbers, erecting barriers across the roads, hoping to hem Rane in somewhere.

There was only one thing to do.

He spotted an inn in the middle of the street. The Emperor's Arms was a small townhouse, its name etched in gold lettering across an awning covering the steps. Rane didn't hesitate, bounding up the stairs two at a time. The front doors were open to let in the breeze, and Rane's sudden arrival inside frightened the owner out of his seat at the welcome desk.

"What do you want?" he asked with a shaking voice, eyes darting all over Rane. "I don't have any money worth taking."

Rane held up his hands. "I'm visiting a friend."

"A friend you say? I don't want any trouble." The innkeeper pressed himself against the wall behind him as if he wanted to sink through it. Anything to get away from Rane.

Rane walked past the man to the stairs at the back of the hallway.

"You can't go up there," shouted the innkeeper as Rane walked up the stairs, past one floor, then the next. Then he spotted a ladder fixed to a far wall leading to a hatch above. He clambered up and pushed the hatch open.

A blood red sky welcomed him as he climbed out onto the roof. After the confines of Napolin's streets, it was a welcome change to have space around him. Even the bells seemed quieter now he was above them. A breeze, full of the sea, cooled the sweat on his brow.

Keeping low, he skirted across the rooftop, keeping below the skyline, and made his way along the terrace. He jumped from roof to roof, heading towards the center of the city. Every now and then, he'd check what was going on down in the streets and was happy to see the chaos continued. Still, he didn't take chances. He didn't want to be spotted by an accidental glance. The fast approaching evening offered more and more shadows to flit between.

When he had to cross wider streets, he moved quickly, jumping gaps of some twelve feet that were too far for a normal man but no problem for a Legionnaire. Another sign he was more than human—even if he wasn't Tainted. Yet. His mind kept wandering to what would happen later. He would need all of *Kibon's* strength if he was to free Christoph and his family. He'd not be able to keep the sword in its scabbard. Lives would be taken.

When his old commander, Lord Jefferson, had him imprisoned Orska, he'd given Rane three prisoners to kill. He'd told Rane that would be enough to make him one of the Tainted. But Rane's sword was only blemished, not black. His soul was not yet fully corrupted. But the question remained—how many would die tonight? Would they put him over the edge? Were Christoph and the others worth risking his eternal damnation?

A shingle slipped as he put his weight on it, nearly taking his foot from under him as it slid off the roof. He tried to catch it, but it was already gone, tumbling to the ground below. Even with the commotion going on streets away, the sound of it smashing seemed terrifyingly loud. Rane pressed himself against the roof while he waited for any reaction. Counted the seconds. When he reached ten without any alarm sounded, he eased himself up and moved on, going slower this time, cursing himself for a fool. He had to concentrate on the now, not on the what-ifs. If he got himself killed, Rane wouldn't be able to help anyone.

By the time he reached the city center, night had fallen. He looked down on a large square. The temple to Odason dominated it, taking up nearly the length of the northern side. The Inquisition demanded that a city's temple be built to fit every resident if they wished to attend the same service, and this one certainly looked large enough to accommodate that order. No doubt it had plenty of room for prisoners too.

To one side, five pyres had been assembled around poles. All that was needed were the people to burn and a crowd to cheer. Rane felt his anger rise yet again. What sort of God demanded the death of innocent people? It was the sort of thing the Rastaks would've done, not the five nations. Yet the Inquisition had turned into some of the world's worst torturers.

There were a half dozen of Odason's Children milling about outside. Nothing for Rane to be concerned with. He couldn't see any guns or rifles. They were just armed with swords and clubs.

He jumped onto a roof ledge and quickly climbed down to the street, the big marble stone walls providing more than enough nooks and crevices for handholds. Back on the ground, he drew *Kibon*. The sword howled in his mind, relishing the freedom and the violence that was sure to follow. Black specks marred the length of the steel, and Rane prayed there wouldn't be too many blemishes to come.

With a deep breath, Rane stepped out of the shadows and into the square. The Soldiers of the Inquisition spotted him almost immediately. They shouted warnings as Rane marched towards them, *Kibon* eager for blood.

28

Sarah

All day long injured brothers and sisters had been brought back to the temple. Some were unconscious, while others were very much awake and crying in pain. Whoever had attacked them—and Sarah could only believe it was Nathaniel's work—had broken plenty of bones, but not a single one of Odason's Children was killed.

Mother tried to keep her calm as she sent more soldiers out to track the attacker down and more wounded were brought back. Space became a priority, and Sarah found herself sharing a cramped cell with Christoph and his family and the others who'd been presented to Mother upstairs.

Saphie was coughing, and the small bucket of rancid water in the cell did nothing to ease her throat. But she wasn't the only one suffering before long. The cell was cramped with little air and the temperature quickly began to rise among the press of bodies.

Sarah herself was pressed against a wall near the door with no space to sit or rest. Through the bars in the door, she could see only a limited section of the corridor outside, but that was all.

"What do you think—" said Fion, but Sarah cut her off.

"Don't speak to me, heathen," she snarled. "I don't know you." Her eyes flicked to the door, and she hoped Fion would realize that whoever stood guard outside would be listening in to any conversation.

Fion gave her a curt nod back. "Bitch."

"I'm sorry I got you involved in this," said Christoph to the other man.

"You've done nothing wrong, brother," replied the man.

Christoph glanced over at Sarah. "Let us hope they realize that and set us free." Sarah could see the similarities between the two men. They both had the same eyes and chin, the same hair. Christoph looked older but not by much.

The parents did their best to comfort their children while they waited all squashed together, while Sarah did her best to keep track of what was going on in the rest of the temple.

Time passed in slow, agonizing fashion, and Sarah wished she had slept while she had the luxury of a cell to herself. Her muscles ached no matter how many times she shifted her feet or tried to find another position to stand in. The air grew even more rank as the stench of their sweating bodies mixed with the tang of urine after the children had no choice but to wet themselves.

It may have been late afternoon when something changed. Sarah could hear it in the tone of the conversations in the corridor outside. Then she spotted Brother Finn approaching with two others following. There was a grim set to his face that made Sarah very worried.

"Open up the door," ordered Finn. Bolts screeched to one side, and hands reached in and grabbed Sarah. Her legs were cramped from standing for so long and refused to work when she was dragged out into the corridor. She would've fallen if not for Brother Finn and the others. But they weren't gentle as they hauled her along, happy to knock her into the walls or let her fall enough to bang her legs. Sarah bit her lip, determined not to show them any sign of pain or weakness.

By the time they reached the stairs, she could walk well enough to go up them by herself, and the fingers digging into her merely stopped her from even thinking off running.

She wasn't prepared for what she saw in the temple. Mother, of course, was on her throne, but before her lay dead bodies and the floor was awash in blood.

Finn threw Sarah to the ground in front of Mother. Blood soaked into her robes and covered her hands and legs.

"Look what your monster has done," said Mother. "Look at your brothers and sisters, murdered and mutilated because you failed to do your duty and stop him when you had the chance."

Sarah looked around her in horror. The corpses had been hacked to pieces. Decapitated. Carved and cleaved. Many were missing ears and noses too, and those injuries disturbed Sarah the most. They didn't occur in combat. They were the deliberate actions of someone desecrating the dead.

Dear Odason, what had Nathaniel done?

"I ... I ... I'm sorry ..." Sarah choked on the words, her mind reeling.

Mother was up off her throne and closed the gap between her and Sarah in a heartbeat. "Sorry?" she screeched and struck Sarah with the back of her hand. It sent Sarah sprawling and she fell on top of a headless corpse. Then Mother grabbed her and yanked her back. "Sorry?"

She threw Sarah into another pile of bodies. Blood covered Sarah from head to foot, and there was no stopping the tears then. No escape from the horror around her. And what was worse, she knew Mother was right. She had failed. The monster had seduced her out on the Steppes, tricked her into thinking he was still human, when all he'd wanted was to get to Napolin to kill.

"Bring the others up," shouted Mother. "Put them all on the pyres. We might as well start with his thralls before we catch the monster himself."

"Mother, please," said Sarah.

"Silence!" Mother snatched up *Odason's Wrath* and pointed it at Sarah. "You will be the first to burn!"

They all heard the screams from outside. They all turned to face the doors, listening. Steel rang out against steel, punctuated by more cries. The sound of battle grew closer, louder, more frenzied.

Then silence fell.

The doors to the temple swung open.

The monster Sarah had known as Nathaniel stood in the doorway, blood dripping off his sword.

29

Rane

Rane stood in the doorway to the temple, unable to believe his eyes. Corpses lay everywhere, hacked and chopped to pieces. Sarah was there, lying amongst them, covered in blood, eyes wide and staring at Rane. He recognized Mother Hilik too, standing in front of a throne with a statue of Odason behind her. She had a sword in her hand. Had she murdered her own people just because Rane had felled them in battle?

"What have you done?" he said.

"Monster!" she howled. "Abomination!"

Soldiers of the Inquisition flanked her, all armed and ready to charge.

Before anyone could move, white hot pain flared in Rane's thigh. His leg gave way under him, and he tumbled to the floor.

"What ..?" Someone stood over him. A woman. Rane

blinked, trying to clear his vision. He was imagining things. It couldn't be. Not ...

"Hello, Nathaniel." There was a chuckle in her voice, delight in her eyes. A face from his past. A friend turned enemy. The Tainted legionnaire in Napolin. And he realized the dead in the temple were as a result of her bloody work.

"Myri."

"I've missed you."

"No," gasped Rane. "Don't ..."

But Myri wasn't listening. She rushed into the temple, laughing as she went. Soldiers of the Inquisition rushed to meet her, but they were nothing but fodder for her blade.

Rane lay on the ground, one hand clutching his wound, the other tight around *Kibon,* and watched her slaughter Odason's Children. He'd faced countless Rastaks, fought Bracke, Jotnars, and other monsters, and yet he'd never been as scared as he was then, for she was murder personified. No sword came close to harming her no matter what the soldiers tried.

In the six months since he'd last seen her—since she'd fallen from the castle window in Orska—Myri had only grown stronger and more powerful. She flowed from attack to attack, cleaving men in half with a single strike of her black sword, dancing away from their futile attempts to kill her before darting in to take another life. And she continued to laugh the whole time.

Kibon pulsed in Rane's hand, its magic working hard on the wound Myri had inflicted. He could feel the bleeding slow, the flesh close, but would it heal in time to fight Myri? And even if it did, how could he possibly hope to win? It had taken both Myri and Rane working together to kill Marcus when he'd fallen to the taint, and Myri appeared far stronger than his friend had been.

He had to do something.

Rane moved his bloody hand from his wound to the holster on his leg. Both guns were loaded still. He had a chance to stop her.

Another soldier fell. Only Mother Hilik and Sarah remained alive. Myri turned to face them. Sarah stepped in front of Mother, despite having no weapon of her own.

Rane pulled a pistol free, cocked the weapon and aimed. His hand shook with the weight of the weapon as he lined the barrel up with Myri's back.

Myri drew her black sword back.

Rane pulled the trigger. The gun boomed.

Myri twisted her body in a way no human should be able to, dodging the bullet. It hit Sarah instead. The sister dropped.

Myri laughed as if it was the funniest thing she'd ever seen.

"Monster!" screamed Mother Hilik and ran at her with her sword. Myri ducked under the blow and cleaved Mother Hilik from hip to hip. The priestess stopped and managed to look down before the upper part of her body slipped from the bottom half in a torrent of blood.

"No," said Rane as he dropped his gun.

Myri turned to face him. "No need to thank me, darling. Believe me—it was my absolute pleasure."

"What have you done? What have you become?" Rane replied, finding his voice at last, tears creeping into the corner of his eyes. She looked so beautiful, more so than before. She'd not become twisted and warped like Marcus, but she radiated power, and Rane could only imagine the energy surging through her.

"I've become what we are meant to be," said Myri, walking over to him. Blood speckled her face. "Glorious."

Her voice was so light and playful, yet she stood before him like an angel of Heras with his life in her hand.

"You've become a monster."

"Tssk. You're sounding like them, Nathaniel, and we're nothing like *them*."

"We were meant to help people," replied Rane. Behind Myri, someone moved. Sarah. She wasn't dead. Not yet. Rane couldn't let Myri see her. "We're not murderers."

Myri laughed, shook her head. "Nathaniel, that's all we've ever been. We joined the Legion so we could kill, and we're fucking good at it. The swords have just made us better, helped us reach our potential, freed us from the shackles that held us back."

"We joined the Legion to save people, not murder them. We fought the Rastaks because there was no other choice. We fought to save lives."

"Fool yourself if you want, but not me. The sword opened my eyes, Nathaniel. These people you seem to care about are nothing but cattle, food to be eaten to give us strength. Do you cry when you kill a rabbit to eat? Do you go hungry because its life is sacred? No. You slaughter them without a second thought." Rane tried not to watch the dark blade in her hand, but it drew his eyes with each flicker of movement.

"We're all human. All lives are precious." He kept his voice calm. He'd not let her know how petrified he was. He gripped tighter to *Kibon*, needing its magic. He could feel his wound was all but healed. The sword growled in his mind, eager to fight Myri. Eager to claim her might for its own.

"Do you know what? I knew it was you when I read in the news sheets that a Legionnaire was loose in the city.

Somehow I knew. And I've got to tell you, I've enjoyed watching you run around like a headless chicken all day, trying so hard not to hurt any of these fucking scum. Of course, I had to join in the fun. Not that I played by your rules." Myri shook her head in disapproval. "Sending the zealots back here with broken bones and bumps on their head? Shame on you for being so weak! You should know only blood matters. Only death makes them weak and makes us strong."

"How many have you killed, Myri? Just to amuse yourself?"

"Oh, there was more to it than that, Nathaniel. It's about real power. Power you could have." Myri bent down and stroked Rane's face. "Don't deny your true self. Join me."

"I am not you."

"Always the fool." She pushed his face away and stood up. "I know you're not me. You're only half a man right now. Now use that beautiful sword of yours. Embrace its power. Become a god." Myri stepped to the left, like a shadow drifting, revealing Sarah behind her. Rane's heart lurched. "I've left one for you. Kill her, and let's see what other treats wait for us below."

"I'll never do that."

"Come on, Nathaniel. Stop being weak. They're cattle. Nothing more."

Rane puhed himself up, standing on shaking legs. "Please Myri, I can't let you kill anymore." His feet shifted as he moved *Kibon* into a two-handed grip.

"Oh darling, you can't stop me." She turned, offering her side, sword ready to strike. "Not on your best day." She lunged, aiming straight for Rane's heart, fast like lightning, and he only just managed to bat her blade away.

"Don't do this, Myri," pleaded Rane as she came again.

Myri let her sword do the talking as it swung down, a blow that would split him from shoulder to hip. He acted on instinct, blocking where he thought her sword would be rather than by what he could see. Steel kissed steel again and again as she forced him back towards the altar.

As her sword came down again, Rane jumped to one side, trying to find some breathing room. Myri swept the blade from left to right, and Rane dropped *Kibon* to block. Her sword skidded down Rane's blade until guard locked with guard, their faces all but touching. She pushed down on him, grinning from ear to ear, and Rane buckled under the pressure, falling onto another body. The black blade moved closer to his face. Death only an inch away.

Rane managed to get a foot under himself and used that to twist sideways, breaking free and sending Myri clattering to one side. She was on her feet in an instant, pressing her attack, forcing Rane back once more. He countered her thrust and retreated, fighting for his life, using every bit of skill and knowledge built up over ten years of war.

Myri rushed at him, but he sidestepped and struck with *Kibon*, cutting across her shoulders. She shrugged off the attack as if it were nothing. Her sword swept around, seeking his jugular. Rane threw himself back, feeling the blade pass and the slightest of nicks as it caught his skin just below his Adam's apple. His hand went to it, could feel the warm, wet blood, but he could still breathe—he was still alive.

"Lucky, Nathaniel. Lucky," said Myri, coming at him again.

Rane moved to the left, painfully aware of how little space there was to maneuver. The dead lay everywhere, getting in the way, their blood making the ground treacherous. He deflected the next lunge, parried another, but the third strike drew blood, slicing through cloth and flesh on his arm. He jerked back, dropping his guard, and Myri flicked her blade across his face, cutting him from jaw to cheek.

Rane knew he had to attack, but Myri was too fast to give him any opportunity. He chopped down at her knee, but she swept his sword away almost before he'd begun the move. He followed through with an elbow strike at her face, but found nothing but air as Myri danced away, almost giddy in delight. She punched him as she moved, catching him on the cheek bone. His head shot back and his vision wobbled, but he managed to stay on his feet.

"Come on, Nathaniel. You can do better than this," chuckled Myri. "I thought you were a great warrior. Do you need a moment to catch your breath? Perhaps I should go and have a chat with that little girl over there while you sort yourself out?"

Rane hacked at Myri with all the strength he had left, but she simply knocked his attack aside with her black sword, sending him sprawling. As he pushed himself up onto all fours, she kicked him in the stomach, flipping him onto his back. He gasped for air, trying to get his lungs to work as Myri stood over him.

He swung his sword at her, but Myri simply stepped over it like a child with a skipping rope. She picked him up so he was facing her. "Don't make it too easy for me. Use your sword. Use your gift," she whispered. Rane spat blood and phlegm in her face in reply. Perhaps there was a flicker of disappoint in Myri's features, but Rane was flying through the air again before he was sure. His skull smashed into the side of the throne as he landed. His sword skidded away, and panic forced him on when all he wanted to do was lie down and pass out. He scrambled on his hands and knees after

Kibon, blood dripping into his eyes, mocked by Myri's laughter all the way. He was dead without the sword in his hands. His old wounds would open up if it was more than twelve feet away.

But there it was, lying among the dead. Rane threw himself at it, relief flooding through him as his fingers closed around the hilt once more. There was a faint pulse of magic but barely enough to stave off unconsciousness. *Kibon* begged for blood, promising all the power it had if he just gave in. Though a half-closed eye, he watched Myri turn towards Sarah. Sarah screamed for help, but there was none to be had.

Only Rane could save her.

Rane—beaten, broken, and bloodied.

Rane hauled himself up, steading himself with his sword in his other hand like a walking stick. A wave of nausea hit him as he got to his feet, and he blinked away the black from his mind. Myri had her back to him, no longer concerned with him as any sort of threat. He spat a mouthful of blood onto the floor and took *Kibon* in a two-handed grip. If he was quick, he could stop her. He had a chance while her attention was elsewhere. He ran at Myri, *Kibon* over his shoulder, ready to strike.

Myri barely glanced over her shoulder as she reversed her sword.

Rane almost didn't notice her blade pierce his stomach. It slipped in so easily. He felt it erupt out of his back, though, and screamed.

He looked down at the blade so black. He coughed, spilling more blood down his chin and onto the floor.

Myri turned to face him, as close as only a lover could be, her eyes wide with delight. He could feel her breath on his skin, her lips by his, almost kissing. "Do you like that?"

she said, grinning. "Hurts doesn't it? Took me weeks to recover after you stabbed me in the gut back in Orska, and I promised then that I'd make you suffer when next we met."

Myri twisted the blade.

The pain hit him, intense, blinding, and he screamed. This was it—the moment he was going to die. Already the room began to disintegrate around him, and the world spun.

He pulled his head back, trying to focus on her face. How could it have come to this? All for nothing.

Blood seeped down his back, his life leaking away.

No. Not like this. His hand fumbled for his other pistol on his hip as he screamed once more. The darkness filled his vision. If he could just...

"Dear Nathaniel," Myri whispered. "Your death will make me mightier still."

He pressed the pistol against her chest and pulled the trigger. He rocked with the blast as Myri flew back, spraying him with blood. She hit the ground, coughing and spluttering, clutching her hand to the hole in her torso.

The gun fell from his fingers.

30

Rane

Rane sank to his knees, the black blade protruding from his back. *Kibon* clattered to the floor next to him, and he knew he should pick it up, but his fingers had stopped listening to him.

Someone grabbed him and tried to drag him away from Myri. He flapped out a hand for *Kibon*, managed to hook a finger around it. "My sword," he croaked.

"I've got it," said Sarah, picking *Kibon* up. He snatched it from her as she hauled him along the floor and held it tight. A smear of blood trailed behind him. They were five feet from Myri. Six. Seven. Not yet far enough.

"We've got to get out of here," said Rane. "Get away from her."

"You shot her. She's dead," replied Sarah. Eight. Nine.

"No, she's not," he grunted. A bullet to the torso wouldn't kill her in the same way her sword hadn't killed him. Yet. He needed more distance between himself and Myri, and more distance between her and her blade. Taking it away from her was his only hope of defeating her. If he lived that long. "Help me up."

With Sarah's arms around his waist, she got him upright. The world around him faded in and out of focus, and darkness tried to claim him. They staggered to the main doors of the temple, fifteen, sixteen feet away from where he'd shot Myri. Far enough for her sword's magic to stop working.

Sarah nearly dropped him as she struggled to open a door leading outside, but then cold air hit him as it swung open. He half-fell through the doorway and collapsed on the pavement. Every breath was labored as he pressed *Kibon* to his chest.

"I need a cloth," he wheezed. Blood trickled down his chin.

Sarah ripped the corner of her bloody robe and stuck the strip in Rane's hand.

Holding it, he fumbled for the hilt of Myri's sword and closed his fingers around it. He flinched at the evil in the blade, so strong even though the cloth. It fought with *Kibon* in his mind, both blades desperate for control over Rane.

But he wasn't going to give in to either of them. He pulled the sword, gritting his teeth against the pain.

It slid free inch by inch.

"Let me help you," said Sarah, reaching for the sword.

"No!" He couldn't let Sarah touch the polluted blade. Its poison in his mind was bad enough. He could sense all the lives it had taken. The power it had given Myri—the same power it now promised Rane.

He let thoughts of Kara, his wife, fill his mind instead, a bright star in the dark, love to fight the fear. At least if he died, he'd be with her once more. Would she forgive him for his failings?

He must have passed out at one point because he blinked and found himself cheek-down on the cobbles, spilled blood warm and sticky against his skin. As he sat up, he saw the sword was no longer in him. It lay next to him, just a sheen of solid black reflecting nothing.

Sarah sat opposite him, her robes covered in blood. "How can you still be alive?"

There was another sound too. From inside the temple. An ungodly wail. Myri was still alive.

Rane gripped *Kibon*. He had to get back on his feet. His eyes fluttered as the energy flowed through him, pulsating, almost burning. Dark words whispered in his mind told him to go and finish Myri. Her death would heal him instantly. Her strength would make him mighty.

Tears flowed down his cheeks. He so wanted to give in. He could hear Myri wailing inside, calling his name, cursing him, pleading with him, begging with him. Her screams echoed through the night.

"Nathaniel?" said Sarah, moving towards him. "We need to get you to a doctor."

Rane shook his head. "I have to finish her."

Kibon sent another burst of magic through him at the words, full of glee. His pain faded, his breathing became easier, as he accepted what he had to do. The darkness was gone from his eyes, and he saw the world with a clarity that he'd not had for a long time.

"Nathaniel?" Sarah's voice was full of fear as he climbed to his feet.

He marched back into the temple with *Kibon* in his hand.

He found Myri near the throne looking as near dead as

anything could be. She lay on her back, eyes staring open at the ceiling, mouth open, gasping for air. Countless cuts bled across her face, neck, and on any other part of her skin he could see. Still alive, but barely. Her life was still his to take. He stood over her, placed *Kibon* at her throat. Unlike her sword, his still shone, reflecting the statue of Odason, candlelight dancing along its edge. He turned the blade, until he could see himself in the steel, twisted, distorted. Tainted.

The sight shocked him. He took a step back as if to escape himself and saw the blade for what it was. He retreated another step, feeling the desire to kill, but it no longer felt glorious. Far from it.

His hand fumbled for *Kibon's* scabbard, almost vomiting with the emotions battling away inside him. He forced the blade back inside against its will, fighting its power every inch of the way. It screamed its anger, threatened to take all its power back. Its fury was almost overwhelming, pounding his thoughts. As the scabbard met the guard, there was only silence. Rane sagged with relief. So close. It had been so close.

"You always were so weak." Myri chuckled, then coughed. Her eyes were open, watching Rane. "That's why I'll win. Why I'll always win. Why I'll kill you. I won't even promise to make it quick."

And the truth was she was right. This could only end one way.

There was only one cure for Myri. He reached into his pocket for the kitchen knife he'd taken from Rache's house. "No, you won't." He straddled Myri and looked her in the eyes. "I wish there was another way."

"Don't, Nathaniel," croaked Myri.

Rane bent down and sliced her throat with the knife.

"Is she dead?" asked Sarah from the doorway.

Rane walked over to her, slipping the knife back into his coat pocket. Using the cloth Sarah had given him, he picked up Myri's sword by its hilt and leaned it against the wall. He stamped down, shattering the blade. "She is now."

"And you ..."

"I'm fine. Where are Christoph and the others?"

"Downstairs."

"Show me."

Sarah led him back into the slaughterhouse that was the temple, past Myri's twisted, tainted body. She'd once been the very best the Legion of Swords had, an example for everyone. Only Odason knew how many times she'd saved Rane's life.

They walked slowly down the stairs, but there were no Soldiers of the Inquisition to greet them. There were only the injured Rane had sent back to the temple earlier.

"I'm glad you weren't responsible for the dead upstairs," said Sarah.

"I told you there was a Tainted already in the city," replied Rane.

"Did you know her?"

"We were good friends once."

"I'm sorry."

"She's at peace now."

They found Christoph and his family in one of the cells. Still alive. Still unharmed. Thank Odason.

"Nathaniel, you came," gasped Christoph.

"Rache found me," replied Rane.

"Is she ..?" asked Fion.

"Alive at your brother's house." That was when Rane noticed the other family in the cell. "Your house."

"Thank you," said the man.

"We need to get you out of here before anyone else comes back," said Sarah.

"Cover the children's eyes when we get upstairs," said Rane. "They shouldn't see what's up there."

"No one should," said Sarah.

With the parents carrying the children, they headed back upstairs. There were gasps when they saw the carnage, but no one faltered. The doors beckoned them on, and Rane was glad when they were outside once more.

"What happens now?" asked Christoph. "Will the Inquisition come after us?"

Sarah shook her head. "The Tainted is dead inside—along with everyone who knew of you. Her death will satisfy the order."

"Go home," said Rane. "Get Saphie well." He tussled the girl's hair.

"Thank you, my friend," said Christoph. "You've saved us again."

"It was my pleasure." The two men hugged.

"Thank you as well," said Fion to Sarah. "We won't forget you."

"Take care," said the sister.

Rane and Sarah watched the families disappear into the city.

"You better go as well," said Sarah, "before more of my brothers and sisters return."

"I'm sorry for what Myri did. She was a good person once. The best."

Sarah glanced back into the temple. "We should be protecting people from Tainted like her—not becoming monsters ourselves."

"Tell me about it," said Rane.

"How long before you become like her?"

"Hopefully never. Myri didn't know what she was becoming before it was too late. I do. I'm going to find a cure for myself and every Legionnaire that has yet to fall to the taint."

"You're a good man, Nathaniel. I hope you succeed."

Rane smiled. "So do I."

"Goodbye, Nathaniel. May the All-Father look over you." Sarah kissed him on the cheek.

Rane could still feel her lips as he hobbled off into the night. His hand went to the locket on his wrist, and he thought of a beautiful home near a stream in the woods. He thought of his wife and child, lost forever. "I love you both," he whispered to the wind.

Rane hoped that one day he'd be with them. Until then, he had a mage to hunt and monsters still to fight. His war wasn't over yet.

31

Rane

The Four Elms was a run-down inn about ten miles outside of Salvator. Rane stood outside, listening to the laughter within. It had taken him two months to make his way there from Napolin. Two months of hiding from the Inquisition, sleeping in ditches or under bushes, getting soaked to the bone by the winter rains and marching down muddy roads. But he was there now, and he had a promise to keep.

Kibon hummed on his back, excited at their journey's end and who'd they'd find inside.

He was fully healed now—or as healed as he could be from the fight with Myri. She had given him some scars that would never disappear. He kept seeing his friend's face in his dreams, the way she'd smiled as she'd run him through for the second time. Sometimes, he dreamed of her with Marcus as they committed atrocity after atrocity. The worst was when he was with them—one of them—covered in blood, drowning in bodies, full of glee. The dreams lingered for days afterwards, filling him with guilt and fear.

He'd yet to find any clue as to Babayon's whereabouts, but he'd left word with people he knew from the war—people he trusted—to get any news to him.

In the meantime, he had some justice of his own to hand out, a promise to Christoph to keep. It hadn't been hard to track down the men who'd deserted his friend's family on the borders of the Steppes. The men that had stolen Christoph's money.

Rane pushed open the door. As expected, Carl, Harken, Jak, and Droon were sitting at a table, laughing their heads off, flagons of ale in their hands. By the looks of things, they weren't on their first drinks of the night.

What did take him by surprise was who else was drinking in the inn. The three Rastaks, who'd caused trouble in the inn where he'd first met Christoph, were sitting with the others. Shaved Head and the two dark eyes were drinking just as hard. It made sense seeing them there. They were all thieves, working together. No doubt Rane had ruined their initial plan that night when he'd broken the Rastak's wrist.

None of the men noticed Rane in the doorway though. They didn't even look up when he walked over to the table. Rane got their attention though when he slammed a knife through Jak's hand.

Jak wailed as he tried to pull Rane's knife free, but the blade had gone right through the table. The wagon driver wasn't going anywhere.

The others all jumped to their feet, pulling knives off their own.

"I don't want any trouble," shouted the innkeeper, but it

was too late for that.

Rane smiled. "You gentlemen stole from a friend of mine. I've come to take it all back."

AFTERWORD

I hope you enjoyed the adventures of Nathaniel Rane. If you did, please leave a review on Amazon or on Goodreads. Reviews really help every author and make a massive difference.

To find out more about Nathaniel Rane and all my other books Visit my website www.mikemorrisauthor.com PLUS, if you sign up for my mailing list, you can get a free copy of CRY WITCH, an adventure featuring my other hero, Jack Frey.

Nathaniel Rane will return in ONCE A HERO. Order your copy today

Made in the USA
Middletown, DE
03 December 2021

54093584R00159